# SERPENTS OF THE DAWN

ADALINE WINTERS

Copyright © 2023 by Adaline Winters

All rights reserved

No part of this book may be reproduced, stored in a retrieval system, or transmitted by any means, electronic, mechanical, photocopying, recording or otherwise without the express written permission from the author.

Cover design
by
Liberty Champion

*For my fellow witches who have found their possessive alpha. Good job.*

*For my fellow witches who are still searching for theirs. They are out there, never settle for less than you deserve.*

VI

# Chapter One

*I'll never be able to look at moussaka again.*

It had been a long day, and it was about to get even longer. The wards surrounding my property clanged in my head, warning me of newcomers. Probably some new folks settling into my bed and breakfast for the night. There were a million things I would rather be doing than contemplating my outfit and sorting through neutral topics of conversation for a pack of violent shifters who saw me as an evil interloper intent on ensnaring their illustrious leader. Perhaps they wanted to discuss the weather? It was a few degrees warmer than average for the festive season. White Castle, a small town located in the Pelican State of Louisiana, was home to just under two thousand folks, many of whom belonged to one of the three supernatural factions: vampires, shapeshifters, and elementals. The latter being me, an elemental with the power to control water. I was also half angel, thanks to my dear old dad who was the angel of death, making me the daughter of death. Lucky me.

Harry shot into my room and hovered three inches off the floor. In life, Harry had been an upstanding vampire, helping run a church support group which enabled vampires to live less murderous lives. In death, he'd refused the call of the light and instead, pledged his afterlife loyalty to me. There was a lot to unpack in that statement. Contrary to popular belief, vampires weren't an abomination. They didn't explode on hallowed ground, they could walk in the daylight, and even occasionally enjoyed a good Italian meal laced with garlic. Sure, they drank human blood, but that never resulted in a turning. The only way to actually become a vampire was to be born one.

Harry's brow crinkled. "I believe you have a last minute appointment in your office."

Below the three-story plantation house was my office and examination room. I was a fully qualified medical doctor who offered my services to the factions because the local emergency room was ill-equipped to deal with ailments that affected the supernatural community. Certain human powers knew of our existence, but for the majority of humanity, we were fantasy fiction. While the world was changing, becoming more accepting of differences and uniqueness, it was not a stretch of the imagination to think that a war would break out should our existence be revealed. The problem was, the head of The Order, who governed the elementals, was threatening our way of life. She was maneuvering the political landscape to drive us head first into a war. Eloise was her name, but I knew her better as grandmother.

I sighed. Whoever it was that darkened my doorstep would have to wait. I had a date with The Principal and his strongest alphas, which spanned the differing species.

I flung open my door and came face-to-face with Rebecca, my longest resident and vampire princess in hiding. She was the epitome of ethereal royalty, all long slender limbs, golden hair, and stunning blue eyes.

"There's a pair of vampires waiting for you in your office," she declared.

"So I heard."

Her eyes flicked over my shoulder. She couldn't see the dead—few could—but she knew of Harry's existence. "He is always beating me to the news."

I shut the door behind me. "It's not a competition."

Harry floated through the wall and appeared in front of us. "And if it were, I would win," he declared.

I rolled my eyes and began my descent down the stairs. I bypassed The Principal's room. Hudson Abbott had moved himself into my home, declaring that as his mate, we should be living under the same roof. That was a month ago and he was negotiating his time between running the pack and driving me nuts. It wasn't that I didn't want him or love him even, but he had hurt me, and my heart needed time to repair the damage he'd caused. So I kept him at arm's length where I could, but the meal with the pack's alphas was long overdue. I was owed a chewing out for my part in the showdown that happened on my grounds where no fewer than fifty-six shifters had met an ugly and pointless end. Also, I wasn't a pretty little docile shifter who would be popping out furry babies for them to dote on. I had no idea what kind of babies we would make. A Nephilim and a prehistoric shifter would be an interesting genetic mix. Ugh,

I needed to not be thinking of babies with Hudson. In order for babies we needed to be having sex, and that would involve me taking him firmly out of the dog house, which I wasn't ready to do.

Hopefully, I could wrap this appointment up quickly. If not, then I would reschedule it for the morning, ensuring I could meet Hudson in the parlor in exactly—I glanced at the grandfather clock—ten minutes. That was ample time for most medical issues facing vampires.

Maggie waved at me from her perch on the reception desk. I pointed at the chair. "We aren't running a bar, sit in the seat I provided."

She huffed in true teenager fashion, but slid off the desk and into the chair with all the feline grace her animal afforded her, her brunette hair bouncing like her mood. Maggie was incapable of remaining mad at anyone—she was like a ray of sunshine everywhere she walked.

I left my supernatural friends on the main floor and descended to the basement. The office door was wedged open and soft mumblings of male voices floated out to greet me. I stepped through and paused to take in my clients. Both were clad in fashionable skinny jeans and cashmere sweaters. I hadn't met them before, which wasn't unusual in itself as there wasn't a great call for a doctor among vampire kind. They didn't suffer from viral infections or common ailments. Broken bones did occur, but given they were as strong as steel, it was rare, and more often than not, they healed at a rapid rate—sometimes so much so, the bone needed to be rebroken and set correctly.

The rounder of the two males stood with his arms folded but was hunched over slightly, like he was in pain. His white blond hair fell over his gray eyes and his lips were pressed into a tight line, making them almost as pale as his skin. The other, a red haired slim male with hazel eyes, swiveled on my client chair to face me.

"We have been kept waiting long enough, when will The Undertaker be here?" he snapped.

Ugh, that nickname was the bane of my life. I was five foot two in heels, with flaming copper hair and pouty pink lips. No one believed I was The Undertaker, the famed supernatural doctor of death. I rounded the desk and sat in the executive chair.

"My office hours are eight till four. My receptionist can make you an appointment for tomorrow as you leave."

"Young lady, this is no time for dress up," the vampire across from me said.

My gaze snapped to his and I leveled him with the Roberts' stare I'd learned from my grandmother. The vampire shrunk away from me. Smart man. His monster sensed mine and recognized it was severely outmatched.

The blond-haired vampire let out a small groan and clutched his stomach. "I cannot bear this pain for another night."

I frowned. What on earth was wrong with him? Vampires didn't get stomach aches. "What happened?" I asked.

The vampire in the chair grimaced. "There was an accident."

"We were cooking moussaka," the pained one added in a rush.

Last I checked, Greek food was not poisonous to vampires. "Ewan slipped," the one across from me stated.

"On what?"

"The eggplant." Oh no. I glanced at the clock on the wall. This was going to take longer than the six minutes remaining before Hudson came to investigate where his mate was, but I couldn't leave him in this state.

"Was it whole?" I asked.

The vampires' gazes locked on each other as they silently communicated. They should know if the damn vegetable was whole when it *slipped*. "Spit it out, Morgan," Ewan said through a grimace. "She's a doctor so patient-doctor confidentiality applies, right?" he checked.

I nodded. "Of course, and it would go much easier and quicker if you were honest with me. It will also make a difference in how I approach the problem."

Morgan sighed and ran a hand through his hair. "It was whole, stalk end first."

I resisted the urge to lecture them on the practices of safe sex, because this experience would deter them from making the same mistakes. With the large and wide variety of toys on the market, there was really no need to experiment with vegetables these days, and I mean large as in eggplant sized.

"How long?" I ask.

Morgan tilted his head and moved his hands about a foot apart. Wow, um, no. They clearly didn't purchase their vegetables at the local Walmart, because I had never seen an eggplant that big. Perhaps they shopped at the organic farmers market that visited every other Monday? I'd been meaning to try it out. "I mean how long has it been in there?" I clarified.

Morgan flushed pink. "Oh, since Wednesday evening."

Today was Friday. No wonder he was in pain. "Can you help me?" Ewan pleaded.

With the eggplant? Yes. With his dignity? Unlikely. That said, literally hundreds of people presented with this problem up and down the country at the local emergency room. Not specifically eggplants, although they were among the long and wide things that people seemed to slip on, accidentally impaling themselves.

I nodded and pushed to my feet. "Follow me," I told him. Morgan stood, and I pointed at him. "Not you. Let's leave a little mystery intact for your relationship."

Morgan plonked himself back in the chair looking relieved as Ewan shuffled to follow me. I let the door bang closed, sealing us inside my examination room. "If you could drop your jeans and then lie on your left side please."

The pain was clearly more persistent than his dignity, because Ewan's jeans hit the floor faster than I could blink. He bent to unlace his sneakers, giving me a wonderful view of his tighty whities. He groaned and leaned on the long black cushioned table. I bent and undid his shoes for him, his ass pressing against my head. I pulled them off, followed by his jeans, and finally his underwear, then helped him into position on his side.

"You're stronger than you look," he commented between groans as he curled into himself, giving me perfect access.

"Looks can be deceiving," I uttered while opening a new box of gloves and snapping on a pair. I blinked at the little Rudolph's dotted on them. Clearly, Maggie had been in charge of ordering supplies this month, because there was no way I had ordered festive-themed medical gloves. Considering where I was about to shove Rudolph's big nose, I didn't think they were appropriate.

I rummaged in my baby delivery kit drawer, finding the instruments I needed along with some numbing cream which would help the passage of the vegetable.

"What are you going to do?" Ewan muttered, trying to look over his shoulder. I put a firm hand on his back.

"You need to keep in this exact position for me."

He tensed and stared straight ahead. "Okay."

I squirted some of the cream onto my finger and began massaging it into his anus. Did it say something about me that I would rather be doing this than sharing a meal with the pack? Definitely. I thought of Dangerous Dave, the pack's head of security, and the never-ending suspicious looks he gave me every time he was over at my house, which was often, given his boss had holed up here.

I placed a firm hand on Ewan's hip and did a little internal investigation. It wasn't in too deep, and the rounded end meant I could try to use the less invasive equipment. "Do you feel it?" Ewan asked.

I blinked. Did I feel the foot long eggplant lodged in his ass? *No Ewan, it has gone for a wander through your intestines. Good news though, it will sprout out of your mouth in the next few days.*

"I do. Don't worry, I will have it out in a minute or two."

I glanced at the clock on the wall. Ugh, I was now late. Hudson wasn't the most patient male, he would come looking for me sooner rather than later.

I withdrew my finger. The cream had both a numbing and relaxing effect on the muscle. Good thing too, given the width of this unfortunate vegetable that would never see its potential as an ingredient. What a waste.

Maneuvering the little plastic cup so it gripped the base of the eggplant, I made sure it had a good seal. "Okay, Ewan, I need you to stay relaxed and concentrate on keeping your breathing nice and steady for me."

His hand gripped the side of the table and he made a big show of breathing loudly. Luckily, the cream had done its job and was helping his anus to stay relaxed, otherwise this would result in a trip to the emergency room where they could sedate him.

I gripped his hip and gently started to pull. The deep purple vegetable slowly made its appearance into the world, and it kept coming, and coming. I caught the end of the vegetable before it smashed to the floor.

"Is it out?" Ewan grumbled.

"It certainly is." I examined the vegetable. "And good news, it's intact—stalk and all." Cora Roberts—rescuer of wayward vegetables.

He glanced over his shoulder at me. "Thank you, doctor."

I nodded, a little in awe of the fact that this had been lodged inside of him. It was more than a foot long. Definitely not a Walmart purchase. "Do you go to the farmers market?" I asked as Ewan dropped his feet to the floor and began dressing.

"Every other Monday, the organic fruit and veg is sublime."

I detached the Ventouse cap traditionally used to help the delivery of babies and waved the eggplant at him. "You want this?"

His eyebrows climbed off his face. "Um, no, you may dispose of that."

"You sure? You can't moussaka without eggplant."

"We have another."

Oh boy. "Put it in the dish this time."

"Don't worry doctor, my lesson has been learned." He slips on his sneakers and looks around the room. "Um."

"Pay Maggie on the main floor as you leave. Standard consult fee only."

Someone rapped their knuckles against the door. Ewan opened it and came face-to-face with Hudson. They stared at each other for a hot minute, then Hudson stepped back and allowed Ewan to leave. Hudson's fitted shirt flirted with his muscles like a koala wrapped around a tree. His blue stonewashed jeans had the same issue. A perpetual five o'clock shadow gave his strong jaw line definition. He was the epitome of everything masculine, and being a red blooded female, I paid attention. That said, he was still semi in the dog house, and he was proving to me day by day that he was sorry. I'd put the brakes on our budding relationship because he'd reversed his feelings over concerns about his political standing and the optics of dating the granddaughter of a rival faction. Then the idiot had jumped into a Hell hole to save me. It was complicated. His deep set hazel eyes were trained on me as he squinted at the offending vegetable still in my hand. Right, the pack meal.

"Traditionally, guests bring wine, flowers, or chocolates." His voice rumbled and caused a little shiver to dance down my spine.

"I'm hardly a traditional type of girl. But this isn't fit for consumption."

I turned and dropped the eggplant into a clinical waste bin along with my Rudolph gloves. Then I began scrubbing my hands in the metal sink.

"You look pretty," he said, edging closer. I looked okay, I was in a silver dress rather than jeans and a t-shirt, or if it was a big day at the office, slacks and a blouse. My hair was twisted into a simple updo, rather than the standard ponytail.

A splash of makeup made my pixie features a little more mature.

I raised a brow and glanced at him, the warning in my gaze clear. I might be attending a meal with the pack's heavyweights, but that was to try to smooth over the rift caused by the loss of life on my land. Regardless of our relationship status, this meal would be necessary. He was trying to read more into it than I was willing to give.

"Thank you," I said, wiping my hands on a towel. I stalked out of my examination room and into my office. I yanked open the desk drawer and withdrew a bottle of whiskey.

Hudson whistled low as he twisted the bottle to face him. "Balblair's. Now that's a gift worth celebrating."

Not too flashy, but not cheap either, being the perfect gift for a group of people who appreciate their food and drink. I pushed the drawer shut with my hip and led the way up the stairs, finding the vampires had already left. Maggie grinned at me and waved.

I turned toward her to collect my final part of the gift. She lifted a round tin from under the counter and handed it toward me. Maggie's cooking was not for the faint of heart, but her cookies? To die for.

"I made triple chocolate chip, oatmeal, and lemon."

"Thank you, I'll be back in a few hours. Call me if you need anything."

"I won't need anything."

Ugh, *please* need something. I spun and faced The Principal who was holding the front door open for us both. "After you," he said with a grin, which spoke as to how much he was enjoying watching me squirm.

The cool night air made goosebumps erupt on my arms. "Why is my Bugatti parked out front?" I wondered. Technically, it was Sebastian's Bugatti. He was my best friend, the vampire Crown Prince of North America, and he kept losing his baby to me in bets.

"I thought you might like to drive?" Hudson said as we descended the steps and he dangled the keys in my face. He knew I would be nervous about the meal and had decided to let me drive my sports car to take my mind off it. A car he hated, given his large frame. He also detested letting anyone else drive, unless it was Dave. He was a control freak.

I swapped my gifts for the keys and with a huff, got into the driver's side. I slid the seat forward and pumped it up. Damn oaf. Hudson watched me reposition the chair with barely contained amusement. Two could play at that game. My foot hit the gas and we peeled out of the driveway at breakneck speed. Hudson cursed a blue streak and I smiled. Never underestimate a Roberts woman, we always got the last laugh.

# Chapter Two

*Have Mercy on my soul, because I would not be forgiving.*

The Pit was White Castle's answer to anything entertainment related. Quiz nights, speed dating, 70's themed disco—you name it, Karen, the owner, had thought of it. She was a whiz at reinventing her premises to keep it up to date with the trends. That said, its sticky carpets and chipped tables needed a major overhaul to not make you feel like you were going to catch a new and suspicious disease.

The Pit was neutral territory, something Hudson had insisted on for this dinner that I had successfully avoided four times, given it was a weekly occurrence that he attended with his alphas. This was the forum for the different shifter species to iron out any issues overseen by The Principal who ruled them all.

It was clear that their major grievance wasn't with each other, but rather with me. That was okay, I was a big girl—I could handle some alphas. After all, I put up with Hudson's domineering ass on a daily basis.

"You ready for this?" he asked as I cut the engine.

I squeezed the steering wheel before turning to him. "How angry are they?"

"Stick with the story, you'll be fine."

Right, the fictitious tale of how Lucifer had tried to commandeer the pack from Hudson by taking control of the shifters and when Hudson had refused to bow to his rule, Lucifer had murdered the shifters to try to get him to bend to their will. There were so many damn holes in that story, but he'd been spinning it for the last month. Hopefully, this meal would be a lot of hot air and anger.

I chewed my bottom lip and dragged in a breath, I couldn't avoid it forever. I opened the door and was still climbing out of the car when Hudson appeared at my side and offered me his hand. I took it, grateful for the support of the biggest, baddest shifter around. I was pissed at him, not stupid.

He threaded his fingers through mine and we set off toward the entrance. Laughter peeled out the door. Great, we were late. Way to make a good impression. Hudson kept propelling us forward until we emerged inside the main room. Tonight, the lights were on bright and the dance floor had been used to house the tables shoved together to make one long dining table. Around it was a crowd of ten shifters who paused their conversations and swept their gazes toward us.

The hairs on my arms lifted. Magic splashed around the room, powerful flares of invisible lightning that humans would put down to that creepy feeling that raised the hair on their napes and made them run up the stairs to the safety of their beds. A mix of male and female, their gazes ranged from curious to hostile.

Hudson guided me toward the head of the table, where two empty chairs awaited us. He pulled out the one next to Dave and I sat in it, grateful to be next to a friendly face. Dave glanced at me. Okay, so not friendly, but familiar.

Hudson sat at the head and placed the whiskey and cookie tin down on the table like he had had the forethought to bring a gift. Bah, thanks for making me look bad.

"From us," he declared. Okay, now that was some smart maneuvering. I could deny they were from us, making me look like I hadn't brought anything at all, or I could remain quiet and reinforce the fact he was parading me around like I was his mate. That status had yet to be confirmed.

Dave arched a brow but kept silent. Smart man. The female opposite me on Hudson's left I already knew. Mercy Stephenson was a tall, blonde, blue-eyed devil who had tried hooking her claws into Hudson's heart. He had made it clear that he was not interested and she persisted like dog shit inside the grips of sneakers. No amount of washing could get rid of the smell, but it would eventually fall away the more you trod it into the ground. Mercy leaned forward and I was in momentary fear of her boobs making an appearance on the table. She'd clearly forgotten a bra this evening, because there was no way she could be wearing one under the tiny scraps of black material covering her nipples. I knew she was an alpha, but I hadn't taken her for one of the pack leaders. I wondered if she was always at these weekly meetings or if this was a special occasion where she came to flaunt her familiarity with Hudson in my face, like those boobs.

"Good to finally see you here, Cora," she breathed. Her voice was a tinkling bell in the air that made me want to punch her in her pert little nose. So she has been here every week. I glanced at Hudson, would it have killed him to let me know? Indigo chose that moment to raise her head and peer at the bitch across from me.

*"Can I eat her?"* Indigo asked in my mind. Mercy jerked back in her seat, and her fingers made a hasty retreat from their path to Hudson's arm. They couldn't hear Indigo, but another animal instinctively knew when a bigger beast was in their midst.

*"No. Not yet anyway."*

My beast existed in an uneasy alliance inside me. For much of my life, I had hid the separate soul-sucking being, wrapping her up in chains and protection spells to prevent her from appearing. But since the showdown with my father, she'd broken free and now there was no putting her back in her cage. She'd claimed Hudson's animal, Keverin, as a mate, and as she explained to me on a regular basis, they were waiting for us idiots to catch up to the inevitable. A prehistoric saber-toothed tiger and the daughter of death? What could possibly go wrong?

Mercy blinked and a dash of color pinked her cheeks. If anything, the blush made her even prettier. A strong hand wrapped around my knee under the table, and I glanced at Hudson, who gave me an amused smirk. Indigo settled but didn't slumber, she thought she was being challenged for her mate and would answer the call in a swift and bloody manner that wouldn't endear the pack to me.

Another male stood, stationed in the middle of the table. "Miss Roberts, we have been eagerly awaiting your attendance at our weekly meals so that we may welcome you into the pack."

My gaze narrowed. This felt like an ambush, not a meal. Hudson opened his mouth, no doubt to inform me who was addressing me. "Good evening, Gordon. How is your youngest, Hatti? Has her broken arm mended okay?"

Hudson's mouth snapped closed. I still held some secrets it seemed. Some of which included treating the pack's ailments when their resident doctor was too busy or needed more specialized equipment. I glanced at Norbert, my fellow medical professional. He'd patched me up a time or two.

"She is recovered, thank you, Cora," Gordon muttered before sitting in his chair. I was not going to be bullied by a bunch of hot air blowing shifters.

"I've not had the pleasure of meeting you," an older woman said, leaning around Gordon from the other side. "I'm Keira."

"Benedict's wife and co-alpha of the cats," I stated with a nod. The rest of the table introduced themselves, a little taken aback at my knowledge of their identities. I hadn't been raised by just anyone; Eloise Roberts was the elemental in charge. She'd taught me to know both my enemy and allies alike, because you never knew when one could turn into the other. Right now, I wasn't entirely sure what the pack was to me. I was poised to become their leader's mate, but I wasn't one of them and never would be.

The door to the kitchen flung open and an army of teenage shifters appeared with plate after plate of steaming food. They placed them in a line down the center of the table and then departed, leaving us to make small talk as we passed food around and spooned it onto our plates. I'd been doing a little more in-depth research about the social customs and feeding rituals of the pack, in particular the cats, given I'd made an oopsie when I let Hudson cook for me. Norbert had been a great help when picking apart the complexities. Mercy met my eyes and picked up the empty plate from in front of Hudson. Oh I don't think so. Sneaky little wolf. A flare of possessiveness soured my stomach. I wasn't the type of woman to fight for a man. I'd made that clear to Hudson—I didn't play games. But it occurred to me then and there, that even if me and him didn't entertain the games, others would most certainly try to draw us into them. Like this wolf that needed putting in her place.

Hudson's mouth opened and I squeezed his hand on my knee in a silent plea to let me deal with this. If he kept coming to my defense, she would keep coming at me. I let her pile it with some of the sliced meat. She lifted it and I intercepted the plate before it could land back in front of him. Her fingers tightened around the edge and our gazes clashed. "Thank you for the food," I told her. In animal speak, she had tried to feed the alpha male, basically making a pass at him and suggesting I wasn't capable of feeding my mate. But by taking the plate from her, I was ensuring she knew her place was below me. The chatter died as the shifters looked on with curiosity. No one moved to intervene or help as this was a pivotal moment. We hadn't gotten to their lost loved ones yet, but if I couldn't hold my own against a she wolf flaunting herself at my mate, then I wouldn't be worth their time.

Mercy blinked. I let my magic crash against her in a wave of warning. I might not have claws, but I wasn't weak. *"I have claws,"* Indigo reminded me. *"They would shred through her heart like hot steel against butter."* Now that was a comforting thought.

She swallowed and with a nod released the plate. I placed it in front of me, swapping it out for my own plate. I then piled that one high before handing it to Hudson. His eyes were wide and he looked like he was going to wrestle me to the floor, strip me naked, and perform the adult tango. I'd declared my intentions in front of the pack's heavyweights who would disseminate it through the ranks. They were like a gossiping granny knitting group.

Hudson took the plate from my hands and with relish began to devour the food. I caught Mercy giving me the evil eye a time or two but ignored her. She'd tried to undermine me on her own terms and had lost. Perhaps she would retract her claws from Hudson now. Her gaze hardened, ugh, fat chance.

"So let's get this out there," Gordon declared as he finished the last of his food and sat back in his chair. "We lost a lot of people in this war you have going on with Lucifer."

I placed my knife and fork down, having forced down every last morsel that Mercy had put on the plate. If I hadn't finished it, the shifters would see it as an insult. My stomach felt huge.

"The battle for control of the pack took place on my premises, yes," I answered. "Perhaps because your Principal had chosen to reside on my lands?"

"Because you refuse to move to the pack house," Keira snapped. "If you hadn't been so difficult you wouldn't have left us exposed like that."

I channeled my inner Eloise Roberts and leveled her with a stare. She held her ground, but blinked several times like she was trying to break the connection. She licked her lips. Doc Norbert sighed. "Without Cora's intervention, none of us would have survived."

"And what intervention was that exactly?" the shorter guy next to Norbert asked. Jessy was the alpha of the aviation shifters. That's right, they had bird shifters. Not pretty little doves, these things were carnivorous eagles and hawks. Scary birds straight out of a Hitchcock movie. I resisted the urge to shiver.

"We've been over this, Jessy," Hudson stated blandly. "A blow by blow account given to you by myself and the doc. Are you doubting our version of events?" Hudson sipped at his water as the weight of his words descended down the table. He'd laid down the challenge, let's see if anyone was stupid enough to take him up on it.

"No, of course not Principal, it is still a little hard to come to terms with our massive losses. Forgive me, it was not a challenge, merely a quest to understand that fateful night."

"There is no understanding evil," I uttered. "True evil does not abide by the rules that the rest of us live our lives by. There is no honor, no purpose, no love, no passion. It is a useless endeavor to rationalize the things evil people do."

"Why would the Devil pick your place for such senseless endeavors?" Gordon asked.

Dave stiffened next to me, being one of the few at the table who understood most of the story. He was in on the lies we had spun to cover up my true identity and the real reason Summer Grove House had become the epicenter of supernatural chaos. The portal to Heaven had been a beacon for my uncle Lucifer to try to invade his homeland. My father arrived and snapped it closed, but not before the sacrifice of shifters which fed the magic opened a Hell hole in the middle of my lawn. The air was charged with mistrust and deceit, but they would have to call their leader a liar to air their thoughts.

"I understand your pain," Hudson said with a small snarl. Oh boy. "But you will not continue to challenge my mate on this matter. The discussion is closed."

All eyes shot to me. "You claim him as your mate?" Keira asked. They all leaned a little closer while they waited for my answer.

I knew this was coming. It was why I'd put off the dinner, I needed a little reprieve from pack politics while I got my head straight, and if truth be told, I was giving Hudson the chance to reverse his decision once again to be with me. He hadn't, but I would understand once the knowledge of who he welcomed into his bed had sunk in. I gave him too little credit, because he'd been nothing but attentive this last month. While I tried to push a wedge between us, he smashed it to pieces with acts of kindness and care.

I swallowed and glanced at Hudson. My fate was sealed, and I prayed he wouldn't hurt me again. "I do."

# CHAPTER THREE

*Kissing me until I comply is a solid strategy.*

The shock splashed through the shifters like they'd been electrocuted. I don't know why it was such a surprise—their Principal had been relentless in his pursuit of me for months. Moving into my rented stables, then when it had been leveled flat by my father and his little display of power, Hudson had rented a room in my bed and breakfast claiming his *mate* lived with him. The more I pushed him away, the closer he came. Honestly, I couldn't see myself with anyone but him, but my heart had a long memory.

"Christmas is an excellent time for a mating ceremony," Keira said with a nod. "We can make it work."

I blinked. "What? No, no mating ceremony."

"The pack will never accept her," Mercy sneered.

"The pack will do as they're damn well told," Hudson snapped. "And you will cease this smear campaign against Cora immediately."

Mercy blanched and sat back, trying to make herself smaller, her gaze downcast to the floor. "Yes, Principal."

That was enough. I could fight my own battles, and being cast as the helpless damsel wasn't going to help my case. "Mercy, look at me," I demanded. Her long eyelashes fluttered up and her blue eyes brewed with a hatred reserved for the worst of enemies. "I am not your enemy. You harbor affection for the man I love, unrequited affection, and that is a pain I would not wish on anyone."

She stiffened and opened her mouth. I held my hand up. "But if you continue to try to undermine me, to play games when witnesses around the table can attest to the shifter faux pas that you continue to try to pull, then I will be forced to assert myself. Nobody wants to see that because I will always win."

She gave me a stiff nod, but I doubted it was the last of it. Mercy Stephenson wouldn't give up her desire to be Consort Royal. But for now, the gossiping powers of the pack had clearly seen I wasn't backing down.

"Are we going to discuss who she is?" Jessy asked. "Because last I checked, we don't need the granddaughter of Eloise Roberts inside our pack. I don't trust that woman, and by extension, I don't trust you." Jessy's eyes flash green.

"Don't tarnish me with the sins of my ancestors," I snap. "I am not perfect, but I do not have plans to maneuver the pack to my advantage. If anything, I think I have proven tonight that I am here for one reason and one reason alone—Hudson."

"We cannot trust an elemental," Jessy sneers.

Dave sucks in a breath and everyone stills. "I can attest that Cora's loyalty is not with her grandmother. Our Principal has chosen his mate and tonight you bore witness to her acceptance of his claim. If I hear one rumor of dissension, I will not hesitate to deal with the cause."

The pack's chief of security had spoken. I had his blessing, and they would be stupid to go against him and Hudson. The air in the room sizzled with restrained magic.

If a fight broke out now, and I had to help put these shifters in their place, it would only solidify their assertion that I was bad news for the pack.

Keira drew in a breath. "I accept the Consort Royal. The cats will not oppose the match."

Gordon leaned forward. "The Equidaes will support the Principal's choice."

"I will need to discuss this with my people," Jessy huffed.

"You do that," Hudson growled.

I kept my breathing deep and even as the shifters faced off. You could feel the tension in the air.

"Is anyone going to open those cookies?" Gordon asked, eyeing the tin. "Because this surely calls for a celebration."

Apart from his declaration, Dave had been silent this entire time. That didn't mean he wasn't paying attention, in fact, it was the complete opposite. Dave soaked in information like a dry sponge and used it later to obliterate you if needed. He reached for the tin and popped the lid. The scent of cookies floated around us and snapped the tension in the room. Dave snagged a lemon cookie for himself as Hudson opened the whiskey and poured us both a glass before sending it around the table. Cookie in one hand, whiskey in the other, the shifters raised their glasses in the air.

"To Hudson and Cora," Dave growled. "Our Principal and Consort Royal." Oh boy.

The shifters howled, whistled, and growled. Karen poked her head out from the kitchen, possibly to check that a brawl wasn't about to break out. It was a good thing she was one of the few humans to be in the know. I'm sure owning the only bar in town meant she'd seen some weird shit.

"These are good cookies," Jessy declared. "Your mate is an excellent cook."

Hudson shot me an amused look. I was a terrible cook and could not claim any responsibility for the sugary goodness. "Cora is many things," Hudson said, cutting off my protest.

The shifters munched their cookies with relish, washing them down with reasonably expensive whiskey. "Do you want the tin back?" Gordon asked, turning the decorative Hershey's chocolate tin around. "Because Martha would appreciate such a fine tin."

"Keep it," I told him as I polished off my own cookie. Maggie would be excited to know that the shifters enjoyed her cookies. Perhaps one day she would venture into the pack and bond with some of her own kind. She had been a very young eighteen when she arrived on my doorstep, terrified of the forced mating her father was dragging her toward. Hudson had outlawed arranged matings, but Maggie's father had missed the memo, at least until he'd received a personal visit from the Principal.

Now Maggie was a beautiful young woman with a bright future ahead of her, however, the lingering doubt caused her to avoid the pack. I'd only recently gotten her to stop running out of the room the second Dave or Hudson turned up. It was progress.

"Now that we have cleared the air," Jessy said, "can we move the pack meals back to the pack house?"

Keira leaned her elbows on the table and looked at Hudson and I. "I guess that depends on if the Principal and his mate are going to relocate?"

"My business requires me to be on the premises," I reasoned.

"We've not discussed this yet," Hudson added.

My head snapped to him. Um, yes, we had, and I had made it crystal clear that I was not moving from Summer Grove House. His eyes bored into mine, begging me to not argue with him in front of his pack mates. With a mental reserve I didn't realize I owned, I kept my mouth shut and let the matter hang. Hudson's gaze glinted with amusement. There was a mountain of differences between us, and while I knew I needed to meet him halfway, I would not be leaving my home. It was non-negotiable.

The shifters cleared the table in record time and exited The Pit buzzing with talks of a mating ceremony I had not agreed to. I folded myself into the Bugatti and sighed. Hudson was suspiciously silent as I drove us home while nibbling on the inside of my cheek until I tasted blood. The tension was making me jittery, but I wouldn't be breaking it any time soon. In fact, as I spun the car onto the drive, I was planning my escape. I didn't want to have the inevitable conversation or deal with the consequences of accepting Hudson's mate claim.

I swung open the door and made it inside without the Principal intervening. Perhaps he also needed time. I waved at Rebecca who was sharing a cake with a male vampire guest. My steps faltered, then I carried myself up the stairs. I wouldn't be handing out unsolicited relationship advice this evening. Nope, they were adults and they could make their own mistakes.

I didn't hear him, but I felt him. Power, masculine and absolute, radiated along my spine. I twisted the handle of the door to my room. Hudson had given me space these last weeks, not pushing, not pursuing, simply being present. He kept to his rented room on the floor below mine and checked in with me in the public areas. My reprieve, I realized, was over.

His breath stirred the hair on the nape of my neck as I stepped inside my room, the door clicking closed behind us. I pressed my lips together as I made my way to the small kitchen and opened the refrigerator.

"Drink?" I asked as I grabbed a juice box.

Silence was my answer as I grabbed another for him. I didn't even know if he liked juice boxes and we were meant to be spending our lives together. Apple or orange? These were important things I should know. I picked out one of each because I liked both, then I fiddled with the tiny straws, finally poking them inside the cartons. Nothing left to do now, unless I tried cooking something, then it would be obvious. I almost laughed, like he didn't already know I was avoiding looking at him.

"Look at me," he rumbled. My fingers tightened around the apple juice and a little squirted over my hand. Damn it. Gentle but firm hands gripped my shoulders and spun me around before I could declare I needed an hour to shower off the sticky liquid. His fingers tipped my head back so I could no longer avoid his eyes. "I know you are scared of the future, how it will look, what you may need to give up to make this work. But we are a partnership, we will both have to make some changes to find our new normal. Change isn't necessarily bad, and I would never ask you to give up anything that makes your soul sing."

My eyes fluttered closed and I sucked in a breath. "You're wrong. I'm not scared, I'm terrified."

He crowded me against the counter and picked me up, making my eyes fly open as he slid my ass onto the cool kitchen worktop so we were eye level. He took the juice boxes out of my hands and placed them in the sink before sliding between my legs and placing his hands on either side of my hips. He tilted his head and stared at me like I was the only woman on the planet. It's both intoxicating and unnerving to have someone look at you like you hold their entire world in the palm of your hands. I didn't want to be responsible for another's happiness, I was one hundred percent sure that my future would be bathed in crimson and soaked in horror. There was no happy conclusion to my life; too many people were pulling at my strings, and it would eventually tear me to pieces. I didn't want to take this magnificent man down with me.

"Whatever you are thinking right now, stop," he whispered. "You are having a silent argument with your own mind. I have no hope of trying to reason with you if you don't talk to me or share what you are feeling. I cannot help you."

"We've never even been on a date," I mumbled. I was reaching for excuses for this to not happen. They were feeble excuses, but for some inexplicable reason, it was important to point this out.

He tilted his head. "We attended the vampires' ball together."

"I came as your date, it wasn't an actual date."

"What about the blueberry pancakes?"

I blushed. "It wasn't meant to be a date."

He grinned. "It was certainly going in that direction, before all the growling and problematic shifters."

"You see, you are proving my point."

"So you want the flowers, chocolates, the romance? I can do that."

I shook my head. "It shouldn't be something I have to ask for."

He frowned. "You are being impossible. Relationships take work, communication, and trust. I can give you what you need, but you have to trust me enough to tell me."

I swallowed the lump in my throat. I was being unfair. I didn't need big romantic gestures. I only needed his arms to come home to at night. For someone to care enough to make sure I'm okay, to check in and ask how my day was and make me blueberry pancakes in the morning when I drag myself from my bed.

He was here, he showed up, he was giving all that and I was being a fool for throwing it back in his face.

My heart was ping-ponging around in my chest. One second I'd committed to him in front of his most powerful leaders, the next I was looking for a way to extricate myself from this relationship. I needed to pick a lane and stay in it. I opened my mouth and he covered it with his own, stealing my breath and the words poised on my lips. My mind went blank as a shot of need pulsed through me. After weeks of barely touching, the sensation was staggering. A shiver raced down my spine and settled low. His lips and tongue did a complete exploration of my mouth like he was trying to imprint himself into my flesh. With each sweep of his tongue, he dissolved my doubts and worries until they were dust being carried out of the open window and into the night air. He replaced them with hopes and wishes. He wrapped me in his arms and drew me close. My body went lax and I sunk against him.

"You've done this alone for long enough," he said against my ear before leaning back. "It's time to let me in and allow me to help you. Together we are stronger. If you need to cry, I will hold you, if you need to scream, then you can do it in my arms. Your enemies become my enemies and we will wage war on them together. If Indigo needs a soul, we will find a suitable source. Starting now, it's no longer you, alone against the world. I will be at your side."

"I don't want you to get hurt," I whispered my greatest fear. "I'd never forgive myself."

He leaned back and his lips kicked up to the side. "I'm stronger than I look. You are offending Keverin by telling him he can't handle it."

My mouth popped open and he covered my concerns with more kisses. He buried his hands in my hair and tugged a little, emphasizing his need. "Damn, I missed this mouth," he groaned. "I know what it cost you to accept that you are my mate tonight, but I have never been happier. You are it for me, Cora. This isn't a tumble in the sheets, or the thrill of the chase. Have I not proved that to you these last weeks?"

Yes, he had. Even predators who liked the chase would have given up by now, and we'd already had a tumble in the sheets, so it wasn't that that kept him interested. No, for some unfathomable reason, Hudson Abbot, the Terror of Tennessee, The Principal, had chosen me to become his mate. He had accepted my darkness and even with death as my constant companion, it didn't scare him. But it should.

# Chapter Four

*Hormonal teenagers should not be mistaken for*

*possessed ones.*

I'd set two broken limbs, treated one suspicious rash, and was readying myself for my final appointment before lunch. Last night, Hudson had retreated to his own room after landing me with the 'come hell or high water we are in this together' speech. I was in love with him. That was undisputed, but I worried about the impact of my political ties. Some of the alphas had pledged their loyalty to us as a mated pair, but there were others—like Jessy—who we needed to get on board to make this work.

Rebecca opened the door to my office and I stood from behind my desk to greet a curvy woman and a tiny wide-eyed girl. I'd place her under ten, except the devious glint in her gaze suggested she'd hit puberty. The girl was dressed in a cornflower blue dress that fell to her knees, while the woman was in a simple, yet expensive, slacks and blouse. The jacket she wore was fitted without drawing attention to her body. They had matching honey blonde hair and big brown eyes. The woman wore hers in elegant waves, while the girl had a long braid that fell over her shoulder, but there was no doubting what they were. Vampires. I glanced at my appointment planner. Maggie had failed to mention I had a vampire client today. Normally I marked their faction next to their names so I had an idea of what I might be facing. Vampires made up less than ten percent of my client list. They tend to be more reserved and therefore less prone to accidents, which makes their afflictions more interesting.

Rebecca's gaze snagged on mine. I gave her a nod, dismissing her. She closed the door and I waved at the two high-backed chairs in front of my desk. "Please take a seat."

The woman folded herself into the chair and pointed at the one next to her. The child jumped into it and swung her legs back and forth.

"My name is Wendy," the curvy woman announced with a catwalk-worthy hair flick. "And this is my daughter, Rachel."

I scribbled down their names on my notepad and raised an expectant brow at Wendy. "How can I help you today?"

Wendy sighed and side-eyed her daughter. "She's possessed."

I blinked and my pen paused in its note taking. "Excuse me?"

"My beautiful, calm, good-natured daughter is possessed."

"And what makes you believe that?"

"She bit the family dog."

Rachel smiled, revealing sharp teeth. Oh boy.

"I see. Anything else?"

"She refuses to eat her meals and is difficult for the tutors." Wendy leaned forward and dropped her voice. "She claims to have seen the Devil and communicates with spirits.

Girls are said to be more susceptible to possession during their change from girl to womanhood."

It was unlikely Rachel was communicating with my uncle or had ever seen him. He didn't sully himself with matters on earth. As for seeing spirits, that was a very rare gift that no one wanted, it made you an outcast among your own faction. They didn't understand it, so declared it as unnatural. I clasped my hands together. "It is natural for children to test boundaries during this transition," I told her. "Along with the rush of hormones, Rachel will have been dealing with the complexities of the blood cravings." Before puberty, vampire children were fed a small amount of blood to keep them nourished, but their instincts to hunt and bite matured with the hormonal change and it could be a shock to a family. We often suppressed our own memories of puberty, the child and parents recalling very different experiences of the same time period.

Wendy leaned back and her eyes hardened. "I know my daughter, Miss Roberts, and she is not herself. I was told you could exorcise such demons from the flesh."

Damn gossiping supernaturals. You do one exorcism and suddenly everyone wants one. I could no sooner cure someone of hormones than any human doctor. Perhaps I could regulate them though. "What kind of blood are you supplementing her diet with?" I asked. The different factions offered very different experiences. If you stuck with humans, then it was solid on nutritional value. However, if they had ventured to shifter or elemental blood, which had a drugging quality to it, that was dangerous and addictive.

"We have a variety of tutors, each of whom offer a bloodletting on a monthly basis."

I glared at Wendy. "What faction?"

She swallowed as she put together what might be happening to her daughter, and it had nothing to do with the Devil. "Bryan is a shifter, he teaches her science and math. Jean is a vampire, who lectures her on languages, and Victor is an elemental, he delivers education on the world and politics."

I pinched the bridge of my nose. She hadn't only hooked her daughter on one type of supernatural blood, she'd done all three. "We only drink human at meal times," Wendy tried to reason. "My husband believes early exposure to the different types would make her less likely to become dependent on them."

"You have basically made your child a drug addict," I informed her. "You have her hooked on the equivalent of meth, ecstasy, and LSD. It is little wonder that she is acting possessed and speaking to imaginary demons? You should count yourself lucky that all she has bitten is the family dog."

Wendy paled under her layer of makeup and darted her gaze to her daughter. "What do I do? Stop her feeding?"

I shook my head and Rachel snarled in warning. "Cold turkey for one so young is dangerous. You'll need to wean her off the supernatural blood one faction at a time. I would start with the elemental. Gradually work down to half, then a quarter, then none. Then move on to the shifter, and finally the vampire."

"That will take months."

"A year," I corrected. No point in sugarcoating it.

"Is there nothing you can do?" Wendy asked. "I'm not certain we can survive a year of Rachel being like this."

Rachel twisted a lock of her hair between her fingers. The White Furry Menace slunk into the room and paused to eyeball my patient and her mother. Rachel hissed. The White Furry Menace's fur stood on end and she arched her back, growling in return. I sighed. There was something I could do, but it wasn't advisable, and it wasn't pleasant.

"You are holding back," Wendy observed. "There is something you can do for us. For my daughter."

I leveled her with my hard assed Roberts' stare. "Rachel has approximately three liters of blood in her body. In order to purge her of the effects of the supernatural blood she has ingested she would need a complete transfusion of human blood."

"Easily done," Wendy snapped, jumping on the fix she believed was easy.

"Twelve times," I finished. "Over a one month period."

Wendy's eyes glazed over as she did the math. That's right, I would need thirty-six liters of human blood. "And if I could provide the blood you can do the procedure?"

I sucked in a sharp breath. I didn't want to focus on where she would be getting that amount of blood from when there was a national shortage in the hospitals. "I can complete the transfusions." Wendy's eyes lit up and she leaned toward me. I held up my hand. "The aim of the process is to tear the magic she's ingested from the supernatural blood from her bones. It will be painful. She will scream, she will fight, and between transfusions she will waver close to death as her body fights to keep the magic and power it has become accustomed to.

"You have made your daughter an addict, Wendy. The road to recovery is difficult no matter the route you take, but the slow method is safer."

Wendy blinked. "Are you sure she isn't possessed?"

I resisted the urge to roll my eyes as I yanked open my desk drawer and grabbed a small glass vial filled with clear liquid. I uncapped it and threw it on Rachel's face. She blinked. "Definitely not possessed," I declared.

"What was that?" Wendy screeched.

"Holy water."

I placed the now empty vial onto my desk and made a quick note on my pad to refill it later. You never knew when it would come in handy. Harry floated through the ceiling, sort of like a weird descending angel. He's been experimenting with his entrances lately. The floating up through the floor was a classic. "Pineapples, Miss Roberts," he exclaimed, pulling on his tie like he meant business.

I blinked. The last time he'd declared a pineapple situation was the explosion of shifters in my house that led to a Hell mouth opening on my lawn. I hoped it wasn't that bad. Maybe we needed a pineapple rating? Ranging from one for *danger is lurking in the house,* to five, *everyone is about to die.*

Rachel turned her head toward Harry and scanned him up and down. "There's one here right now," Rachel said. "I can sense them."

Oh, okay, color me surprised, she was a sensitive. Perhaps she couldn't fully see Harry or hear him.

Harry froze and eyeballed the tiny teenager. "Can she see me?"

Rachel tilted her head. "He's wearing a suit and looks worried."

Wendy reached out and gripped her daughter's hand. "I'm sorry, we will fix this. Safely. I will be with you every step of the way." Good, she'd taken the safer, albeit more difficult, route. There was hope for Rachel yet. "And before you know it, those demons and spirits will be something in the past."

I rubbed my temple. This was now a delicate matter. I'd somehow backed myself into a corner accusing Rachel of being an addict—which I believed was also in play—but how to tell her mother that she could also see ghosts? Ugh.

"I would like to see you for a monitoring visit each month," I told Wendy.

She nodded. "Of course, Miss Roberts, we will be back next month." She gripped Rachel's arm and urged her up. Rachel stepped around Harry, confirming she knew exactly where he hovered. I would break the news of their darling daughter's gift to them in the coming months. I had to get them on the withdrawal program first.

I wrote a quick script out for some meds which would help with the tremors and handed it to Wendy. "For when the night sweats and shakes get too bad."

Wendy folded it into her brown leather handbag and ushered Rachel out of the room. I turn to Harry. "What's wrong?"

He swallowed. "There's someone here to see you."

I arched a brow and leaned against my desk. "That's hardly a pineapple situation. Perhaps we need to go over the guidelines."

Harry shook his head. "There's an issue with this visitor."

Oh no, please don't tell me my grandmother had arrived for an impromptu visit. But my wards hadn't clanged in my mind in warning, and my grandmother's power packed a punch. I would have known.

"What's the issue?" I asked.

Another male ghost with bloodshot eyes and scraggly brown hair, floated through the door, somehow stumbling over nothing. Impressive, when you could literally pass through anything.

"The issue, Miss Roberts, is he's dead."

# Chapter Five

*When everyone close to you has a pre packed bag, what does it say about you?*

It had been weeks since I'd seen another ghost that wasn't Harry. It wasn't that people weren't dying, because that would be a naive belief. It was that I didn't have a beacon of heavenly light drawing the deceased to my premises. I'd also stashed the soul stone which held some power over the dead in the Roberts' family vaults. Which meant the only way the dead would find me is if someone directed them to me.

I folded my arms and leaned against my desk. "Who are you?" I asked.

The guy ran his hands through his hair. The strands didn't move when his fingers disappeared inside his head, and I resisted the urge to grimace as he all but stroked his phantom brain. "My name is—" He shook his head like he could shake loose the information. He was most definitely recently departed. Sometimes they were a little confused at first, clarity came with time and acceptance. Occasionally they failed to understand that they were even dead.

Harry floated closer to me, a look of mistrust plastered on his face. "It's okay," I said to the mystery ghost. "Can you tell me how you got here? Or who sent you?"

The guy's eyes snapped to mine. "I was sent by a man with power." Okay, that hardly narrowed it down. Every second person in this town had some kind of power.

"Are you from White Castle?"

His brows furrowed and he lurched forward, his hands passing through my face as he tried to clasp my cheeks. I sighed. The sensation wasn't particularly pleasant. There was a reason people attributed random cold spots to ghosts. Spirits were here but existed in an alternate frequency to us.

In an attempt to warn us that something otherworldly was nearby, our bodies registered the changes in temperature which lifted the hairs on your arms.

"I don't think so," the guy answered. "No, not White Castle, that's where I've been sent."

"Try to concentrate on one thing at a time, it will help with the confusion."

"I don't trust him," Harry stated.

"If he meant me harm, he would have never gotten through the wards."

"Just because he isn't having murderous thoughts, doesn't mean he isn't dangerous."

I shrugged. "True, but for a ghost struggling to remember his own name, I'm feeling pretty safe right now."

"No one is safe," the mysterious guy whispered.

Wonderful, we had a fatalist in our midst. I'm not sure I had the mental fortitude to deal with him right now. "Focus. What is your name?" I tried again. If I could find out his name, I could use the wonder that is the internet to search for his location and cause of death. Ghosts didn't turn up at my house out of the blue, he'd been sent here for a reason and I needed to ferret out why.

A fierce frown appeared on his face and then his eyes lit up. Here we go. "My name is Caleb Duckstein."

"Hi Caleb, I'm Cora and this is my friend, Harry."

Caleb glanced at Harry. "Are you like me?"

"Dead? Very much so."

"I'm dead?"

Why me? "Yes, you are dead, Caleb Duckstein, and we need to figure out why you were sent to me."

We didn't have time to deal with a deceased freak out, I needed to move this along. Duckstein was an unusual name—so unusual, it should make the search for him pretty easy. I sat in my office chair and flipped open my laptop. It whirred and beeped. I needed to update this ancient piece of equipment, I'm pretty sure laptops don't beep anymore.

Harry and Caleb hovered at my back, their collective spiritual energy making my skin zing with electricity. I typed Caleb's name into the search bar and found him on the second hit. A photo of a younger Caleb declared him as the school's star quarterback. He was bright-eyed and bronzed, a far cry from his current state. That was four years ago. I clicked the photo and noted the school, then searched for it.

"Looks like you are from Peach Tree, a small town located a few hundred miles west of here."

"That's right, Peach Tree," Caleb agreed.

I clicked on a few more news links but couldn't find anything about his death. It should at least be in the obituaries unless it was recent. Small towns like Peach Tree reported on everything because there was little else to talk about. Which meant he died in the last day or so.

I spun in my chair to face him. "So why have you been sent to me?"

His eyes suddenly focused, lighting with clarity, and I knew as sure as the sun would rise tomorrow that I would not like his answer.

"The man sent me because they're dead," he said.

"We already know you are dead," Harry stated.

"Who's dead?" I asked.

Caleb's eyes met mine. "Everyone. Everyone in Peach Tree is dead."

A shiver ran down my spine. Perhaps I should play the lottery today given my ability to predict the future?

"And you were sent by a mysterious man to inform me of this? Do you know who he was?"

"No, I'd never seen him before, but he guided me here."

I sighed. I guess I was going to Peach Tree. I snapped my laptop shut and placed it inside my desk drawer before stalking through to my lab. I grabbed my emergency black bag containing a variety of potions, a change of clothing, and items that one might need when venturing off to view dead bodies and unknown crazy situations. I'd put it together recently, due to the fact my life seemed to regularly involve solving crime.

I trotted up the stairs and nearly ran straight into Dave who was hovering at the doorway like a creeper. I arched a brow as I grabbed my car keys from behind the desk and smiled at Maggie. She handed me today's mail.

I shuffled through the white envelopes. Bill, bill, insurance. A small black card with a single vertical gold line decorating the left side stood out among the demands. I flipped it over. The words 'You are invited' sat in elegant script, the letters shining like molten gold.

"Who delivered this?" I asked Maggie.

She tilted her head. "The mailman."

Ugh, help me now with these teenagers. "It doesn't have an address."

"Maybe it's one of those mass mail drops that everyone gets?"

I studied the card. "That would be logical if it told us what I was being invited to and didn't have a faint trace of magic on it."

Maggie plucked the card out of my fingers and glared at it like she could force it to reveal its secrets. Nothing happened. Perhaps she needed to reevaluate her glowering skills. "Put it downstairs on my desk," I instructed. I didn't think the small bit of magic on the card was dangerous, but until I understood what it was, I wouldn't take any chances. Fortune might favor the brave, but life favored the cautious. "I'll most likely be gone at least a day," I told her. "You'll need to get some more bread and coffee from the store. Get Rebecca to mind the desk while you are out. The Richards couple extended their stay by two days. They've already paid, but please ensure you change their towels today and give their room a quick clean."

Maggie nodded and jotted down my instructions. "Got it. What should I tell The Principal?"

I glanced over my shoulder at Dave. Ugh, just my luck that the pack's chief busybody was lurking when I needed to escape. "Hudson isn't here?" I checked.

Maggie tapped her pen on the pad. "No, he left an hour ago, pack business. But he left him behind." She nodded at Dave. Could my day get any worse?

Sebastian threw open the front door. My vampire best friend was here, oh goodie. Now it was a party. He eyed the duffle bag in my hand and raised a brow. "Going somewhere?"

Since when did I need to announce what I was doing and where I was going? Nobody owned me. Wait, everyone owned me. My grandmother was in the background trying to pull my strings, my father had declared me the go-between for Heaven and the prevention of an all-out war with humans, and Hudson had claimed me as his mate in front of the pack. Everyone owned me.

"Road trip, I need to visit a town called Peach Tree."

"I'll get my bag," he said as he swiveled on his heel and waltzed out of the house. Apparently my vampire friend also had a go bag, it was a sign of the times.

"Tell Hudson to call me when he gets a moment," I told Dave. He folded his arms and stepped in front of the door, blocking my exit. I raised my eyebrow and leveled him with a stare that would make my grandmother proud. "Move out of my way."

He looked back at me unimpressed and undeterred. I should know better than to try this on the guy whose nickname was Dangerous Dave. "Are you seriously holding me hostage in my own home? You do not want to test me, Dave."

His jaw ticked. Oh, he didn't like it pointed out how ludicrous his actions were. *Suck it up, buttercup, because I wasn't sugarcoating it.* "Why are you going to Peach Tree?" he growled.

I jerked my head at the door, not wanting the other supernaturals to overhear my tale from the departed. Dave sighed and swung it open. I stepped through and trotted down the steps onto my driveway. Sebastian was heading toward us with an almost identical duffle bag. Dave scowled at the vampire.

"There's a spirit here," I whispered.

Dave tensed and looked around, his wide gaze passing right over Caleb and Harry on his left. I resisted the urge to roll my eyes. He's never been able to see ghosts, why would he think that had suddenly changed?

"What does it want?" Dave snarled low. He was always snarling, this was a little less than a growl.

"He wants me to go to Peach Tree because he believes everyone is dead."

Dave jerked back. "Everyone?"

I nodded as Sebastian sidled up to me and wrapped his arm around my shoulders. Ugh, save me now, he was determined to wind Dave up. "Don't fret, wolf, I will keep her safe."

My eyes fluttered closed. Idiot vampire. "Hudson can't accompany you, so I will."

Great going, Sebastian. "I will be fine, plus there's no room in my car."

"We will take my car," Dave said. He snatched my car keys out of my hand and turned on his heel before stalking to his Escalade.

"We might be gone for longer than a day and I don't have time for you to stop off and pack your underwear and toothbrush."

He grinned at me as he opened the driver's door. "I have a bag in the car already."

My shoulders slumped as Sebastian took my duffle bag and threw it into the back seat along with his own before sliding in beside them.

What did it say about us that we all had ready bags? I climbed into the passenger seat and slammed the door closed before clipping my seat belt on. I glanced over my shoulder, finding Harry in the middle of the back seat and Caleb next to him. Two ghosts, one shifter, a vampire, and an elemental in a car. What could possibly go wrong? Everything. Everything *could* go wrong. The trouble is, *could* seemed to be in my future more often than not and now I had witnesses to my demise. Lucky me.

# Chapter Six

*What I would give to have a simple life filled with the simple pleasures of cookies and snuggles.*

I'd known Dave for years, but in all of that time, he'd never insisted on accompanying me anywhere.

"Why were you at my house?" I asked him after I'd ruminated for over an hour in silence.

Dave side-eyed me for a second before switching his attention back to the road. That look said a million things. "Because Hudson couldn't be," he answered.

That's what I thought. "He doesn't trust me."

"He trusts you. It's everyone else he doesn't trust."

"Oh shit," Sebastian muttered from the backseat.

"The Principal has misjudged this particular move," Harry agreed.

"Who?" Caleb asked.

I shook my head. I really didn't need the peanut gallery weighing in on my relationship.

"You are the Consort Royal," Dave said by way of explanation. "You agreed to the mating last night and by now the entire pack will know of the happy news." His tone implied the news was anything but happy.

"You agreed to what?" Sebastian asked.

"This is most certainly news we should have all been aware of," Harry said. Since when did I need to publicize my relationship status? This isn't a democracy. I ignored my friends and focused on Dave.

"How does that translate to me needing a babysitter?"

"Not babysitting, protection."

My hands ball into fists. Hudson had seen what I could do. There wasn't any need for protection. Unless it wasn't protection for me, but against me. "Am I under threat from the pack?" I checked.

"News of your nuptials has caused a ripple of uncertainty in the pack. There are purists among us that don't believe he should be mating outside of the pack."

I hadn't agreed to marry Hudson, but mating was considered a lifetime deal. If one of the mates died, the other would not take a new mate. "How did Hudson respond to that?"

Dave smiled. It wasn't a pleasant one, and if I had the room, I'd have taken a step back. "He explained that his choice of mate wasn't any of their business and they were welcome to take their leave if they no longer desired to be part of the pack that he had brought together."

I blinked. He'd basically told them to suck it up or become loners. Wow. I unclenched my fists and forced my hands to relax while rolling my shoulders. My gaze darted over my shoulder to Sebastian, and he met my stare with a raised brow. That's right, I hadn't explained to my best friend that I'd agreed to Hudson's claim. If the pack was pushing back now, they had no clue who their Principal had let into their midst and who she brought with her. But Hudson knew, and that was the important thing.

"That explains the protection detail," I muttered.

"You need to call him," Dave instructed. "He plans to return to your house later today and will not be too happy that we've disappeared."

I opened my mouth to decline. Being part of a pair was going to take some getting used to. Dave beat me to it and instructed his fancy ass car to call 'The Principal'. The phone rang once, twice, three times from the car speakers and I had high hopes I was going to escape with a hasty voicemail. Reality struck true and hard once again.

"What's wrong?" Hudson answered.

"Who answers the phone like that?" I wondered.

"Cora? Why do you have Dave's phone?"

"Well, you left Dave protecting me—and we will be discussing personal boundaries later—but right now, I'm on my way to Peach Tree because Caleb, a spirit, turned up and informed me that everyone is dead."

The silence that coated the car was thick with tension. Saying it out loud seemed to make my actions more ridiculous. "Just to be clear," Hudson drawled. "A dead guy told you to go to his town where he claims everyone is dead and you didn't question it?"

"He's dead, it's not like he's lying about that fact. It's pretty hard to fake."

"Who sent him? How did he find you?"

I glanced at Caleb and sighed. "He's not got clarity yet. He's clear a man sent him, but he's a little lost on the details."

Dave smirked and I rolled my eyes. I didn't have to explain to anyone where I was going or why.

"Have you considered this could be a trap?" Hudson asked.

"By whom and why?"

"There are very few people who know what you can do."

A shiver worked its way down my spine as I considered what he was saying. Four people knew, and two of those people were sitting in this car, and one was on the phone. Rebecca was the other. I trusted each and every one of them. Wait. No, there were more, except they didn't reside on Earth. My father and his cadre of angels knew, but also my uncle and his horde of demons in Hell. That was concerning.

"That's true, but I can't ignore the fact a ghost turned up and declared that everyone was dead."

"Everyone," Caleb agreed.

"Everyone as in his family?" Hudson asked. "Surely that is a case for the local law enforcement?"

"Everyone is dead," Caleb reminded me.

Harry frowned at Caleb and then shrugged his shoulders as his stare turned toward me.

"Yeah, the *everyone* is yet to be defined. Someone sent him my way for a reason. If it's a trap, I have a Dave and a Vampire Prince with me. Plus, I'm hardly defenseless."

A heavy pause came from the speaker. I glanced at the screen—nope, we were still connected. "Sebastian is there?" Hudson growled.

Ugh. Dave's smile widened like he was enjoying my pain. "He's my best friend."

"So you called him before me?"

I squeezed my eyes closed and rubbed my throbbing left temple. I was starting to get a headache. "No, I didn't call him at all. He was already there."

"I was reminding Cora of our prior engagement," Sebastian said. His tone was neutral but it was still delivered with the tact of an atomic bomb. Thank you, Sebastian.

"I see," Hudson said in an equally neutral yet scary tone. If they were in the same space, Hudson's hackles would be up and Sebastian would be baring his pointy teeth. This is my life. Supernatural passive aggression at its finest.

"There's nothing you need to worry about, Principal," Sebastian said. "And your attack dog is here. Unless you don't trust your mate?"

Wow, way to twist the narrative. I was outmatched by these political superpowers. I wanted to help the dead, eat cookies, and snuggle with my mate. I was a simple woman.

"I trust my mate, it is you I don't trust. Try not to trip and give her your blood."

The pounding in my temples trebled in intensity. "Stop, both of you. Just stop. I will call you with an update once we arrive at Peach Tree and understand better what is happening."

"Do that. Are you driving straight through or stopping to rest?"

I glanced at Dave who gave a stiff nod. Right, the man of many words. "Straight through, we can take shifts if need be."

"Cora?" Hudson adds before I can press the red end call button on the screen.

"Yes?"

"If you need to protect yourself, you let her out."

"Will do." My voice raised an octave, making me clench my teeth.

"Just so we are clear, if the bloodsucker feeds you his blood, I will kill him, consequences be damned."

"Glad we cleared that up," Sebastian grumbled as the call was cut off.

"You could have helped," I pointed out to Dave.

He grinned like he'd enjoyed my squirming far too much. Lord help me, I was surrounded by difficult males who delighted in winding each other up.

We drove through the day, stopping for snacks and fast food that made Dave grumble about the quality of the burgers. Apparently 100% beef didn't mean 100% quality beef, and his explanation ruined perfectly good burgers for me for life. Sebastian happily devoured mine.

According to Wikipedia, Peach Tree had an aging population of around four hundred people, with one school which catered from kindergarten through twelfth grade. It had a library, a store, two diners, a police station, doctor's office, and one church which the majority of the townsfolk flocked to every Sunday morning. Those not retired were employed by local farms or traveled to bigger towns.

As the name suggested, the streets were lined with peach trees and every garden had one. I bet they made a good cobbler here. Dave couldn't ruin that for me. Our car rolled down the main street, and the sun was beginning to dip into the horizon, casting an array of pinks, lilacs, and oranges that backlit the fluffy clouds beginning to roll in with the dusk. I twisted to ask Caleb where we should go first. But he'd disappeared.

Harry shrugged like he had no clue where his spirit companion had gone.

"Where to?" Dave asked.

Great, now I had to admit that I had lost Caleb. "Police station?"

"Is your ghost not clear?"

"My ghost has disappeared."

"That's not suspicious at all," Dave drawled as our car made a slow trek through the town. Scattered between the few businesses there were pretty three story townhouses.

I wound my window down and sniffed the air. "You feel that?" I asked.

Dave frowned and tilted his head. "I feel nothing."

"Exactly," I whispered. "Pull over."

Dave angled the car to the side of the road and put the brake on. I unclipped my belt and jumped out of the car.

I glanced up and down the street, eyeballing the dark windows in the houses and the empty street.

Dave and Sebastian joined me on the sidewalk. "I don't get it," Sebastian said as he shoved his hands in his trouser pockets. Dave sniffed the air, his nostrils flaring like he could scent any nefarious creatures. If anyone could, it would be him.

"Where is everyone? There are no cars, no lights, no sounds, nothing."

Sebastian frowned and Dave scanned the street. A cold hand of warning slid down my spine and settled like a lead weight in my gut.

Caleb reappeared before me. "Like I said, everyone is dead."

# Chapter Seven

*I am not broke.*

Death not only had a smell, it had a feeling. Ask anyone who has ever visited a relative in the funeral home. There was an eerie sensation that prickled over your flesh and stirred an ancient instinct held deep within you. Death. Danger. Run.

Unless you were the literal daughter of death, then that awareness stalked your every waking moment and you learned to get comfortable with it. I knew death wasn't an end destination but an inevitable stopping point on your journey to the next life, whatever that might hold. Nobody was infallible, but how you lived your life, your intentions, your actions—that is what colored your soul and determined whether you went up or down.

All living beings held magic. Some more than others. The supernatural factions held more than humans, and humans held more than the animal kingdom. That magic was left behind after death occurred, you didn't need that currency in Heaven or Hell. It would eventually be returned to the Earth, but until the funeral rites had been performed and the body laid into the ground, whether that be as scattered ashes or full body burial, the magic clung to the air.

Magic saturated the air in Peach Tree. Unless a god had died here recently, a lot of death had occurred all at once and none of those victims were buried.

"Where is everyone?" I asked Caleb.

Caleb frowned and looked up and down the street. He was still confused. When death happened suddenly and unexpectedly, the soul struggled to catch up to what had happened to them. Caleb knew he was dead, so that was a step in the right direction and he remembered he had a mission to find me. Caleb looked up and down the empty street as Harry came to float next to him. Caleb shook his head. "There's a river of blood and an ocean of pain, a mountain of torment and a world of suffering awaiting you."

Then he disappeared, leaving me with that ominous statement. I sighed. Caleb clearly favored the dramatic but without specifics, I couldn't find it in me to be worried.

"He's a rather unhelpful fellow," Harry commented.

I pointed toward a crossroads about two hundred feet in the distance. "Let's head to the town center and then we can split up and try to find someone who knows what is happening here."

Dave's car beeped, engaging the locks. A little pointless given that I suspected when Caleb said they were all dead, he meant it in a literal sense. But what could kill an entire town? A gas leak? It seemed unlikely that everyone would be in the same place though. Rounding up an entire town's population, even one as small as this, was impressive.

Our trio trudged down the sidewalk with Harry floating silently behind us. The crossroads were defined by a café with overflowing flowery window boxes. Peachy Corner had a slate sign outside which boasted the best peach cobbler in the country. Across from that was a red brick building with a set of stone steps and arches which declared it as the library.

On the northern side was a smaller building with a big heavy wooden door. Dr. Lauren Forde was etched into a shiny gold rectangular metal plate on the wall. One doctor for the whole of the town? She must be a superwoman. Or perhaps not, if what Caleb said was true and everyone is indeed dead.

A breeze rustled the leafy peach trees. Dave lifted his head and his nostrils flared. His eyes narrowed down the western street. "Do you smell that?" he asked.

Honeysuckle, sweet and heavy, drifted like a spell on the wind. It was heady and intoxicating and so very wrong. A long ago memory surfaced of wandering the greenhouses kept by The Order's herbal and potion masters. "I think I know what it is." I prayed I was wrong, but as the universe kept proving, worse case scenarios were my life.

Sebastian lifted his head and stared down the street in the direction of the heavy scent. "There's something wrong with the smell. It's laced with—"

"Death," I finished for him, my feet already scurrying along the sidewalk like a predator scenting her next meal. Indigo raised her head, her senses locking onto the foul unnatural stench. She snarled her disgust. Great, the soul hungry daughter of death was turning her nose up at whatever awaited us. This should be fun. Dave and Sebastian flanked my sides as we stalked down the shadowy, quiet street while Harry floated behind us. We passed empty shops, dark homes, and closed doors. I dug into my coat pocket and pulled out a set of medical gloves before snapping them on.

Sebastian raised a brow. "Are you expecting a body?"

"Well, the dead guy didn't poof out of nowhere."

We crossed a road, and the scent deepened, along with the ominous sensation that skittered over my flesh. I pulled my coat tighter around me as the chill increased with the departure of the sun.

Our footsteps stalled on the edge of a neatly manicured lawn. A sign hammered into the lawn glowed with the words *'I will give you the keys to the kingdom of heaven'*. There were small piles of fresh soil around the wooden posts. It was newly erected and the words seemed familiar. I knew it was a bible reference, but something stirred in a memory about this specific quote.

"No way," Sebastian muttered. "If this is some Kool-Aid kind of situation, we need to let the authorities deal with it."

"Don't be a baby," I muttered as I took the first step toward the white building. A wooden cross was nailed above the closed door bearing a plaque which read, 'The church of the Peach Tree welcomes all.'

"How inclusive," Dave muttered. The pressure of the expelled magic was suffocating and we weren't even in the building. Dave stepped in front of me and pushed open the door. "Stay behind me," he instructed. Harry floated in ahead of Dave, uncaring that the pack's head of security had issued a mandate.

My head tipped back and I groaned. This would not do. I couldn't have a shifter getting in my way every time they suspected danger. I couldn't function like this. Hudson and I needed to set some ground rules.

The air was so still as we stepped into the church, the specks of dust were highlighted by the hundreds of candles that littered the floor, making them glitter as if they were suspended in time. The patrons were statues facing the pulpit. All we could see was the back of their heads, like they were waiting for the pastor to make his entrance. I froze and Sebastian swore a blue streak that his mother would have clipped him around his head for while promising to wash his dirty mouth out with soap. However, given the spectacle we were facing, she may have forgiven him. The pastor was kneeling on the floor, his hands together and raised in a sign of prayer. Perhaps his maker had taken pity on him before he lost his life.

I tried to make sense of the unsettling scene before us. Dave took a step down the center aisle and I followed, glancing at the townsfolk propped up in the pews.

"This is some next level shit," Sebastian said from behind me. I paused and leaned toward a middle-aged bald man sporting pale blue corduroy pants and a crisp white shirt. There was nothing amiss except his eyes and his heartbeat. He had neither.

Two burned-out sockets stood in place of the eyes he had once seen the world through. I gazed down the row, noting that identical black, ashen holes were sunk into each person's face. I spun. Every single person here had lost their eyes. No, not lost, they'd been burned from their skulls.

"This is disturbing," Harry agreed as he glided around the room looking at the people.

"I guess the cause of death is pretty obvious," Sebastian stated.

My gloved fingers carefully probed the cold man's face. He was as stiff as a board. "Is it?" I asked.

"They are missing their eyes."

"True, but there's no blood," I mumbled. "The eye removal was done post mortem and they've been dead long enough for rigor mortis to set in, but not long enough for it to subside—so less than two days." What I was super curious about was how they were all still upright, as if someone had held them that way until rigor mortis had frozen them in this position.

I stepped back and spun in a circle. The people here were all adults, at a guess, nobody below the age of twenty years. This was certainly not the entire town, which begged the question—where the hell was everyone else?

Dave paused in front of the pastor, his big body hiding the kneeling leader. "Cora, what do you make of this?" he asked. I stalked toward the raised area and side stepped Dave to view the pastor. "That's weird, right?"

I tilted my head. "Someone arranged him like this, waited for his body to lock into a position of prayer, which would take hours. Weird seems to be our motto."

"I thought our motto was fangs before claws?" Sebastian muttered.

Dave raised a brow at him. If Sebastian thought he was going to get a rise out of the pack's head of security, he hadn't been paying attention.

"I wasn't referring to the pastor. Look at the book open at his knees."

"The Bible is hardly a weird thing for a pastor," Sebastian scoffed.

I stepped onto the raised area and looked over the shoulder of the pastor so I could view the open book in front of him. My gaze scanned the text, it was Latin. I was no expert, but I was one hundred percent sure this was no Bible. The odd word or two stood out to me—'diaboli', meaning devil. Not unusual in itself, there were plenty of references to the Devil in the Bible. But teamed with the words 'rex' and 'salvator', meaning King and Savior, this was most likely some kind of grimoire which worshiped the darker side of the afterlife. What had the little town of Peach Tree gotten itself into?

"Devil worshiping?" Dave asked. Clearly, he too had a little Latin knowledge.

"It appears that way."

"What's that?" Sebastian asked, pointing at a little symbol at the bottom of the page. I squinted at the loops and curves. A circle in the center with another butted against it, but not interlocking. To the right was a curve, but broken with a straight line, like the letter G.

I blinked and my heart sank as I gazed out at the parishioners. The words on the sign outside the church suddenly made sense. "I think it's the letters C O G."

"Cog?" Dave asked.

"No, not cog the word. It's an acronym."

"For what?"

"The Children of God."

"The sex cult?" Sebastian muttered.

"Seems like they've branched out into Satanism," Dave said.

"No, I don't believe so. This is a sloppy cover up for something much more sinister."

"Like what?"

"These people were dead long before their eyes were removed, and the sign outside was freshly erected. This book, while creepy, I don't believe holds any actual power to call the Devil."

"You'd know," Dave mumbled.

"What was that?" I snapped. "Speak clearer if you are going to start pointing fingers."

"I said you would know what has the power to call the Devil."

Sebastian looked between the two of us. "What is he talking about?"

I rolled my eyes. "Nothing, Dave's being a bigot. All elementals are evil—even the one his boss is engaged to."

"If I believed you were evil, I would have taken you out already."

Indigo itched against my skin, she was burning to get out and show Dave exactly how outmatched he was. "Try it," I said with a smile that was a little of me and a lot of the psycho bitch I housed inside me. Dave froze, a predator weighing up the strength of another. If he was in animal form, his teeth would be bared and his hackles would be raised. I didn't want a fight, but I wasn't going to back down and act the meek little elemental.

Dave inclined his head. It was a small victory, and I'm sure he had weighed up the fallout from Hudson should he try anything with his mate.

"So this is a setup?" Sebastian checked.

I shook my head. "No, not a setup, a cover up. Whatever went down here was hastily twisted into a cult-lead activity, but it is sloppy work. The Children of God no longer exist, they are now called The Family. As far as I know, they aren't into Devil worship and never have been."

"Why take their eyes?" Dave asked.

I stepped off the stage, passed in front of the victims, and sat in the front pew to the left. Underneath the stench of death and burned flesh, lingered the cloying honeysuckle scent. There were no other obvious wounds or causes of death. I snapped my glove off my hand. "Do you have the juice?" I checked with Sebastian.

He nodded once and pulled a juice box out of his pants pocket. Like a boy scout, always prepared. "Is this a good idea?" Dave asked, folding his arms. "We don't know the motivation. You haven't exactly had the best history with your gift. Blindness, psychic bombs, evil presences tracking you..."

My hand paused a few inches from the bare shoulder of a woman with ice blonde hair. She was wearing a white dress with tiny embroidered strawberries. "We can't cover up this amount of death. This will go to the human authorities because as far as I can tell, these people are all human."

I glanced over my shoulder and Dave gave a sharp nod as he unfolded his arms. "Agreed, what's your point?"

"My point is—once those authorities take control, we will have lost our window of opportunity to figure out if this is something that affects us. Caleb was sent to me for a reason. The quickest way to determine what killed them is for me to do a read."

Dave drew in a long breath. He no doubt had orders from Hudson to protect me at all costs. Hadn't the fool learned by now that I didn't need to be saved? If anything, the world needed saving from me. But that was another problem for another time. I quit stalling and grasped the cold flesh of the woman and closed my eyes while I waited for her death to speak to me. The seconds ticked by, then a minute, then two. I flicked my eyes open and gazed at the woman before switching my hand to the forehead of the squat man with a round belly next to her. Nothing.

"Maybe try your other hand?" Dave suggested.

I gritted my teeth and yanked the glove off my other hand before touching the entire row of dead parishioners. Nothing. No death echoes, no violence, no memories.

"Are you broken?" Dave asked. "Have you lost your connection with the dead?" Harry paled, clearly I had not lost my connection.

"I am not broken."

"When was the last time you did a successful read?"

"Last week, with Bernard from the west side of town. Remember, you brought him to me?"

Dave huffed an agreement as I moved down the rows and touched each and every person before glancing back at Sebastian and Dave in disbelief. "I'm broken."

# CHAPTER EIGHT

*What does it sound like when the Devil blows his*

*trumpet?*

The Children of God were now called The Family, and while they had questionable practices and beliefs, it had never been suggested that they worshiped the Devil. This was a stage set to throw the limelight on the elusive Satan-worshiping cults, and if it succeeded, it might ignite the 1980's public panic we saw surrounding the shrouded world of Satanic rituals. Last time, twelve thousand reports poured into the authorities—unsubstantiated, but also due to their volume, unmanageable. The Order had stepped in and assisted the human law enforcement with weeding out that which would take a more supernatural angle to resolve.

"This is a clumsy attempt to reject Christianity and condemn the residents of Peach Tree for Satanism?" Dave asked. We'd not yet left the church, we were checking everywhere to see what other clues the guilty had left to fool the authorities.

"Actually," I began, ducking to check under the pews. The only thing suspicious was Harry's booted feet hovering a few inches off the ground. "If you consider Satanism to be the rebellion of Christianity, to worship a being derived from Christianity, then you must accept that Christianity is, in fact, the true worldview."

"Without God, the Devil cannot exist, and without the Devil, God cannot exist?" Sebastian concluded. Not technically true, I'm sure God would go on existing if my uncle met his demise.

I stood, finding nothing amiss on the floor. "A very simplistic view, but essentially, yes. But one thing is clear, this is not Satanism and this is a small fraction of the town."

"So where is everyone else?" Dave asked.

"I'm not sure. Caleb isn't among the dead here, so they must be somewhere in town. Somewhere big enough to house a town full of bodies."

"I cannot sense him," Harry added.

I stalked to the front of the church and debated picking up the book masquerading as an evil tome that led these parishioners to doom. If we let the lie live, then we give the authorities something to focus on while we try to uncover what, or rather whom, is behind this. I spun and sighed as my two companions stared at me for direction.

"I think if we leave the staged scene, the authorities will most likely call The Order for guidance anyway."

"And then your grandmother will call you?" Dave asked. It wasn't accusing, merely curious.

*Very clever, Dave.* He was trying to figure out where I fitted into my grandmother's organization. I shook my head. "Unlikely, there are dedicated teams who work these kinds of cases. But like us, they will figure out very quickly this is a lie meant to redirect."

"How long do we have before they arrive?"

"A day, perhaps two. Law enforcement always tries to figure this shit out first and only when their reports start to hit technology does it raise a red flag to people in the inner circle."

"Let's find the rest of the townsfolk, then take it from there," Dave suggested as he began to open the door to the outside.

The sun had now set into the horizon, leaving behind a scattering of twinkling stars dotting the inky sky. I scanned the street. Where would be big enough for hundreds of bodies? The library was a large building, but wasn't conducive to stacking bodies. We began walking toward the crossroads back into the center of town. The café promising the best peach pie came into view along with a celebratory sign for the football match which took place two days ago. A sinking heavy weight settled in my stomach. The church was a perversion, but the school—that would be unthinkable.

"Which direction is the school?" I asked. Dave pulled his phone out of his pocket. It was the latest model, in pristine condition, but the bigger version and he pulled it close to his face, narrowing his eyes. "Do you need glasses?"

His gaze flickered to mine. "No."

Okay, then. A woman's voice boomed from his phone and informed us to turn right at the crossroads.

He raised a brow as we followed the instructions. "What?"

I shrugged. "Never took you for someone who followed technology."

"Our enemies utilize technology, I would be a fool to not level the playing field."

Sebastian chuckles next to me as we continue down the silent street. It's as if the place has been abandoned, but not in a disorganized way. There are no open doors, no TVs blaring, and no forgotten bicycles on the lawns of the pretty houses. Wherever everyone went, it was planned.

The school is a complex series of buildings set back from the main road. They showed a passage through architectural time, as it clearly had been added to as the town grew. The smallest building declared itself as an elementary school, with a little white picket fence and some playground equipment. The biggest building, a two story glass-fronted affair, seemed to be the newest addition.

I nodded to the doors. "I think we need to find the sports hall."

Dave slid his phone into his pocket and we entered the unlocked doors of the school. The honeysuckle smell hit us hard and made my stomach flip.

"What is that?" Dave grumbled as his nose twitched. Shifter noses were far more sensitive than mine, and I was already longing for clear air. The sign pinned to the wall had an arrow pointing to the left for the sports hall.

"I'm not sure," I answered as we followed the arrows through the hallways to a set of double doors painted royal blue. Caleb appeared before us.

"You found me," he whispered, making Harry jerk. Ha, it took someone special to scare a ghost.

"Prepare yourselves," I instructed as my hands tightened at my sides.

Dave pushed on the metal bar and the doors gave way. Darkness awaited us. A deep, hidden, and ominous presence coated the air. It was stifling, it seized my lungs and wrung them tight in my chest. The menace paused inside the room and turned its attention to us.

Sebastian was frozen next to me. "You feel that?" he asked.

I swallowed the knot of fear lodged in my throat. "I do, but this scene isn't going to investigate itself." I forced my feet forward, it was like moving through mud. Once over the threshold of the hall, I felt around on the wall for a light switch. Things never seemed as bad in the light.

My fingers brushed a circular switch and I pushed it. The lights flickered on. Oh, how very wrong I was. This scene was most certainly better in the dark, it hid the atrocity that had taken place.

Lying in concentric circles were bodies stacked on top of one another. The youngest victims were in the center, working to the outside no more than a foot in front of us, was the eldest. Nobody had been spared, from babies to grandparents. Generations of Peach Tree residents had been torn from the world.

I squared my shoulders, sucked in another breath of the cloying honeysuckle scent, and started walking around the edge of the bodies. I spotted Caleb's body in the third ring, his spirit hanging out next to me.

"What happened?" I asked Caleb. Perhaps now he had fulfilled his task of retrieving me, he would gain a little clarity. At least these people had retained their eyes. I could live an eternity and it would still be too soon to see that again.

Caleb shook his head. "It rained fire, swept us away in a violent wave, a tornado blew through, and then the ground shook violently."

Okay, so he was still confused. Perhaps these bodies would talk to me. I knelt and placed my hand against the cheek of an elderly lady with tight silver curls. Nothing. It was like touching the living, they didn't want to tell me their secrets. I tried a few more to be sure.

"Guess we are working this the old-fashioned way," Dave muttered.

"What's the old-fashioned way?" Sebastian asked.

"The basics of a crime, motivation, means, and opportunity."

"On the surface, this looks exactly like a Kool-Aid situation."

I rolled my eyes. "Give up, this is not a Kool-Aid situation."

"Should we take a body for further observation?" Dave asked.

When the authorities arrived, they would be matching the deceased with a town census. It would take time, perhaps days, to figure out everyone's identity. We could slip the body back before anyone noticed. But I couldn't hide the autopsy marks, and that would confuse the humans.

"No, it's too risky, we get what we can tonight, then if we need to look at a body further, it will need to be after the coroner has examined it."

"I can stay with the bodies and report back to you with what the authorities are leaning toward," Harry suggested.

"That's really helpful, thank you." I relayed Harry's message to Sebastian and Dave.

Dave jerked his head and we started scouring the room. Inch by inch we searched for clues, Caleb mumbled nonsense in my ear about flames. I ignored him the best I could while I tried to make sense of why these folks were dead. They seemed to have simply laid down in perfect circles and died. Unlikely.

Indigo pushed against my senses. She heightened my smell and crystallized my vision. Dave's eyes narrowed on me from across the room, like he could sense my deadly alter ego pushing to break free, but there was no danger and there were certainly no souls to eat. She nudged me to focus on the third circle. I carefully stepped over the first few circles and stopped in front of a twenty-something woman with a swollen stomach. Damn. No one was safe from what happened here.

I tilted my head and spotted something white clutched in her hands. Bending, I reach for her clasped fingers. They didn't budge. Ugh. Rigor mortis was my enemy. I knelt and pried her fingers apart as carefully as I could. A loud snap echoed in the room. Hopefully the coroner would put it down to poor handling of the bodies and not a nosy person removing evidence.

"What is it?" Dave asked.

I lifted the white silky material from her hand and then dropped it. The sickly scent suddenly made sense. I grabbed a glove from my pocket and snapped it on before picking up the flower once more. I twisted it around, making sure I was correct. Unfortunately, I was.

"It's a Datura," I explained. "More commonly known as the devil's trumpet. Highly toxic."

"To the point of death?" Dave asked.

"Absolutely. It is hallucinogenic if ingested but almost always deadly. It might lend a clue as to why my ghost is very confused."

"It doesn't answer why you can't get a read on their deaths," Sebastian stated, frowning at the bodies. "It begs the question, did the murderer know you would be coming and did they do something to prevent you from using your gift?"

I stood and began making my way through the bodies to the edge of the room with the flower in my hand. "That, I do not know the answer to."

"Is that flower responsible for the heavy floral scent saturating the air?"

I spun the flower between my fingers. "This one flower? No. That scent is the result of a mighty crop of devil's trumpets."

"I think we figured out how they died," Dave said. "And given they are a small close-knit town, who band together for events, they would have been an easy target."

"We have the means and opportunity," Sebastian said. "Now we need the motive."

I sighed as I scanned the room. Why would someone kill an entire town with deadly flowers and then try to clumsily cover it up? We were missing something. Perhaps following the clues would lead us to the motive, because standing here and gazing at the sea of bodies wasn't getting us anywhere.

"We need to find the source of the flowers," I said as I began striding toward the doors. One thing was for certain, these people had died not by their own hand, but by a cruel and sadistic murderer, and we needed to bring them to justice no matter the consequences.

# Chapter Nine

*If the cat gets the cream, does he stick around for seconds or go looking for his next bowl?*

Three hours. That's how long it took for us to scour the town. There weren't any crops of poisonous devil's trumpet growing in anyone's backyard. That was both a good thing and a bad thing. Good, because to get rid of it, I would need to call The Order for help. Bad, because we hadn't figured out where the hell it had come from. It clearly wasn't an accidental ingestion, this had been planned. I couldn't fathom why, and for someone to plant evidence directing the police to cult activities—it didn't add up.

We'd left Harry with Caleb and the bodies. He had strict instructions to report back to me as soon as the authorities arrived and what their initial findings were.

Dave glided the Escalade down the empty highway, passing the odd trucker as we sped toward White Castle. I'd managed to find a plastic bag to store the flower in. Sebastian was snoozing in the back as I contemplated my next move. Perhaps finding the origin of the flower would lead us to the perpetrator.

Dave's phone rang through the speakers of the car. I glared at the screen as 'The Principal' flashed. Dave clicked a button on the steering wheel.

"What's happening?" Hudson boomed.

Sebastian jerked awake. "Bloody overgrown cat," he grumbled low.

Hudson either didn't hear him or chose to ignore him. "Cora?"

"I'm here. It's a long story, but in summary, the whole population of Peach Tree is dead."

"How?"

I glanced at the flower in the bag on my lap. "Poison. But they tried to cover it up with planted evidence pointing the finger at a cult."

"That's concerning."

"Cora has a sample of the flower that she thinks was used to murder the residents," Dave said.

"Will that help?" Hudson asked.

I pressed my lips together. If I could find the source perhaps. "I'll take it to Rockhard and Lenson. They might be able to shed some light on it, if Dave can drop me off in town."

"I'll meet you there," Hudson stated.

I opened my mouth to tell him not to bother but the call cut off. So that's how we were going to play this? Deliver instructions and then duck out before a meaningful conversation could take place? Hudson needed a reminder of who his chosen mate was. Big clue, I was not some submissive kitty waiting for the attention of her big muscly mate. Ugh. Boundaries needed to be set.

Dave side-eyed me. "You are grumbling incoherently."

"Your boss is a dick. Was that clear enough?" Sebastian chuckled, and I glanced over my shoulder at him.

"Calm down, he simply missed you," Dave replied, trying to smooth things over.

"Unlikely, he's a domineering, arrogant asshole."

"That too. A word of advice, if I may?" Dave said.

Now I was getting relationship advice from Mr. Stoic? Oh boy—how the mighty have fallen. This should be fun.

"Hit me."

"Hudson is an alpha—*the* alpha."

"This isn't news."

"He's also a cat."

"Again, not news."

"Stop trying to deal with him on human terms, or even elemental ones."

"I'm not following."

Dave sighed like he was explaining the core concepts of addition to an adult who couldn't grasp simple arithmetic. "He's not yet secure in his mating. You have kept him at arm's length for weeks. Out of your business and out of your bed."

"Because he ditched her," Sebastian added. It wasn't necessary, everyone knew he ditched me.

"He made a mistake," Dave said.

"That's not the issue here. We aren't debating who made a mistake and when," I said. "I need to know how to tame a tiger with a god complex without losing myself in the process. I'm not going to roll over and show him my belly."

"That would be a surefire way to lose him," Dave said as he tapped his thumbs on the steering wheel. "Hudson needs someone who challenges him, who holds him accountable. Someone who doesn't take his bullshit."

"I believe I am already that woman."

"Agreed, but you are pushing him too far away. He also needs to know that no matter how much you disagree or argue, you will be his partner. That you will back him and let him back you."

"So he needs to be the cat that got the cream?"

"That's a visual analogy I could have done without," Sebastian muttered.

Dave ignored Sebastian and carried on. "The reason he is being overbearing right now is because he's unsure where he stands. Perhaps it is time to cement your future."

"I agreed to be his mate in front of the pack's heavyweights—what more does he need?"

"Have you told your family this?" Dave's eyes flickered to Sebastian in the rearview mirror. "Your friends?"

I swallowed the knot in my throat as Sebastian stayed silent and hung me out to dry. "No."

"Can you see it from his perspective?" Dave pushed.

"Yes," I gritted out. Nobody liked their shortcomings in a relationship pointed out to them, but he was right; I was keeping Hudson at a distance. I'd already made that commitment on his turf, with his people, but now it was time to go all in. It was time to take that leap. "How does one meet on cat terms?"

Dave smiled, and that, more than any weird cult references or a town full of dead people, freaked me out. "Easy, Cora. You stop fighting and let him sweep you off your feet."

"I'm hardly a blushing princess. My feet are firmly planted on the floor."

Dave huffed. "Listen to him. Make his words count and enjoy his company. Take an interest in his life. That is how you make a cat comfortable."

My phone buzzed in my pocket. I gripped it and tipped my head back against the seat with a groan. Sebastian looked over my shoulder. "Oh shit, granny Roberts is calling."

I contemplated ignoring the call, but my grandmother was an insistent creature, and not knowing what she wanted would stir anxiety in my body that I didn't need right now. I pressed the green circle and pressed the phone against my ear.

"Grandmother," I uttered.

"Where are you?" she asked.

I squeezed my eyes closed. I should have predicted that question and planned a response before I accepted her call. *Stupid Cora, your attention is slipping.* "I was investigating a death with Dave," I explained. There, no lies. Hopefully, she would conclude that the person was a shifter. "We are on our way back to White Castle."

"A death outside of White Castle?" my grandmother asked. Her words were crisp icicles, sharp enough to cut.

Ugh, that was unusual. "That's correct."

Dave glanced at me, and I shrugged. The silence stretched, making me check the phone. She was still there. Probably working through the information and deciding what political angle she could use to further her agenda. I might be related to this woman, but her heritage was isolated to creating a granddaughter whom she could manipulate for her own gain.

"Is the cat still wooing you?" she asked, proving my point.

My hand tightened around the phone. "Hudson is still at Summer Grove House, yes."

"And are you still keeping him out of your bed?"

Dave's eyebrows rose. Oh wonderful, now he thought my holding out was a political one, not me protecting my heart. Thank you, grandmother. "That's correct."

"Keep it that way, beasts like Hudson like the chase, the second he feels you are fully won, he will lose interest."

First relationship advice from Mr. Stoic and now from Miss Cold and Heartless. Let me think for a moment as to whether I would be following it—er, no. "Understood," I responded. There was no reasoning with her, I had tried many times in the past and failed. "Did you call for something specific?" I wanted to get her off the phone as soon as possible.

"Yes. I will be visiting you the day after tomorrow."

Ugh, grandmother visits. Yippee. She rarely announced it, so what gives today?

"Of course, will you need a room prepared?" Please say no, please say no.

"No."

Thank you universe.

"But I will need you to start the spell to unlock the Roberts' third vault."

And the universe just slapped me in the face. "The third?" I checked. I was itching to ask her what she wanted, but I bit my tongue.

"Correct."

"Ok."

The phone cut off and I exhaled a sigh and closed my eyes.

"Your grandmother seems invested in you keeping Hudson on the hook," Dave said.

"She continues to try to manipulate me."

"Is she succeeding?"

I opened my left eye and looked at Dave. "If she was, do you think I would be stupid enough to accept her call in a car full of supernaturals with supersonic hearing?"

"I think you are savvier than you let on."

"I'm too tired to play political mind games."

Sebastian leaned forward and stretched between the front seats. "Leave her alone, she is being transparent in her dealings with her grandmother, can you say the same?" Dave's jaw ticked.

I glanced at Sebastian. "Aren't you going to put in your two cents worth on my relationship?"

He grinned, showcasing his pearly white slightly too sharp teeth. "Of course. The solution to all your problems is very simple."

"Let's hear it."

"Run. Don't stop to pack, don't tell anyone where you are going. Get on a flight with me today and we will disappear into the sky and no one will be able to track us. I hear the food is good in Hawaii or what about Alaska? No one goes there."

I chuckled even as a part of my soul tugged at the promise of freedom from all this responsibility. "I'll keep that as my backup plan," I joked. Well, I was mostly joking. Sebastian was running away from his reality for his own reasons.

I settled back and chewed my bottom lip. What on earth did my grandmother want from the third vault? We had a number of them in the cellar under my home, containing treasures we'd accumulated over the years. The third vault was reserved for the most dangerous of items, and as such, the process to open it was a slow one. It protected it from being ransacked by people, and even under duress, the process to open it could not be rushed.

"What's in the third vault?" Dave asked.

Glad to know the supernaturals in the car weren't above eavesdropping. "Lots of things."

"And what is your grandmother likely to be after?"

I pressed my lips together and stared at the rapidly rising sun. It could be so many things. There was an unwritten rule among the Roberts women regarding the third vault. You don't ask, you don't query, you accept the need to store something inside there and don't go snooping at shit that wasn't yours. That said, I wasn't stupid—I had fail safes no one knew about. I had to, for the sake of the dangerous items tucked away in there.

"It could be anything, I'm not being deliberately obtuse. Without knowing what she's up to, I can't know what she would be retrieving."

"Can you get in there earlier?" Sebastian asked. "To check out what's inside before she arrives?"

A smile spread on my face. "There's no need, I know exactly what's in there."

Dave glanced at me, his features twisting in surprise at whatever he sees there. Everyone kept underestimating me. It was my greatest weapon and would be their greatest downfall.

# Chapter Ten

*The pertinent question is, did you taste their peach pie?*

The day had well and truly broken by the time we pulled into town and Dave slid the car to a halt in front of Hudson. He was looking as delicious as always. I'm not sure the man has even heard of a bad hair day. His muscles are defined under the thin cotton of his pale green T-shirt, and his arresting hazel eyes, like molten pools of gold, tracked me as I opened the door and snatched the bag containing the flower from the floor.

Dave jumped out of the car, leaving Sebastian sitting in the back. "This is the end of the road, vampire," Dave drawled as he threw the car keys to Hudson. Sebastian rolled his eyes and climbed out of the Escalade.

"I'll see you in a couple of days," Sebastian said to me before he started strolling down the street away from us.

"Could you not have dropped him back at his car?" I snapped at Dave.

He raised an eyebrow. "No, I'm leaving you and Hudson with the car. I have business in town. The vampire is all grown up, he can find his own way home."

"That's not in question, but your manners are."

"My manners don't extend to the fanged population." Then he strode away from us in the opposite direction of Sebastian. "Tell Hudson about your grandmother's visit," he called out over his shoulder.

Hudson reached for me and wrapped his possessive arms around my waist, drawing me closer. I made sure the bag with the flower hung from my hand at the side. I didn't want to accidentally poison us or destroy the evidence I'd stolen from a crime scene. "I missed you," he mumbled into my hair.

I tipped my head back to stare into his eyes. His gaze caressed my lips before slowly bending his head, giving me plenty of time to avoid his kiss. His mouth settled over mine and I leaned into him. I didn't want to hide from this anymore. All the death and horror I'd seen in the last twenty-four hours made me eager to hold on to something warm and alive, so I returned his kiss with enthusiasm. He broke away, panting.

"As much as I'm wanting to see where that kiss is going, I think you have something more pressing to deal with first."

My hand tightened on the bag. I did have more pressing issues, but the promise of fire in his eyes was a seductive pull that made me want to say fuck it to the world. Surely somebody else could deal with the trouble brewing in a town hundreds of miles away? Hudson's lips twitched. "If I were a lesser man, I would act on the promise of pleasure in your eyes, but you would beat yourself up for it later. So let's solve this new mystery you have landed in the middle of, then perhaps, we can pick this up later."

He was right, I would beat myself up for it, and him recognizing that only solidified his place in my heart.

"My grandmother is coming to visit in a couple of days to retrieve something from the vaults."

"Do you know what?"

"No, but I can figure out what she took once she leaves."

He tucked a curl behind my ear. "Why are you and Sebastian seeing each other in a couple of days?"

"He is about to take a stand against his parents, and I said I would be there for support."

A growl rumbled in his chest. "I don't like you near Leon."

"I don't like being near Leon, but Sebastian earned my friendship and loyalty. Also, in the interest of full disclosure, my grandmother wants me to continue to keep you out of my bed. She thinks you will lose interest."

"Your grandmother is a piece of work."

"Good thing I didn't take relationship advice from her then."

His thumb traced my bottom lip. "Yes, that is a good thing."

I was reluctant to break this fragile bubble we had around us, but the quicker we could sort out this Peach Tree mess, the quicker we could move forward in our relationship. I sucked in a breath and stepped back, breaking the contact. He grabbed my hand and threaded his fingers through it, earning him some more brownie points and a big smile.

We walked down the alley toward the pharmacy. I pushed open the door and the bell tinkled, announcing our arrival to Rockhard and Lenson. A light floral scent floated around the store, indicating they'd been brewing something in their labs which had leaked. Hudson sneezed, making me blink. Allergies? The Terror of Tennessee had allergies? Seriously?

A heavy-set man appeared from the back room, busily finishing off a jelly donut and licking the sugar from his fingers. His gray eyes widened behind the thick-rimmed glasses perched on his nose. "Cora," Rockhard bellowed as he lifted the opening in the counter and swept me up into a bear hug. "Lenson, get your ass out here. Cora's here with the burly shifter."

I choked a little from the squeeze Rockhard gave me as his life partner appeared through the door. He was a balding slim guy, dressed in a pink shirt and an apron with a cloud and unicorn print on it.

A deep growl emitted from Hudson. I patted Rockhard on the back. "Best let me go, big guy, before he explodes into fur and snarls at us all menacingly."

"I am menacing," Hudson snaps as Rockhard lets me go.

"I'm not afraid of the big bad cat," Rockhard declared with a wink. "I hope you made him work for your forgiveness."

A smile pulled at my lips. "I did."

Lenson leaned across the counter and eyed Hudson. "If you hurt her again, expect retribution, Principal. I don't care who you are, or what you think you can do." Ugh, save me now, my surrogate protective fathers were giving Hudson *the talk*.

Hudson nodded once. "Understood."

"Now we've cleared that up," I said, waving the bag in my hand. "Can you confirm what this is, please?"

Rockhard plucked the bag out of my hand and opened it. He sniffed and jerked his head back. "Lock the door," he said as he pushed past Lenson into the back room. I raised a brow at Hudson, who got the hint and went to twist the lock on the front door.

"Flip the back soon sign," I instructed, and Hudson obeyed. I raised a brow, the corner of my mouth lifting in astonishment. How long would this last? Hudson doing as he was told?

We followed Lenson into the back room in time to see Rockhard pulling the flower from the bag with a pair of tweezers. "Where did you find a devil's trumpet?" Lenson asked as he grabbed a glass beaker and slid it in front of Rockhard.

The flower dropped inside of the clear container. "From a crime scene in Peach Tree."

"Did you get a slice of their pie?" Rockhard asked. He pursed his lips and made a kissing noise against his fingers. "It is divine."

"No to the pie, because the whole town is dead."

Rockhard blinked at me then stared at the flower. "That's a crying shame, but one lone flower would not be powerful enough to kill a whole town."

Lenson grabbed a few bottles of varying liquids. They had no labels on, but I was confident they knew exactly what was in each of them. Rockhard and Lenson were more commonly known as The Scientists. Their knowledge of potions and spells was unparalleled in North America, so much so, my grandmother had tried to recruit them numerous times to The Order. They preferred to remain independent of the politics and were picky about who they helped.

"Is there something different about this flower?" I wondered as I took a step back and watched them work.

Lenson raised a jar half full of sapphire liquid and held it up to Rockhard. Rockhard shook his head. "Let's do that last in case it destroys the bloom."

"What can you tell us about the flower?" Hudson asked as he leaned against a metal worktop.

Lenson glanced over his shoulder as Rockhard spooned some gray powder into a clay bowl. "Datura is its Latin name."

"Something I can't get from Google," Hudson pushed.

"Datura is poisonous. Ingested, it causes a number of symptoms including hallucinations." The knowledge snapped in my mind at what he was hinting at. Oh, boy. I was a stupid elemental for not putting this together. This was magic 101.

"Which means?" Hudson asked.

"It means they are carriers of spells. They are a great deliverance item for powerful magic."

"The air was heavy with expelled magic in Peach Tree," I confirmed. "Under the death and the false evidence pointing toward Satanism, a great deal of magic hung in the air."

"Is there a way of telling if the flower was part of such a system?" Hudson asked. I didn't need confirmation, it was the only thing that had made sense in the last twenty-four hours.

Rockhard pushed the tweezers inside the jar and pulled a petal from the flower. He dropped it in the clay bowl and ground it together with the powder.

"Stand back," Rockhard muttered as he pulled a helmet over his face and slid the visor down. I stepped back and pressed myself against Hudson. Lenson pulled on a gas mask.

"Should we leave?" Hudson muttered in my ear.

"Um, not unless they say."

Rockhard nodded once at Lenson, who tipped a little pale green liquid that smelled like urine into the bowl. For a second nothing happened. Then *boom*. An explosion which shook the walls echoed around us. Hudson yanked me against him and hit the floor. I was squashed under two hundred pounds of hard shifter. I tapped my hand on the floor.

"Let me up," I grumbled.

Hudson's hands had protected my head from cracking against the floor, but he was still crushing me like a buffoon. "Is it safe?"

"Yes," Lenson said.

Hudson leapt to his feet and offered me his hand. I launched up and spun to find the walls splattered with different colors of magic. It was a rainbow of power, and the remnants were still glittering in the air. I sucked in a breath and spun.

"What does it mean?" I asked.

"Right here, you have the big four," Rockhard said, snapping his visor up to stare at the display. "Water," he said, pointing to a deep blue streak. "Fire." He waved a hand through a faint reddish glitter in the air.

"Earth," Lenson added, motioning at a green swirl.

"And air," I finished, hovering my hand over a splat of silver on the wall.

"Elemental magic did this?" Hudson said with a scowl.

"Yes, that bloom was trying to deliver elemental magic," Lenson said as he poked at the rest of the flower in the jar with a scalpel. "And a whopping dose of it too."

"For what purpose?" Hudson asked, taking a step closer to the table.

Rockhard shrugged. "We are scientists, not psychics."

"How much would be needed to affect the whole town?" I asked. "Because there were hundreds of bodies."

"The whole town?" Rockhard said with a tilt of his head. "Fields and fields of Datura. The heavier the magic, the more flowers needed to deliver it, and this shit was heavy."

Fields full of Datura? I've never heard of such a thing. Where would one grow fields of a highly poisonous flower?

"Do you know of such a place?" I asked. If anyone knew, it would be them.

Rockhard's eyes narrowed like he was scanning a map of the earth. "No."

"Helpful," Hudson muttered.

"We don't know of somewhere," Lenson said. "But we can locate the origins of this flower, and if that flower grew in those fields—"

"Then it will lead us to the source," I finished. "Very clever."

Rockhard's chest swelled with pride. "Flattery will get you everywhere."

"He's not lying, it really will get you everywhere with him." Lenson winked.

"How long until you have a location?" I asked, causing Hudson to snap his head toward me. "What, you thought it was a little hocus pocus and boom the coordinates would land in our lap?"

"Clearly, I underestimated the simplicity of the spell."

"This isn't like scrying for someone whose life force leaves an imprint on the earth," Rockhard explained. "This is finding the root of this flower that is essentially dead."

"It's a delicate spell, it will take time and patience," Lenson muttered. "Give me twenty-four hours, and I'll have your location."

"What's the price?" I asked. They might be like family, but there was always a price.

"An invite," Rockhard said, rubbing his hands together.

I folded my arms. "To what?"

Rockhard's lips twitched. "Your impending nuptials, of course."

I squeezed my eyes closed and pinched the bridge of my nose. "How do you know?"

"You declared your intentions at The Pit and expect it to stay quiet?"

"Good point."

"So an invite?" Lenson said.

"Done. We have to go," Hudson growled as he grasped my hand and tugged me out of the back room and through the store. After he unlocked the door and swung it open, I flipped the sign to 'open'. He pointed the keys at the car and opened the passenger door. I slid in and eyeballed him as he jogged around the front and climbed into the seat next to me.

"What's the rush?" I asked.

"The rush, if you haven't already worked it out, is that only one organization is likely behind a conspiracy of elemental magic. The rush is ensuring you beat your grandmother home, because even though she said she was coming in a few days, this should be the startling evidence you need to prove that you cannot, and should not, trust her."

I frowned as he started up the car and did a one-eighty in the road to head toward my house. If my grandmother was behind this travesty, accountable for hundreds of human deaths, she would have every reason to cover it up and every reason to ward against my gift. What was the purpose though? Something didn't add up. *What are you up to grandmother? And what do you need out of the third vault?* An ominous feeling settled in my gut. So help me, I would not hold back on account of blood if she was responsible for this. Humanity needed to be cherished, not abused. It was agreed by the three factions, and if my grandmother had been playing with our most sacred law, she would be at the mercy of all the supernaturals—with me leading the fray.

# Chapter Eleven

*Mysterious strangers who sweep unflappable vampire princesses off their feet are a rare occurrence, so pay attention.*

"Stop at the gates," I told Hudson as my home came into view.

"Why?"

"I want to check the wards, I think it would be prudent to put up extra protection."

"I'll come with you," he said as he paused the car past the gates.

My eyes slid over to him. "You have to let me work. I have spent the last twenty-something years protecting myself. I know there has to be some compromise between us, but I have to maintain my independence. Don't smother me, it won't end well."

Hudson's hands tightened on the steering wheel. "Fine, don't be long."

I leaned over the center console to kiss his cheek, but he turned his head at the last second and captured my lips. Little tiny sparks of heat spread over my body. I pulled back a little breathless and tumbled out of the car. Hudson gave me a wink as I slammed the door closed. *Oh, well played, Principal, making me rush to get back to your lips was a clever technique.*

He sped off toward the house and I began making a circle of the property boundary. I strengthened my wards against evil intent to anyone inside the house, extending it from only me. In hindsight, that was a little selfish. I also reinstated the ward which clanged in my head every time someone crossed the boundary. I'd altered it to only wrap around the house when Hudson had moved into my now flattened stables.

Times were uncertain, and I felt sure I would appreciate the early visitor warning.

I came full circle and pulled the mail out of the box nailed to a post alongside the gate. I started flipping through the pile as I walked toward the house. Bill, bill, more bills. Luckily, they were getting easier to pay. The bed and breakfast was doing well, and my reputation as a supernatural doctor had strengthened with an endorsement from the pack's chief medic—Norbert. The final item was a magazine. I twisted it as a flush crept up my neck. I would murder Maggie and Rebecca.

I took the first steps up to the house and paused as a new black card fell from between the pages of the offending magazine. I glanced over my shoulder and scanned the quiet scene. Birds twittered in the trees, the light breeze rustled the leaves, but there was no sneaky, creepy character delivering odd mail. I kept going as I studied the card, the faint magic seeping from the words. 'Do you dare?' was printed on one side this time. On the other, another line in approximately the same position as the other one, except it was shorter and at a forty-five degree angle.

The door swung open and Rebecca appeared before me. She'd curled her ice-blonde hair and was wearing a knee-length red dress with gold buttons all the way up the center. She smiled at me.

I waved the magazine at her. "You are in big trouble, missy."

She had the audacity to look innocent. *Yeah right, I believe you.* "What's that?" Hudson asked as his head appeared from behind a tree he and Dave were erecting in the corner of the parlor, while The White Furry Menace was eyeballing the large tree like she was considering attacking it. I'd come to learn Bella liked to hide in trees.

I jerked the magazine behind my back. "Nothing."

Maggie's eyes widened as she scuttled past me with a jingling box of ornaments. *That's right, run from me.*

Hudson's gaze narrowed. No way was I showing him the freaking bridal magazine one of these meddling supernatural idiots had subscribed me to. No way.

"Just in time," she declared.

I frowned and stepped past her into utter glittery chaos. "It can't be that time already," I muttered, spinning in a circle. "We had Thanksgiving a few days ago."

"Two weeks ago," Rebecca clarified. "It's now officially Christmas."

Some of the guests were joining in with the decorating while helping themselves to freshly baked cookies.

Aunt Liz appeared from the kitchen and jerked her head at me to follow her. I gladly welcomed the distraction and practically ran toward her.

"When did you get here?" I wondered as we escaped to the kitchen and I dropped the magazine displaying a beautiful festive bride.

She smirked at me and gestured to the table where a plate of sandwiches waited. My stomach rumbled as I sat and began demolishing the yummy goodness. Damn, I didn't realize how hungry I was.

"Dave called me from Peach Tree. He updated me on what you found and thought you might need some elemental back-up."

Dangerous Dave needed to keep his dangerous mouth shut. "Rockhard and Lenson tested the devil's trumpet flower. It was used to deliver elemental magic, but the reason remains a mystery."

Her forehead crumpled into a frown as she slid into the seat across from me with a mug of tea clutched between her hands. "They suspect elemental involvement?"

I would need to tread carefully. Liz might be my aunt, and I adored her, but Eloise was her mother, and accusing the head of The Order was akin to treason.

"An extremely powerful elemental would need to be involved."

She blinked. "You think my mother is involved?"

Okay, so careful had been knocked on its head, but not by me. "I don't know, but she's commanded me to open the third vault."

Aunt Liz sucked in a breath. "I see."

She didn't ask what my grandmother wanted. It was an unwritten rule among the Roberts women. But the fact she wanted in the third vault after a truck-load of magic had been expended in Peach Tree killing the residents, was a coincidence we couldn't overlook.

"You need to be very careful," Liz said. "Your grandmother is a force to be reckoned with. I don't doubt she loves you, but ultimately, if it comes down to you or The Order, I don't like your chances."

"Me either." It wasn't news, but it still stung.

"What are you going to do?"

I glanced out the window at the peaceful morning sunshine. "Rockhard and Lenson are trying to locate where the flower originated from. If they are successful, I'll go and investigate the area, see if I can figure out who is behind it and what they are trying to achieve."

"And the vault?"

"I can't deny her access. I'll start the process today."

"I wonder what she wants. Knowing that would give us perspective on whether she's truly involved."

I steadied my expression. I had done the unthinkable and it would not be forgiven by my family. Aunt Liz stared at me and I struggled to hold my ground. Her gaze narrowed. "I see," she finally said. "Do what you must. If she is breaking the number one law, then she must be held accountable."

Okay, remind me never to play poker with this woman. A raucous sound came from down the hallway and I raised an eyebrow at the unfamiliar deep male voice.

"Rebecca's latest conquest," Aunt Liz said as she scooped up the empty plate and rinsed it in the sink. I shot up from my seat and hurried down the hallway. I had expressly stated time and time again that she should not have romantic engagements with the guests. I knew I was being unfair given that the Crown Vampire Princess of the United Kingdom was in hiding and never left the grounds, so really, where was she meant to make such connections? But the fall-out was always that the males fell in love with her after one night and she lost interest.

I skidded to a halt as a rugged man wrapped in leather trousers and a matching vest spun Rebecca, dipped her back, and planted a passionate kiss on her mouth. I blinked and stared like everyone else in the room who had paused their Christmas spirit to watch the romantic liaison taking place. Rebecca slammed her fists against his chest and he dragged a hand through her hair and tugged until she relented and let him devour her. I wanted to look away, but I couldn't. Neither could anyone else.

He finally broke away from her and pulled her upright. Rebecca swayed slightly. Oh wow, the unflappable princess had met her match.

"I'll be seeing you real soon, princess." His startling blue eyes glanced at me and he pushed a lock of his dark wavy hair behind his ear. Not a vampire, a shifter. "Miss Roberts I presume?" he drawled. I nodded. "Thank you for the most welcoming and enticing stay at your fine establishment. I will return and will definitely recommend it." With that, he sauntered out of the front door. Everyone stood very still for a few moments, soaking up the fact that Rebecca had been kissed senseless.

Rebecca ghosted her fingers over her lips. I caught Hudson looking at me with a small smile on his stupidly handsome face. *Yes, yes, you have that effect on me. It's hardly front page news.* I knew exactly what a kiss like that did to a person.

"Don't you have a tree to decorate?" I snapped at the gang and the few guests who had stopped to watch the show.

I grabbed Rebecca's arm and tugged her toward the stairs which led down to my office. "I need your help," I muttered, eyeballing a frowning Hudson on my way past. "I'll be back soon," I informed him before he could think to follow me.

I ushered a still-dazed Rebecca downstairs and out through the door, before swinging around into the cellar where the family vaults were located. The air smelled a little damp down here, and there was always a chill to the air, no matter the time of year or weather.

I pointed to the stool and Rebecca sat on it while I proceeded to open the first lock on the vault using the handle to hit the exact number of degrees which gave the unlocking combination. It popped open and I pulled the door back.

Rebecca's glazed vision cleared as she peered inside. "What the hell? How long have I lived here and didn't know you were hoarding treasure a dragon would be envious of?"

I smirked at her over my shoulder as I stepped inside. "Welcome back to the land of the living. I will tell you all about the vaults, if you confess who gave you that kiss."

Rebecca grimaced, but the allure of pretty, shiny things beat her embarrassment as she followed me inside the vault. "Don't touch anything," I instructed as her hand grazed over the head of the statue of Buddha proudly displayed on a white stand.

"Why, what does it do?" she asked, peering at it.

"That one grants wishes." She blinked. "But don't expect to feel grateful. If you wished for good health, you would get it, but at the same time, all your loved ones might die in a car crash."

She snapped her hand back and grimaced. "That sucks."

"Which is why it's here, safe from the clueless public. So who is he?"

"Ezra Edge," she breathed and got that dreamy look again.

I snapped my fingers in front of her face. "That's quite the name."

"He's quite the guy."

"He's a shifter."

A smile pulled at her lips. "I know. He's a lion, a predator." Oh boy, I did not want to know how she knew. What happened behind closed doors in my bed and breakfast should stay sacred. Especially if it involved turning furry.

"And has said lion swept you off your feet?" I asked as I opened a trunk and retrieved the circular metal plate and ceremonial dagger.

"He's—" she paused like she was searching for the words.

"Good looking?" I tried.

She scowled at me. "He's sex on a stick, Cora, but that isn't why I'm still thinking about him."

"Do not start to describe his bedroom skills," I said. "Please."

"But he does this thing with his teeth."

I slapped my hands over my ears. "La la la."

Rebecca rolled her eyes and followed me out of the vault. I stopped my insistent rambling which was saving my ears from being burned with Rebecca's sex exploits.

"It's not like you haven't bedded capable men before now. What makes him so different?"

I walked up to the heavy circular door of the third vault. It didn't outwardly look any different to the other doors in the room. In fact, it made every effort to blend in. Which was the point. Nothing remarkable to see here, move along.

Rebecca leaned her shoulder against the wall and folded her arms. "He isn't listening to me," she said.

"I'm sorry, are you saying it took a man not listening to you to get you to fall head over heels?"

Placing the metal disc into the center of the vault door, it clicked as the grips engaged. "No, you don't understand. I can push and manipulate males, I snap my fingers and they appear with their tongues lolling and eager eyes."

I glanced at her. "This isn't painting you in a flattering light."

"I'm pretty in any light."

I snorted as I took the dagger and scored my left palm from my middle finger to my wrist, drawing blood to the surface. It wasn't an overly complex ritual to open the door. But if one thing wasn't just so, then the process would fail. If I placed the disc in the wrong way, or didn't use my left hand, if I drew blood from my wrist to my finger instead of the other way around, then the door would remain sealed.

"So Ezra didn't bend to your will and that is all it took?" I checked.

"No, there's a complex set of criteria. But not being bullied around by me has a certain appeal. Nobody wants a doormat."

I chuckled as I placed my hand on the disc and let my blood seep into the grooves. The other thing about this vault? Only Roberts' blood could open it. "You fell for the bad boy? How very ordinary of you."

"Ezra is hardly ordinary. Plus, I would have thought you would understand. Are you telling me some of your attraction to Hudson is not even a little because he doesn't take any of your shit?"

No, I couldn't tell her that, because a lot of my attraction was built on the fact he pushed me to do better, be better. There was something uniquely attractive about a man that challenged you but didn't rule you. It was a fine balance few had learned, but those who had, could wield it to bring any woman to their knees. It's also why I've been holding off for so long. He could crush me, I was one hundred percent sure of that, and it takes a hell of a lot of trust to give someone that power over you.

The metal plate warmed beneath my palm and I checked to make sure I'd fed all the grooves before removing my hand. Rebecca wrinkled her nose. "Why are these things always creepy blood rituals?" she muttered.

"This from the being that has to drink blood to sustain life," I grumbled.

"I only ingest the smallest amount possible, and even then it is through baggies."

Rebecca Lexington, ladies and gentlemen, the only known vegetarian vampire in existence, and I was being judged.

"Perhaps Ezra could help you with that," I teased as I wiped my hand on a towel. "I think he'd be willing to let you bite him, he might even enjoy it."

Rebecca's cheeks flushed. "Shut up."

I was still laughing as we strode up the stairs to the parlor where it looked like a unicorn had thrown up. Bella was eyeballing the sparkly baubles like she was numbering their days.

I was feeling far more jovial than what I had when I went downstairs and even smiled at Hudson as he wrapped an arm around my back.

Harry shot through the ceiling. "Pineapples, pineapples, pineapples," he shouted and then disappeared. I should've known better than to think I could have a moment's peace. It was the law of the universe to usurp any such thoughts, and I was a fool for forgetting it.

# CHAPTER TWELVE

*Everyone needs to believe in something.*

There's a superstitious belief that bad things come in threes. You find people saying things like, 'that's my third, nothing else can happen now'. Numbers hold a special significance in many cultures, including the Bible, where important words are often repeated three times. Three gifts were presented to Jesus on His birth; gold, frankincense, and myrrh. Jesus conquered death and rose after three days, and of course, the holy trinity encompasses God—the Father, the Son, and the Holy Spirit.

In witchcraft, the triple goddess is made up of the maid, the mother, and the crone. In mathematics, a triangle has three sides and signifies balance. Even Pythagoras thought three was the first true number.

Common sayings also include 'third time lucky' or 'third time's a charm', which is a direct opposition to this ominous and disturbing notion that our bad luck will occur in threes. So why do people persist with this notion? I believe it stems from the human need to draw a dark time in our lives to a close, that there is a certain point where bad things will stop happening.

So while Harry floats up and down my room in a ghostly version of pacing, mumbling about pineapples, I contemplate if the incident at Peach Tree is the first instance of bad luck and my grandmother's impending visit is the second, then whatever had Harry worked up would be the third. That means by this unsubstantiated and unrealistic law of the universe, my bad luck would be over.

Hudson stretched his legs out and placed them on my coffee table. I slapped his thigh. "Feet off the furniture," I grumbled from my place next to him on my sofa. It was hard enough letting him inside my private space. This was my sanctuary, my one place of safety to escape all the demands of life.

"You don't have a TV in here," he observed.

"No. So you can't watch your alien shows here." I'd discovered his guilty pleasure was watching conspiracy programs about the unexplained. He and Dave religiously watched the long-running show which claimed that aliens were pretty much responsible for everything. If that wasn't airing, they always managed to find something else, like the theory that we were living in a form of *The Matrix*. You'd think shifters would be more down-to-earth.

It's not as if it's the first time he has been in here—he once broke into my room in the middle of the night, and there was that time we were being attacked by wild shifters led by the Devil. Then he and Dave had repaired my roof, and again after the pack meal where he kissed me senseless. But simply sitting in my space, taking in his surroundings? That hadn't happened before, and surprisingly I felt okay with it, with him, here soaking up my personal rooms with things I had chosen to surround myself with.

He glanced at the floor-to-ceiling bookshelf which took up half a wall. "You read?"

"Whenever I get the time, which lately has been a rarity."

"You need a vacation."

I chuckled as I played with the tassel of the cushion between us. I did need a vacation, but with the threat of my grandmother trying to dominate the world and my father's declaration that it was on my shoulders to bear the responsibility of humanity's continued ignorance of the supernatural world, I couldn't see lazy days spent reading on a sandy beach in my future any time soon.

"Is Harry going to let us know what the emergency is any time soon?" Hudson drawled.

"Being dead means you get confused more often than the living. Trauma and emergencies can take time to work through. If I try to pry it will likely set him back."

"So you are saying we have to have patience?"

"Yup."

"I hate patience."

Harry stopped his floating and spun to face me. "Peach Tree," he started.

I leaned forward with a nod of my head. "Yes."

"The police came, then an hour later they came."

"What's he saying?" Hudson asked.

I shushed him. "Who came?" I asked Harry.

"There was a black van with a white logo on the side. A swirl."

"That's the chalice. The Order's symbol."

"The Order is already in Peach Tree?" Hudson asked.

"What happened?" I asked Harry.

Harry ran a ghostly hand through his hair. It was an unconscious movement, because he had no influence on his hair.

"There were five men. Their leader was a tall man, with midnight hair and white eyes. It was most unsettling."

"The Hound," I whispered. "My grandmother sent her best team led by her most ruthless elemental to Peach Tree."

"They took over the scene and pressured the authorities to make reports supporting the cult theory."

I relayed this message to Hudson. "They don't stand a chance against The Hound."

"Why is he called that?" Hudson asked.

I blinked as a painful memory tried to surface. "Because once he scents you, once you become his prey, there is nowhere you can run, nowhere you can hide. The Hound will find you and he is an expert at torture which leaves no scars."

A growl rumbled from Hudson. "He hurt you?"

I chewed the inside of my cheek, the last thing I needed was The Terror of Tennessee launching retribution on an elemental because of a buried hurt.

"It was part of my training when I visited my grandmother. Don't blame the tool."

Hudson snarled and it cut through the room, causing the hairs on my arms to rise. His tiger was showing. "I blame your grandmother. She is your family. She is meant to protect and cherish you, not put you through exercises which would break a weaker person."

"That's not the end of it," Harry said. "Caleb was next to me one minute, then *poof* he was gone. Never to be seen again."

Ah, so that's what had Harry so riled up, he'd witnessed the afterlife coming for someone like him. Did that mean he was ready to follow them? Or was he terrified that he would be caught in the white light?

"I'm sorry," I said softly. "That must have been traumatic."

Harry nodded. "They burned the bodies."

I frowned. "Like cremation?"

"No, they took the ones in the church and threw them in the school, and then they set the school alight. "

Why do that? If The Order had staged the scene in the first place, why go to this extreme to then cover it up? Unless…

"They burned the bodies," I whispered. "I don't think this is sanctioned activity by The Order."

"But massive elemental magic was delivered to the people of Peach Tree," Hudson reminded me.

"I know, but then it was covered up—poorly enough that I would see through it, but good enough that the authorities wouldn't."

"Perhaps they didn't expect you to investigate?"

"Then why ward against my gift?"

Hudson leaned forward and rested his elbows on his knees. "That, I don't know."

There were too many moving parts. I could try to use my contacts within The Order to see what was officially being said about Peach Tree. My stomach twisted, I was missing something important. Perhaps my grandmother's visit would shed some light, but if she didn't want me to know, then I wouldn't know. She wasn't the head of The Order because she folded under scrutiny.

My phone buzzed on the coffee table and I glared at it for a second. If it was my grandmother, I couldn't be held responsible for my actions. It wasn't. I let out a sigh of relief and picked up the phone.

"Boys, what do you have for me?" I asked.

"We have a location," Lenson said.

"Excellent."

"I'll send you the coordinates."

"Thank you."

"But Cora, you should go prepared."

"I'm always prepared."

"Tell her about the concentration," Rockhard shouted.

"You're on speaker phone, you idiot, no need to shout, she can hear you," Lenson grumbled.

"What about the concentration," I prompted.

"We couldn't get a definite lock on the location, only a general area. So we did a concentration incantation to look for large amounts of Datura."

"That's very clever."

"Thank you. It worked, but the scale of the crop—it's big. You'll need protection. Gloves, masks, boots."

"I can sort that," I told them.

"Okay, good luck," Lenson said and then the call went silent. I glanced at the phone. He'd hung up.

"I need to rest," Harry said and disappeared through the floor. Rest? Where did ghosts go to rest? They were meant to be eternally resting, but he'd given that up by ignoring the white light calling his name. Perhaps he was exhausted from being my spirit sidekick—I could hardly blame him. Maybe I could negotiate a deal with my father to allow Harry the chance to be welcomed into Heaven.

My phone dinged with a new text message. I opened it and clicked on the link sent by Lenson. It took us to a map. Hudson looked over my shoulder. "Chicot state park, I know the area, it's about two hours' drive from here. If we set off now we can be there before the sun sets."

I guess that meant I'd swapped my ghost sidekick for my shifter one. "I'll grab the safety equipment we might need."

"Okay, what can I do?"

"I already have a bag packed, it's in your car. Maybe grab a change of clothing for yourself?"

"I have a bag ready. Are we expecting to get dirty?" A wide grin spread across his face, causing me to roll my eyes. Ha-ha, very witty.

"Dirty? Me?" I said with mock innocence. "Oh, Principal, you haven't seen my dirty side."

He blinked and I saw that as a win as I exited my rooms and swanned down the stairs. He didn't follow, I apparently stunned him into silence. Score one for me.

*Cora Roberts—Tamer of prehistoric cats.*

# Chapter Thirteen

*New life policy. Bad guys don't always equal snacks.*

It is amazing what you learn about someone on a road trip. For instance, I now know Hudson prefers classic rock, and that is something we have in common. But he also enjoys more recent bands, as well as the occasional 80's pop song.

I also found out he is as picky as Dave when it comes to his burgers. Lucky for me, he knew a little local diner off the beaten track, and I can confirm it is the best damn burger I have ever eaten. Remind me to let him do the barbeques at the house.

The GPS informed us we would be taking the next right. I glanced at the screen. We were less than thirty minutes out from the coordinates Lenson had sent. The well-worn road gave way to dirt and the suspension began to be put to use, causing me to grab the handle and grit my teeth.

Hudson cast a glance my way. "What's the plan when we get there?"

I twisted my lips to the side as I pondered it. "If it's as large as Lenson thinks, then I would expect it to be guarded. Then again, if it's away from populated areas, and it isn't Order owned land, it may just be left. Growing the plant isn't illegal, so there's no recourse should it be found, and it could be attributed to wild and natural growth."

"What you are saying is—you don't have a plan?"

I nodded. "That's about right, yes."

We settled into silence again and I watched the GPS count down the minutes until we came to the end of the road. There were thick trees blocking us from proceeding any further, and Hudson brought the car to a stop. The sun was still peeking above the trees, but we were losing light rapidly.

"Guess we trek the rest of the way," he muttered, cutting the engine and hopping out of the car. I followed and clicked the trunk open, pulling out some gloves, small for me, large for him, and a couple of masks which I shoved in the bag I had slung over my shoulder.

"Ready?" he asked as I slammed the trunk closed.

I nodded and we began following the voice from my phone which demanded we fight against the thick woodland. It took longer than it should have and it was a while before the trees opened, revealing a field. A field full of blooming Datura. It went on and on, as far as the eye could see. I glanced at Hudson. He looked as stunned as me.

"I can't see any that have been harvested," he muttered.

"Let's make a loop around the edge, see what we are dealing with," I suggested and began walking around the field in a clockwise direction. Hudson trudged after me as we kept a safe distance from the edge. We walked for ten minutes before the scene changed.

"That's where they harvested," I said, pointing at the patch of field that was covered in soil. We strode onto the area and began walking to the other side of the field.

"This is a lot of flowers," Hudson said as he cast his gaze as far as he could see. Maybe a quarter of the place had been used. That was concerning. "Was all of this for Peach Tree?"

I paused and folded my arms. "Honestly, I'm not an expert, so I'm not entirely sure."

"Who would know?"

I was already sliding my phone out of my pocket. Surprisingly, I had a strong signal. I pressed the last number received and switched the call to video.

Lenson answered with safety goggles on. "Cora, is everything okay?"

"I need to show you what we found." I switched the camera around and scanned the area, showing him everything. The sucking in of breath wasn't reassuring. I brought the screen back to myself and Hudson stood behind me.

"That's enough Datura to take down the state," Lenson informed me.

"And the part already harvested?" I asked.

"That's what I'm talking about, Cora. The remaining plants, if used correctly, would be enough to poison half of America." My eyes widened and I swallowed the knot of anxiety working its way up my throat. "However," Lenson continued. A spark of hope flared. "If what we suspect is true, and the Datura isn't being used to kill people, and it's being used as a delivery method for magic, then the potency would be less."

"Meaning it would cover even more people," I concluded. That was bad. "Thank you," I told Lenson.

"Would a sample of the plant help us to understand what they are trying to achieve?" Hudson asked.

Lenson thought it over for a few seconds and then shook his head. "No, the magic would be infused after they picked the plant. It would be too volatile and dangerous to give the plants power while they are left unprotected. We'd need an infused bloom, one that hadn't yet been expended."

Rockhard appeared over Lenson's shoulder. "You need to destroy the crop, that's the safest thing to do right now."

"How?"

"Burn it."

I rubbed my temple. I hadn't come prepared for arson. "Is the smoke harmful?" I asked.

"To you? Perhaps. Shifters in their animal form have a better chance of not succumbing to the poison," Rockhard said, pointedly looking at Hudson. "Once it's burned, you can then douse the area in water."

I promised to keep them up to date and terminated the call.

"I didn't bring anything to start a fire," Hudson grumbled.

I sucked in a breath. "That's okay, I can do it."

"But he said you would be susceptible to the poison, I don't want you anywhere near this when it goes up."

"They don't know about her," I stated and Indigo immediately raised her head. "Time to come out and play," I told her.

She eyeballed the scene. "There aren't any souls."

"You have a one track mind. No, there are no souls. I need your expertise in smiting, to light this place up."

"Fine, then we find a soul."

"I'll do my best."

She pushed at my skin and I gave in, allowing her to transform. My gums ached as my teeth elongated and pain tore down my spine as my wings erupted.

Hudson took a step back. Not through fear, he was simply giving her some room. She grinned at him. I'm sure it wasn't a reassuring look. "Are you safe?" Hudson asked her.

"Of course, mate, the poisons of this world have no effect on us. I would simply expel it from my being."

He nodded and then began his own transformation. A few seconds later, his giant tiger stood beside me. Indigo tilted her head just as Keverin, Hudson's animal, gave her a giant lick on her chest.

"No time for foreplay, mate, I must turn this field to ash. Perhaps later."

Foreplay? Oh my god, save me now. How would that even work? The daughter of death and a prehistoric tiger? Indigo chuckled. "Don't fret, Cora, I would only take him in his human form."

That's encouraging.

Indigo tensed, her wings arched, and we shot into the sky. The field was even more terrifying from this view. She raised her hands and power tumbled through us. A stream of pure energy shot from her palms, and as she circled the field, sparks caught alight and flames erupted. Keverin stalked around the edge of the blaze, snarling as sparks danced onto his fur. The smoke bloomed into the sky, but I could feel my molecules expelling the toxins. It was a little disconcerting; most people weren't aware of their molecules.

"I need access to your element to put out the fire," Indigo stated. That was curious, I didn't realize she couldn't just use it. I reached for my power and fed it through to her. She yanked on the water from the lake nearby, and a cloud formed in the sky across from us. She coaxed it over to the field and with a clap of her hands, the water released onto the ground. The flames died and Keverin growled. Oops, he wasn't a fan of water.

Indigo swooped to the ground just as Keverin shed his fur and an explosion of light revealed a naked Hudson. Indigo perused him and licked her lips.

"Not now," I said.

"It's been too long," she argued.

"We cannot have sex in a burnt field of poisonous plants, you might get a rash."

Power swelled from nowhere. It sucked the breath from my body and made my flesh tighten. Hudson spun in the direction of the trees we'd trekked through, and Indigo crouched, narrowing her gaze.

"What is it?" Hudson growled.

"Bad guys?" Indigo asked me. Ugh, she was asking if they could be snacks.

"Perhaps."

Four elementals spilled from the greenery, two men and two women. I recognized three of them, they each represented a different element. I assumed the fourth unknown wielded earth to make an elemental power quad. All of them wore the insignia of The Order, and the ones I recognized reported directly to my grandmother, which meant I could no longer ignore the fact that she was involved.

Indigo's wings snapped in irritation and they faltered in their approach, clearly unsure of my identity and what I was capable of. "Principal, you are trespassing," the tall guy with ice-blond hair snapped. Wesley Maidstone—top water wielder in The Order. I was better, but I refused to be used by them.

Hudson ignored him.

"The land is not yours to claim," Indigo declared. Her voice came out multilayered and the elementals shifted a little, clearly uncomfortable with her presence.

"That was our crop you just burned," the raven-haired woman said. She was the unknown, but still no match for us.

Indigo shrugged her shoulder. "Oops."

I mentally palmed my face. This was escalating quickly.

"Leave now, and we will let you live," Hudson said. He was deceptively calm, and it was one hundred percent more terrifying than if he had roared the words.

Power pulsed around the elementals. Unusual power. "They are packing something extra," Indigo said to Hudson as I thought the words.

"Agreed."

"Be careful," I warned her. "Wait for them to make the first move, we can be in no doubt if we hurt members of The Order that it was self-defense."

Indigo rolled her eyes.

Wesley gave a subtle jerk of his head and that power coalesced into one force. What the hell? They were combining their efforts. This wasn't to scare us, they planned to murder us among the ashes of their ruined crop. A green ball of power shot toward us. Indigo snapped out her hand, her pure white energy swallowing the green, fizzling it out.

She tilted her head as the elementals looked worried. They should be. If they had any sense they'd be retreating.

"We can't let you leave with the knowledge," Wesley shouted. "Submit to a memory wipe and we can all go about our business."

"Like fuck am I letting you rummage around in my mind," Hudson snarled. I was in complete agreement, they could plant anything in there.

"Then the pack will need to be looking for a new leader before dawn," Wesley snarled. Another flash of power, this time in the form of lightning.

Indigo's chest rattled. What in the ever loving f—

She released the sound and followed it up with a battle cry before diving in front of Keverin and taking the hit of lightning to her chest. It knocked her back and winded us.

"You threaten my mate, you die," she thundered, ignoring the sizzling on her flesh.

Keverin let loose a roar that made the trees tremble. Fire blazed toward us with a push from the air elemental, coming at us fast and hard. I implored her to listen to reason and not commit murder. She ignored me and rampaged toward the elementals. There was no stopping her, no putting the brakes on. Power pulsed from her in threatening thunderous waves. The elementals were tiring as she batted their magic away like she was swatting at flies.

She reached Wesley first, his eyes widening as he looked upon her. He recognized his death and tried to back away. Too late. She tore his head from his body, blood sprayed through the air as she simultaneously dived through his chest and pulled his heart out, still warm. "A little overkill," I muttered.

Keverin launched himself through the air and took the earth elemental to the floor, his teeth tearing into her throat. Ugh, these two were perfectly matched.

"Glad you have now caught on," Indigo said as she snapped her wings out, the left one taking the water elemental to the floor. Indigo slammed her foot through her chest which caved in and killed her.

"Don't kill them all, I need to question them," I instructed.

She eyeballed the final elemental who turned and began sprinting away from us. Indigo snapped her fingers, freezing him in place. "Oh no, I have something special in mind for you. Ask your questions before I eat his soul. He's tainted with the darkness, this man has a one way ticket to Hell. I'm giving him a mercy." She said this aloud to terrify the man as I pushed, she allowed me through. I saw the moment he realized he had been attacking the President's granddaughter. I had no doubt all that awaited him on his return was death, so he was dead either way, but I couldn't let him utter a word of what he'd witnessed here.

"What is the purpose of the magic delivered through the Datura?" I asked.

He blinked. "The purpose? To allow the one true faction to rule all others."

"How would that achieve this goal?" He grimaced and I tilted my head. "You aren't making it out of here alive," I reminded him. "However, your demise can be drawn out, painful and terrifying. Or it can be a swift death that you don't feel. The choice is yours."

He swallowed and glanced at the snarling prehistoric tiger next to me. "Eloise wants complete control as the treaty failed."

"I'm aware."

"So she's looking for a different means to achieve that aim."

"By poisoning whole towns?"

"That was a test run, we miscalculated."

"Miscalculated what?"

He trembled like he was struggling. He was trying to move his mouth and it was like he was being strangled. He'd been gagged. Magically. Damn my grandmother.

"We've got everything we can," I said.

Indigo tore through my flesh once more and snapped her hand into his chest. The sound of his ribs cracking made me a little nauseous, but that was nothing compared to the revulsion when she bit into his heart and blood dribbled down my throat. "That's unsanitary."

She took her sweet time ingesting the soul. It sat like a lead weight in my gut and then the sheer power of it made my knees collapse.

"Cora?"

Indigo sank beneath my flesh once more and I glanced at Hudson. He'd separated from Keverin and they were both looking at me as I fought with the magic I'd ingested. That was no ordinary elemental. He'd been powered up and the effect was dizzying.

Hudson's hand grazed down my naked spine. "Are you okay?"

"Peachy," I breathed, as I focused on drawing in air and releasing it in a steady wave.

"You don't seem peachy."

I raised my head and glared at him. "You try eating someone's souped-up soul and see how it settles inside you."

He gripped my elbow and pulled me upright. My jeans had torn where they'd been stretched by Indigo and my shirt was ripped down the back. The two halves flapped open and the front had been singed by the hit of elemental magic. I prodded the burnt flesh on my stomach and hissed.

Hudson wrapped his arm under my legs and lifted me. "I can walk, you overgrown cat."

"I know, just give me this. You got hurt and I need to reassure myself you are okay." He started walking with me through the dark woods, with the moon as our companion. A naked shifter and a half naked elemental, what must we look like.

"I am okay."

"I know."

He pulled me tighter against his chest and the muscle in his jaw ticked. My fingers trailed along it, trying to coax it to relax. He glanced down at me.

"I'm here, alive. I'm okay. It's going to take a hell of a lot more than some power-drenched elementals to get the better of me."

He squeezed his eyes closed. "You jumped in front of me."

"Technically, Indigo jumped in front of you. They threatened you, her mate."

"Your mate," he corrected.

I nodded, because I could sense from the tremble in his body that he was on the edge and one wrong move from me and I'd be burrowed away in some secret hideout with him. It didn't sound like a terrible idea.

We emerged in front of the car. I lifted my head and dropped a kiss on his lips. He didn't waste time, he delved deeper and twisted me so my legs wrapped around his waist. Pushing me up against the car, his fevered body met mine, every hard ridge was defined for my fingers to explore. From the bunched and tense muscles on his back, to more private regions, Hudson was defined in all the right ways. My fingers threaded through his hair and I tugged. I needed to get closer, it wasn't enough. I tensed my thighs and his chest brushed mine. I hissed at the contact. He jerked away from me and frowned.

"I'm sorry," he said, looking away.

I gripped his chin and dragged his gaze back to mine. "I'm not fragile, Hudson, I won't break. Don't hold back and treat me like some precious princess. This won't work unless you are able to be yourself with me."

He tucked a piece of my wild hair behind my ear and leaned his forehead against mine. "You are precious." I opened my mouth to disagree and he brushed his finger across my lips to silence me. "But like a diamond is precious it's also almost unshatterable. Don't think for one second I don't know you are capable of changing this entire world if you so wished, but it won't hurt you to let me look after you once in a while. Okay?"

What did a woman say when her man treated her like a flower, but respected her strength? Nothing. Because without trying, he'd become exceptional, and nothing I could say would come close to the beauty of his words. I was lost to him, untethered in a raging storm, but he would always lead me to safety.

# Chapter Fourteen

*Acceptance is the greatest gift of humanity, which is why rejection burns so deep.*

Hudson turned on the lights of the car to give us better light. Then he unzipped my bag and rummaged around for the pot of healing balm. He unscrewed the lid and scrunched his nose up at the smell. According to him, it smelled like ass, but it was a powerful substance I always kept with me.

He swept his fingers into the jar and I lifted my top to reveal the burned flesh. With a steady hand, he began applying the clear gooey substance. I gritted my teeth and suppressed the scream building in my throat.

"I'll be passed out in five minutes," I warned him. "I best get in the car before that happens."

"Yes, I don't want a swooning princess at my feet."

I rolled my eyes and climbed into the passenger side, my eyes already heavy with the pull of sleep which would hasten the healing process. Hudson started the engine and then we were off. I curled on my side and gazed at the man that stole my heart before succumbing to the lull of oblivion. Unlike before, I didn't feel vulnerable or threatened in his presence. I was safe. Hudson had torn through my defenses and for the first time in my life, someone knew my secrets and had accepted me for all I am. The horror, the ugly, the good, and all the complexities of my heritage. He was my mate, and I knew in my heart I would tear the world apart if anything happened to him. That thought was both terrifying and comforting.

*Rolling green fields separated by a lazy river filled every direction. The sun warmed my skin and coaxed a smile to spread on my face.*

*"Do you hear it?" Hudson asked from next to me. We were lying on a large soft picnic blanket with an array of fruit and sandwiches between us.*

*"Hear what?"*

*"The battle cry of your future."*

*My life was a battle, but I didn't hear it cry. "No."*

*He gazed out across the scenery. "There's something coming."*

*"Something?" I felt like an idiot repeating his words back to him, but he wasn't making any sense.*

*He jerked his head toward a bend in the river. The blue sky darkened and a storm cloud billowed in the air. Lightning cracked and electrified the river. The crystal water turned crimson and a shadow moved in front of the sun. An eclipse.*

*The grassy hills withered and turned gray. I stood and took a step back.*

*Hudson was behind me and wrapped his arms around me. "It's coming, Cora. Your future, your fate, your freedom filled with death, darkness, and decay."*

*I shook my head and heavy tears welled in my eyes. "No, this is not my future."*

*"This is the witching hour, and you are its master. Decide your next steps carefully—you hold the key to the future of those you love."*

*"Will you stand with me?" I whispered as his words shook me to my core.*

*"In the end, we are all alone."*

*His arms disappeared from around me and I twisted to watch him disintegrate into the air. The tree behind me withered, the leaves falling from its branches in a rush before being swept away on a breeze, turning brittle and then to dust. Tears fell from my eyes and landed on the parched ground, which thirstily gobbled up the liquid.*

*I shuddered from the icy wind whipping around me. The silence broke and hundreds—no, thousands—of tortured screams filled my mind. My knees gave way and I collapsed to the ground as my hands clutched my head and I squeezed my eyes closed, trying to block out their pain.*

"Cora," Hudson's voice broke through.

"Hudson? Help me," I gritted through my teeth. If I opened my mouth the tortured screams of the haunted would drown me.

"Cora, wake up."

Wake up? If only. There was no escaping this torment. My teeth rattled as my body shook. I lashed out in panic and a loud growl tore through my mind, pulling me from the nightmare I was stuck in.

My eyes flew open and Hudson's panicked hazel gaze came into view. Blood seeped from the side of his neck and spilled over his chest. My hands clutched his arms. He hissed and I glanced down. My claws were extended and embedded in his flesh. Crimson leaked from between my fingers and slid onto his pants. I tore my hands away, leaving holes in his forearms. My hands covered my face and I shook my head. "I'm sorry."

Strong bloody arms gripped my waist, hauled me over the console, and into his lap. "Don't be ridiculous," he grumbled as he held me against his chest.

"I hurt you." This was everything I feared. What was I thinking? I couldn't take a mate, a partner, I'm too dangerous. One wrong move and I'd kill him. He needed to get as far away from me as possible. I was dangerous, violent, unpredictable.

Hudson pried my hands from my face. I blinked up at him. "This is nothing, the cubs cause more damage than this when they are playing."

I doubted that. His gaze turned molten as he saw me trying to withdraw. "No," he growled. "You don't get to do that with me. You think I don't worry about hurting you? I have a prehistoric temperamental tiger ruling my emotions, but the fact is, we house these beasts and they have claws. As you already stated, you are not a fragile flower, no need to treat me like one either."

He kissed my eyelids, and the tears stopped leaking. I drew in a shaky breath and grounded myself in his presence. I stopped catastrophizing and my claws shrank back. Hudson turned his arms for my inspection; the punctures had stopped leaking. Was this an ominous prediction of our future? Covered in blood with an air of violence whipping around us?

Glancing outside, I saw my house behind us shrouded in darkness. My hand ran over my stomach, no burning, no raised flesh. I'd healed quickly, a positive effect of having Indigo out of her chains.

"What were you dreaming about?" Hudson asked, grasping my chin and turning my head back to him.

I didn't want to lie to him, but I wasn't ready to speak about the horror of my psyche either. "It was just a dream," I answered.

He tilted his head and his forehead crumpled into a frown. "A dream where you screamed aloud?"

"A nightmare, then."

A heavy sigh expanded his chest. "I'll be here when you are ready to share."

I leaned into him, and covered his mouth with mine. The kiss, a promise of trust and a prayer of thanks that he wasn't pushing me. Something tapped against the window and we jerked apart.

"Fucking vampire," Hudson growled as Sebastian waved from the outside.

"We have a prior engagement," Sebastian said with a frown at the blood covering us both. "Are you hurt?"

If only that were the case. But this time, it was me doing the hurting. I shook my head. "I'm fine, it's Hudson who is hurt."

Sebastian's face relaxed. Apparently, that was acceptable.

"Engagement?" Hudson asked like I'd promised Sebastian my hand in marriage.

I patted his chest. "No need for jealousy, Principal, I'm a one tiger girl. I told you about this already. My best friend needs my support to face down his parents. He's about to give them some home truths, and I don't expect it to be pleasant."

"If Leon lays one finger on you, I will destroy him," Hudson growled. Ha, this was quite the turnaround from the politically-driven motivation that had caused us to separate not so long ago. This was the devotion I needed, and I was going to covet it like Gollum and his precious.

"Let's get you cleaned up first," I told Hudson. I expected him to fight me, but apparently, me putting him before Sebastian made him more amenable.

Sebastian entered the house first and sat in the empty parlor, shrouded in darkness. Maggie was busy checking in a dainty female vampire with long dark hair. Rebecca poked her head out of the kitchen.

"Can you keep Sebastian company?" I asked.

She raised a brow at my state. "Are you okay?"

"It's not mine," I reassured her as I dragged Hudson down the stairs and into my office. I pointed at my chair. "Sit."

He did as I instructed and I retrieved some antiseptic and dressings. I slid between his legs, and his hands wrapped around my thighs, holding me close as I began bathing the worst of his wounds on his neck.

"I'm sorry," I whispered. No apology cut it. There was no excuse.

"I think you need to let Indigo out more often," Hudson said carefully, causing me to scowl.

"What possessed you to make that conclusion?"

"You need to become more in tune with her. If she didn't feel oppressed, she wouldn't overreact when she senses you're in danger."

Huh, that made sense I guess, and he did have his own beast to contend with, who he certainly had a better relationship with.

"I'll make time to get to know her," I said as I placed a dressing against his neck and moved to his arms. The puncture marks had almost closed over. I took my time cleaning the blood from his flesh anyway, wanting to erase the pain I'd caused.

Hudson caught my hand as I was repeating the wiping motion to get rid of the blood.

"Stop, I'm okay. I'll be healed before you return with the vampire."

As if on cue, Sebastian strode into the room. "Are you coming?" he snapped.

I rolled my eyes and gave Hudson a quick kiss, the lingering guilt still present between us.

"You can make kissy faces with the cat later. We need to hit the road and get this done before I back out."

"Keep your panties on, I'm coming."

"Not helping, Cora," Hudson grumbled.

A blush filled my cheeks as his words penetrated. *Cora Roberts—mistress of the innocent innuendo.*

Castle Elliot was a lesson in gothic architecture. Built in the seventeenth century, the main building encompassed towers and turrets with gargoyles and arched stained glass windows. The inside had been modernized over the years by Aira, Sebastian's mother, creating a perfect blend of historical and modern. I loved their home. But I hated Leon, he was an arrogant, unfeeling asshole. Vampires often became emotionless over time. I think it was a symptom of their extended lifespan, as they watched generations of humanity fall around them and the rise of new eras.

"You ready?" I asked Sebastian as he opened the front door.

"As I'll ever be," he grumbled. There was a hard set to his lips. He was determined to explain his avoidance of his parents' marriage matches, but I couldn't see this going well.

Aira appeared from the drawing room to the right. Like Rebecca, she was the epitome of royal elegance. Dressed in a simple but expensive black sheath dress, she oozed grace and decorum. Unlike me, whose clumsy feet got her into trouble more often than not.

"Sebastian, Cora, I wasn't expecting you," she said, her voice a tinkling sound. "Is there anything wrong?"

Sebastian shook his head and I stepped a little closer in a show of silent support. "I need to speak to you and father," he said, pushing on through the house and into the drawing room.

Leon was seated in an armchair with an expensive tablet in his hands. The house might be from the dark ages, but the vampires made sure to keep up with the latest technology. Sebastian had once explained to me that if you resisted the progression of technology, then you got left behind. It didn't wait for you, and that meant your enemies, who marched with the masses, would have an advantage over you.

Leon lowered the tablet to the table next to him and raised an expectant brow at us. "The meal is next Saturday, surely you aren't parading the Consort Royal as an excuse for your duties? The lie hardly works now that she is bound to our enemy."

I ghosted my hand over Sebastian's back, offering him my strength and support. Aira perched on the end of the sofa and folded her hands in her lap.

"Well?" Leon spat.

Sebastian trembled a little then straightened his spine and rose a little taller. *That's it,* I silently encouraged. *You got this.*

"I will not be marrying any princess you present to me."

"You will marry, it is your duty," Leon said, rising to his feet. I resisted the urge to roll my eyes at his display of dominance. This moment didn't need my derision.

Sebastian's hands fisted at his sides, and I heard him swallow. "No, father, I won't."

"Why ever not?"

Aira's eyes had softened. She knew, I realized, and had been waiting for her son to open up. Perhaps we should have played this differently, spoken to his mother first who could have cushioned the blow. Too late now.

"Because I'm gay."

You could have heard a pin drop in that castle. Even the servants shuffling around in the other rooms had paused. Leon's face fell in shock. Aira tensed as she eyeballed her husband with a cold stare. She was ready to strike should he become violent, and my opinion of her shot up. I always liked Aira, but couldn't fathom why she tolerated Leon.

"No," Leon whispered as he ran a hand through his hair. "You have dated many numerous women through the years."

"Dated, yes. Slept with, no."

"I cannot conceive of this," Leon said, his voice rising. Here it comes.

"It isn't a matter of what you can conceive," Sebastian stated. "It is whom I am attracted to and the implications are I will never marry a princess."

Leon's arms flew into the air. "So what, you expect us to start a line of princes for your viewing pleasure?"

"That would be more fruitful than the princesses, but I think the time for arranged marriages is over. I am capable of finding my own match without your meddling."

Leon moved so swiftly, he was a blur. Sebastian lunged from his position next to me and the pair slid across the coffee table. The no doubt priceless vase smashed onto the hard tiles as they grappled on the floor. I moved to pull Leon off, but Aira beat me to it, knocking me back as she wrapped her arm around her husband's neck and put him in a choke hold. Sebastian rolled out from underneath Leon. His features had sharpened, showing his supernatural origins. I rarely saw this happen.

Sebastian wiped the blood from his burst lip and glared at his father. "I am not doing this to hurt you," he snarled. "Who I'm attracted to is not a choice."

Leon growled and Aira shook her head. "Let it be, Leon."

"You are no longer welcome in this house." Leon sneered. "While you make these disgusting choices, you are no son of mine. You're dead to me."

Sebastian froze. This was worse than I thought. I knew Leon was hardly going to welcome the news as it fucked up his plans of international relations and power, but—

"That works for me," Sebastian spat.

"Just leave," Aira pleaded. "I will be in touch."

Sebastian gripped my hand and spun us toward the door. He practically pulled me out of his home and down the steps to his car. He threw the passenger door open, bundled me inside, then appeared in the driver's seat next to me. The door thudded closed as he put his foot down and we spun into the darkness.

I kept quiet, because what are the right words when your father doesn't accept an integral part of who you are? I hated Leon for making his son feel like this. Sebastian banged on the steering wheel, and I covered his hand with mine in a show of support.

"You can stay with me," I uttered. "Always."

He side-eyed me, his features twisted with a soul-deep agony. "Thank you."

I nodded and allowed him the space he needed the rest of the way home. We spun into the driveway and Hudson was sitting on the porch swing, reading under the light.

I exited the car and trotted up the stairs, glancing at the book in his hands. Huh, I never took him for a horror fan, but Stephen King could weave a good tale. Hudson's eyes darted to Sebastian who'd followed me up the steps.

"Why is he here?"

Oh boy. "His parents kicked him out. He's going to be staying here."

Hudson rose very slowly and put the open book face down on the arm of the chair, and I winced at the cracked spine. He took a step toward me and glared at my best friend. "No," he said.

"That is not your decision to make. It's my home"

Hudson sucked in a breath. "Like hell is he sleeping under the same roof as you."

"Go inside, the room next to Rebecca's is free," I told Sebastian. He opened the door and made his way inside. I waited until it clicked closed behind him.

I didn't think this through in terms of Hudson's jealousy. I kept forgetting I was dealing with a possessive shifter, but I would not be turning my friend away in his time of need. I guess I needed to compromise, and that compromise would take a leap of faith on my part.

I moved toward Hudson who was staring at the front door like he could murder Sebastian with just a thought. "Would you feel more comfortable if you moved into my room?"

Hudson's gaze snapped to mine and a small smile crept over his lips. It was going to happen sooner rather than later, may as well be now.

"Yes," he growled and swept me into his arms. He darted inside the house and took the stairs two at a time past a startled-looking Maggie and a smirking Rebecca. Why where the supernaturals suddenly up and around in the middle of the night? Ugh, vampire hearing, I had zero secrets in this house.

Hudson threw open my door and made his way to my bedroom. He dropped me on the bed and prowled over me. "Now, little witch, you promised me your dirty side."

# CHAPTER FIFTEEN

*Live a little, for clarity, doesn't mean getting naked on the lawn.*

Hudson's gaze lit from within, his animal was close to the surface and it drew Indigo from my depths. She pushed against my mind, and I allowed her through, becoming the passenger. She didn't shift but I saw the recognition in Hudson's eyes as a worthy predator sat before him. She spun onto her knees and tilted her head.

"You want me?" she purred. Oh, boy.

Hudson's hands snapped out, ready to wrap them around her. She tensed and somersaulted through the air, landing in a crouch behind him on the floor.

*"Don't play games with him,"* I warned.

*"I thought the wolf explained you need to meet him on cat terms, Cora,"* she answered as Hudson spun. His muscles seemed to be bulging against his shirt. He was about to hulk out.

*"Yes, I'm giving him the cream, get back on the bed,"* I instructed.

I felt her lips spread into a feral grin. "If you want me, Principal, you'll have to prove you can catch me."

Hudson's eyes danced with amusement and excitement at the challenge Indigo was laying down. I sighed and tried to roll my eyes, but she was in full control. Hudson became very still, there were a few feet between us, and we had nowhere to run but the sitting room. I was certain this pointless game of chase was going to be over within seconds.

Indigo tensed and then dashed into the sitting room as I predicted. Hudson was a hairsbreadth behind us. Instead of turning to the door to let this insane game play out throughout the house, she spun right and lifted her hands.

The French doors blew open and she dashed for the opening.

There was zero hesitation as she launched herself from the third floor. I knew we wouldn't be hurt, but my stomach still lurched. *"What are you doing?"*

*"Playing the cat. Don't worry, the sex will be worth it."*

I felt the thud behind me and just like that the chase was on. Indigo laughed like a lunatic as she led the way between the trees bordering my property. I sent a silent prayer that nobody had noticed in the house, because sex in my private rooms was one thing, playing games outside was another.

*"Live a little,"* Indigo chastised as she narrowly missed Hudson's hands.

He growled and the hairs on my arms stood on their ends. The footsteps stopped behind us, that feeling of being pursued halted. Somehow, we lost him from our immediate trail—which was suspicious. She spun in a circle, squinting into the darkness which was charged with our energy. There's no way he didn't know where we were. Indigo chuffed in agreement. *What game are you playing, Principal?*

Indigo crouched and her vision became hyper focused, through her I saw the world differently. Heat signatures became clear, from the little mouse scurrying along through the fallen leaves which left a faint orange trail, to the owl, emitting a golden glow from where it sat in the tree opposite me, watching us run around like children.

*"That's seriously cool,"* I told her. I had no idea she could do this, not that I prowled the gardens at night regularly.

*"You haven't seen anything yet,"* she answered as she scanned the shadows for our mate.

She took a steady step forward and then another. We sensed him a split second before he pounced. Her head shot back just in time to see Hudson falling toward us. The damn cat had hidden high in the trees.

He knocked her over but spun during the fall so she landed on top of him, like a cushion—if that cushion was made of hard hot muscle. He rolled over and pinned her hands above her head. Green rolled over his gaze as Indigo struggled beneath him. Our hearts were thumping rapidly with the thrill of the chase and the inevitable explosion.

He leaned down and fused our lips together in a hot, passionate kiss that sent pulses of need to every part of her body. Indigo tried to buck him off, still fighting. Hudson pushed her thighs apart with his knees and used his weight to keep her pinned in place.

Indigo snarled and arched her back. What on earth was she doing? We'd been caught, stop the fighting already. *"You'll see,"* she said as she relaxed underneath him. Keeping our hands pinned to the ground by one of his, he used his free one to grip the neckline of my dress and with a growl, tore it down the middle, revealing my flesh to the cool air and his heated gaze. I was five percent annoyed, and ninety-five percent turned on. I loved this dress, but damn, that was hot. I'd never understood the appeal until this moment.

"You are stunning," he rasped.

He sucked and nibbled down my throat before lathing his hot tongue over the lace of my bra and drawing my nipple into his mouth. Even with Indigo in charge, I could feel everything and was quickly getting lost in the sensations he was delivering.

I felt her intention before she moved. Jerking up against an unsuspecting Hudson, she flipped us, straddling his thighs and shamelessly grinding down on his erection. His gaze lit from within as his animal pressed against him, fighting to be let out. One of his hands gripped my hips and the other tangled in my hair. My heart was pumping, my skin tingling, and my head spinning as he rewrote what passion meant. Nobody would ever compare.

*"Nobody ever needs to compare,"* Indigo reminded me. *"He's ours."*

There was still a niggling doubt, something that was entirely to do with me and not him. It was the evil little voice that whispered I wasn't enough for him. Indigo jerked back from Hudson and stood. He blinked up at us in disbelief, and if he could see my mental face, it would have mirrored his. What was she doing?

She gave Hudson a sultry look, I know because I felt her amusement, and then turned on her heel and sprinted away. *"What are you doing?"* I yelled. *"Turn back, he's on the floor panting for us!"*

*"Wait for it,"* she said while chuckling. Oh no, she was laughing, this was some harebrained plan conceived in the mind of a being born of death and destruction.

The air whooshed out of my lungs and Hudson took us to the ground once more, the roar he released scattering lesser prey. Our knees hit the ground and he gripped the rest of my dress and tore it from my body. My underwear followed and he pushed my head to the floor with one hand while lifting my hips back with another. Then his tongue was against my core as I struggled with the onslaught of sensation whipping through my body and the deep ache he'd created. I twisted my head as he pulled his mouth away, a ripple of shock running through me as his eyes narrowed to vertical slits.

"Don't move," he growled. He unzipped his jeans and then surged inside of me, my breath catching in my throat at the sudden fullness. He moved inside me, chasing away the ache and replacing it with consuming pleasure.

Indigo was retreating, but not before she tugged away from him one last time. He snarled and pulled me up against his body, his hand dropping to where we were joined and he rubbed in fast circles on the bundle of nerves, creating a dizzying spiral of need. His teeth sunk into my left shoulder, and I convulsed around his shaft, screaming into the night at the crescendo of pleasure blazing through me. A smug Indigo disappeared into my mind, leaving me with a provoked and possessive Hudson.

Hudson's rhythm became jerky. "Cora," he whispered like a curse and a prayer. He thrust one last time and held me against him as he spilled himself inside me.

Our heaving chests fell in rhythm, slowing with each passing minute. His tongue suddenly snaked out and licked a hot path over my shoulder. I hissed and turned to inspect the bite. It wasn't too bad, two puncture marks where his fangs must have descended, and a small trickle of blood that he seemed intent on licking.

"I'm sorry," he muttered. He didn't sound that sorry. "She provoked me."

"I'm aware," I muttered. "Don't worry about it."

He withdrew from my body, zipped his jeans back up and then swept me up in his arms. How did I end up naked and he was still fully clothed?

He strode toward the house and whipped open the door. Everyone was in the parlor and reception area looking everywhere but at us. Except Dave, he was leaning against the desk with his arms folded and his right eyebrow cocked.

"Avert your eyes from my naked mate," Hudson snapped.

Dave unfolded his arms and lifted them in the air before sweeping his gaze to the side. I didn't miss the twitch of his lips as we ascended the stairs past a few guests. Their noses twitched. Ugh.

"Pay up," I heard Sebastian say.

"They weren't on the lawn having wild monkey sex," Rebecca sing-songed. My cheeks flushed.

"Really?" Sebastian answered. "Because I'm quite certain that scream was born of pleasure."

I needed to move out, perhaps out of the state. Nobody but Hudson should know what I sound like when I orgasm.

"Agreed, but they were in the wooded area. Next time, be more specific in your bet boundaries."

Hudson's lips twitched. "It's not funny," I grumbled. "They call it bedroom activities because that is where you are meant to stay—in the bedroom."

Hudson shook his head and chuckled as he kicked open the door to our room. "Oh, Cora, I'm going to enjoy corrupting your sweet innocent mind."

"Is that so?"

He throws me on my bed. "Starting with just how naughty we can get in *our* bedroom. Now spread your thighs for me, beautiful, so I can feast on you some more before making you scream."

Oh boy.

# Chapter Sixteen

*Tiptoeing around a grenade doesn't make it any less deadly.*

The sun rose and with it came a new sensation. I was content, loved, and happy. Yes, the world around us was a shit show, and I suspected it was about to get a lot worse, but I was no longer alone. Hudson Abbot had climbed inside my soul and made his home there, but I had also done the same. There was an invisible thread that linked us together, as fine as silk and as strong as steel.

My mind churned over the events of the last few days. I'd missed something fundamental, and now it became solidified, as clear as the Louisiana sunshine.

"What are you thinking?" Hudson asked from next to me. He'd not changed his breathing or opened his eyes. I wasn't even aware he was awake.

I twisted in the sheets to turn to him. He was sexy in the morning with rumpled hair and a relaxed face. My eyes drifted down his body, his very naked body. I was pleasantly achy and totally relaxed, but that feeling was about to disappear. Perhaps this is what life is about? Catching the moments we had and using them to form memories to cling to when shit gets serious. I vowed to make room for as many of these moments as possible.

His eyes flipped open as he caught me ogling him. Bah, I was a red-blooded woman and he was all mine, this wasn't a crime. His mouth curled in a very cat-like grin, self-assured and satisfied.

"The Datura," I started. It was time to return to reality, at least for a little while.

"What about it?"

"We've discovered that it is being used as a delivery method for magic."

"That's right."

"But we aren't asking the fundamental question."

"Who is the magic for and why?"

I shook my head as his fingers trailed patterns over the swell of my breasts. "No, magic is a constant, like energy. And what is the golden rule of energy?"

Hudson's fingers paused and he frowned. "It cannot be created nor destroyed."

"Exactly. So the question is—where is this magic being drawn from? It isn't a small amount you could siphon from nature, this magic packs a punch, big enough to infect an entire town."

"What holds that kind of magic?" he asked.

"The factions. Humans hold a little, vampires more. Shifters share their magic with animals and nature, which puts them higher up on the totem pole. But elementals are at the top."

"You think your grandmother is stealing magic from her own kind?"

I shrugged even as a cold tingling ran its icy fingers down my spine. "That would be the most logical conclusion."

"How would she do that? Kill them?"

I swallowed the knot in my throat and shook my head. "No, that would make the magic hard to contain, it would naturally want to return to the earth."

The horror of what she might be doing made my blood boil. "How then?" Hudson pushed.

"There are rituals, painful and horrific ones, that she can do to remove the magic from the source. If she keeps them alive, their magic will remain in the air, easier to collect and redirect."

"Perhaps that is what she wants from the vaults?"

The wards clanged in my mind and I grimaced. We were about to find out.

Dressed in a pair of navy slacks and a cream blouse, I descended the stairs with trepidation in my heart and determination in my soul. A huge part of me needed to believe that my grandmother would never do something so heinous, but the logical, realistic voice whispered that I was being entirely too optimistic.

I found my grandmother sitting on the sofa in the parlor sipping tea with Rebecca and Sebastian. Huh, where was Hudson? Perhaps he'd made himself unavailable given my grandmother's expectations of our relationship. He trusted me, but didn't need to be playing The Principal with the head of The Order when we were in a silent and deadly war.

I strode into the room like I owned it, because I did. I sat in the armchair and caught Rebecca's eyes. She tensed.

"You must excuse me, Eloise, I have some urgent matters that require my attention," Rebecca said as she stood.

My grandmother nodded. "Of course, dear, let me know your decision."

Rebecca's lips pressed together and she disappeared into the house. What decision? What was my grandmother up to now?

Eloise Roberts was timeless. Her silver hair was swept into an elegant updo and she wore an expensive burgundy skirt suit with the ease of a top politician. She smiled at me as I poured a cup of tea for myself, noting her cup was still half full.

"Can I get you something to eat?" I asked. I was starving after the marathon evening I'd spent in Hudson's arms, but my stomach was tied up in knots and that didn't mix well with food.

"No," she said, taking a sip of her tea. "Where is the Principal?"

Trust my grandmother to cut through the pleasantries and bullshit. "I'm not sure." This was the truth. I had no clue where Hudson was. Perhaps that was his way of protecting me, what I didn't know I couldn't say.

Eloise sighed. It was ingrained in me to feel small in the presence of that sigh of disappointment. I might find her methods and ambitions unsavory, but she was still the grandmother that had created steel in my spine. I guess I had that to thank her for.

She eyed me with the Roberts' stare and I resisted the temptation to look away.

A small smile pulled at her lips, making her look uncomfortable, probably because she rarely smiled. How very sad. I guess she would be free of the wrinkles that plagued the happy and the free.

"You are truly my granddaughter," she said. I didn't realize it was ever in question, but I think she meant it as a compliment. "I'm proud of you."

Despite myself, I let the compliment warm my heart. I didn't need her approval, but like most grandchildren, I craved it, particularly when my own mother was no longer with us, and my father, as far as they were aware, was a nobody.

Sebastian swanned into the room and eyeballed the back of my grandmother's head like he could reverse his course and slink out of the room. My grandmother tilted her head. *Too late, buddy.*

"Sebastian, what is the Vampire Crown Prince of North America doing in my granddaughter's house so early in the morning?" She glanced at me like she was assessing if I was bedding the vampire as well as Hudson.

Resigned, he came further into the room, his slightly rumpled appearance not helping matters. My grandmother's gaze burned through him. This was my fault, I should have organized for him to have some spare clothing. I was a bad friend who had wild monkey sex on the lawn.

"I'm staying here for a little while," Sebastian answered. He didn't sit, indicating he did not welcome a further conversation with the woman.

"Why?" she asked.

Sebastian straightened, slipping into his royal role seamlessly. "I do not answer to The Order, Eloise, and I would watch your tone if you wish to continue to have positive ties with myself."

He'd left his parents out of it, and in the end, Sebastian was their future, regardless as to whether he caved to the pressures of a marriage alliance.

My grandmother swept her gaze over him before turning back to me with a wicked glint. Oh wow, she was seriously considering the possibility of whoring me out to the supernatural elite.

Sebastian gave me an apologetic look before ducking out of the room.

"If the cat is giving you the run around, you might consider a pairing with the vampire. He seems quite taken with you."

"Sebastian is a good friend," I said and patted myself on my back for not breathing fire in her face. The struggle was real. "And Hudson is not giving me the run around."

"No? Then where is he?"

Avoiding you. "I'm unsure of his whereabouts, but that does not make me unsure of his heart."

Her gaze narrowed. "Heart? You think you've ensnared The Principal?"

Interesting that the pack's gossip mill hadn't yet reached her, perhaps her attention was elsewhere. "He's declared me as his mate to the pack."

She blinked. "Have you set a date for the ceremony?"

"No."

"So it's not official?"

"Yes."

She glanced at my hand. Oh right, *if you liked it then you shoulda put a ring on it* sprang into my head, and I had the irrational urge to stand up and start the iconic dance.

My fists clenched, I would not allow my grandmother to wobble my security. Hudson was committed to me, I didn't need a piece of jewelry to prove it. "We've been a little preoccupied with a mass death in Peach Tree."

I'll give it to her, my grandmother had a poker face Vegas would admire—she gave nothing away. "What happened?" she asked.

I studied her pose, slightly too rigid, and just a little too well put together, but her body leaned toward me ever so slightly. She knew exactly what had happened and wanted to figure out what I knew.

"There was an elaborate, yet clumsy cover up trying to pin it on an amateur Satanic cult ritual."

"Did you glean what really happened?"

Ha, she was testing me. Had I uncovered her plans? If I had, I knew too much, and if I hadn't, I would see disappointment on her face, but at least I wouldn't be in danger.

"No."

She hummed. "If you had to hazard a guess?"

*Tread carefully, Cora, remember blood counts for little when dealing with this woman.*

"A spell gone awry perhaps?"

Her brows furrowed. Damn it, too close. "To what end?" she pushed.

I resisted the urge to fidget, it was a tell I'd long since gotten rid of. "That remains to be seen." If I revealed the discovery of the flower, then all bets were off. That key piece of evidence had led us down the trail right to her fields of death, where she'd sent her best elementals to protect the crop, and now they were dead. Shit, shit, shit. The more I thought about it, the more dangerous it became. Perhaps a little deflection?

I leaned toward her. "Whomever committed the crime in Peach Tree knew to ward against my gift, I couldn't get a retro read from any of the dead. There are some in The Order that know of my power, perhaps we should start by looking at them."

My grandmother's face relaxed. "I will see to it myself that they are questioned, if they don't squeal then I'll send in Michael Glaister."

I grimaced. Michael Glaister, The Hound. The Order's terrifying torturer. But I'd won her over by trusting her with this information and putting her in charge of finding the perpetrator. Needlessly, given she had at least given the order and more than likely been present for the massacre.

"Is the vault ready?" my grandmother asked. My shoulders relaxed as I welcomed the change in topic.

"Yes."

"Excellent, I have little time to waste on tea and cookies this visit. Perhaps next time."

I stood and led the way to the vaults. It would need a little more of my blood to complete the opening, because it was my blood that started it. I also had this sick sensation that there would be no next time, because if what I suspected was true, my grandmother was committing crimes I could not overlook.

Everyone in the house was studiously avoiding bumping into us, and I didn't blame them. Being caught in the glare of Eloise Roberts was a disconcerting experience. We made it to the vault uninterrupted and I sliced open my palm once more and held my hand against the plate. The vault clicked.

My grandmother raised a brow at me. Yes, yes, I was leaving. I wasn't dumb. "I'll wait for you upstairs," I said, closing the door to the basement behind me and leaving my grandmother with priceless and powerful artifacts. Knowing what she had taken would be crucial in understanding what her plans were.

Ten minutes later, Eloise Roberts swept through the house with a leather satchel at her side. She cast me a look as she rushed toward the door. My grandmother didn't rush—*anywhere*. What the hell was in that bag?

"I'll be in touch," she said and the door thumped closed behind her.

My friends emerged one by one from the kitchen. So that's where they'd been hiding? Figures. Even my ghostly sidekick hovered behind the group, a frown etched onto his face. However, for the first time in weeks, neither Dave nor Hudson were present. I wondered what was keeping them occupied. Sebastian was brandishing a tray with a plate of fatty goodness on it. Yum, a cooked breakfast. He placed it on my lap and handed me the silverware.

"Now what?" Rebecca asked.

I shoved some sausage in my mouth as a promise to my stomach that more food was on the way.

"Now we discover what she has taken and piece it together with what we know already And just like Columbo, we will have all the answers we need to solve this mystery."

"And just how are you meant to know what has been taken?" Aunt Liz said from behind me. I glanced over my shoulder and grimaced at the disapproving stare.

"I took precautions."

"That vault is meant to be safe from such precautions."

"It is."

"Then what the hell have you done?" Aunt Liz snapped. "My mother is not to be trifled with."

"I have a replica vault." Thick silence coated the room. "It will show us what has changed."

"That's a very dangerous game you are playing, Cora. I hope you know what you are doing."

I scooped up some fluffy scrambled eggs and joined her in that sentiment. I also hoped I knew what I was doing, because this game wasn't only dangerous, it was deadly.

*Cora Roberts—demolisher of eggs and family trust.*

# Chapter Seventeen

*Just when you think things can't get any worse, the universe sucker punches you in the face.*

When you've violated the trust of your family, you have to make sure it was for a damn good reason. I only hoped my grandmother hadn't taken something insignificant from the vault. Otherwise, I could kiss the support of my aunts goodbye.

With Aunt Liz at my back, I opened the first vault, which contained much of my personal collection. We'd left everyone else in the main house. This was primarily Roberts' business.

"How does this show us what she took?" my aunt asked as she gazed at the treasures I'd hoarded over the years.

I stalked to the back of the vault and pushed a cabinet two feet to the left, revealing an unassuming rectangular door. I whispered a chant specific to myself, and the door clicked open, a small gap appearing at the side.

My hands wrapped around the handle and I yanked it open. The lights flared to life, like it was welcoming me home. My aunt followed on my heels.

She spun in a circle, her mouth popping open. "You replicated the entire third vault?"

I nodded at where a faint purple magical signature hovered like a glittery beacon. "I did, and for about three hours afterwards, the room replicates the movements of the visitor, showing what they touched."

I moved toward the glitter and gazed at a book on a waist height wooden pedestal. My grandmother's signature was concentrated in this area, she hadn't been anywhere else. This is what she took.

Aunt Liz peered at the book, a look of foreboding blanketing her features. "Is this just for show, or can we see what the book contains?"

I cast her a look, a smile pulling at my lips. "Since when do I do anything halfhearted, Aunt?"

Her hands trembled a little as she touched the cover. "Nothing good can come from this grimoire."

"Whose is it?"

"Eunice Roberts, your great-grandmother. She was an expert spell caster and the reason I cannot have children, neither can you. It would be a death sentence to the father, and I think you are rather fond of Hudson."

Eunice Roberts was born without elemental power, and she made it her mission to alter the curse placed on the Roberts' bloodline. The first born of each generation would drain their fathers dry of magic and life-force. Technically, my father should be dead, but the curse was no match for an archangel. I suspected I had weakened him, and that's why he stayed out of my life. Also, I technically was a Nephilim, a feared race that were commonly slaughtered at birth. My mother had the common sense to conceal my identity and teach me how to chain my alter ego.

This grimoire would contain all of Eunice's secrets, her darkest spells, and greatest accomplishments. She was both revered and feared in our community, and what the hell my grandmother wanted with her mother's grimoire terrified me.

"This is an exact replica?" Aunt Liz asked.

I nodded. "Down to the crinkled pages and torn edges."

"Can we remove it from here to study it?"

"Yes."

Aunt Liz lifted the large black leather tome in her hands and clutched it to her chest. "Now to figure out what nefarious spell my mother is seeking."

I closed up the room and moved the cabinet back in front of the door before sealing the vault.

"Do you go there often?" Aunt Liz asked. Her voice was steady, but the ice in her tone was unmistakable.

"That was the first time," I assured her as we entered my office.

Aunt Liz cast her gaze over me, like she was assessing my truth. With a sharp nod she said, "Keep it that way."

I sat in my chair and Aunt Liz pulled one of the visitor chairs around the desk to sit next to me. We opened the grimoire, even though this was a copy, the power still clung to the pages like glue.

I frowned at the first spell. "What language is that?" I wondered.

Aunt Liz's brow furrowed. "Russian, maybe?"

"Do you speak Russian?"

"No."

I pulled my phone out from my slacks pocket and typed the first few words into Google Translate. "Not Russian," I muttered. "Kazakh."

We glanced at each other, our eyes colliding in understanding. "Not me," I said with a shake of my head.

Aunt Liz chuckled. "Yes, definitely you."

Hudson burst through the office door. "I don't have the time," I countered.

"And I don't have the patience," Aunt Liz replied. "You are her favorite."

I banged my head on the desk with a groan.

"Why are you doing that?" Hudson growled.

My head shot up and I leveled him with my gaze. "Because Great Aunt Sophia is about to receive a begging call from her grandniece, and it will probably cost me a little of my soul."

"So dramatic," Aunt Liz said. She was smiling now that I'd relented to do the task.

"You have *more* aunts?" Hudson said with a raise of his eyebrows as he slid into the remaining visitor chair across from mine.

"Sophia is my grandmother's younger sister," I grumbled as I scanned my phone for her number. When did we last speak? I glanced at the call list, two months ago. I'd missed our monthly phone call. Oh boy.

"Why are you calling her?" Hudson asked.

I waved at the grimoire in front us. "This is a replica of what my grandmother collected. The problem being that the spells are written in Kazakh, so we don't know what we are dealing with."

"And your aunt just happens to speak it?"

"My great-grandmother had an affair with a Kazakh prince. In order to protect her, she was sent to live on his estate. Kazakh was my Aunt's first language and Kazakhstan her home country."

"Your family has a very colorful history," Hudson observed. A smile pulled at my lips. No one could accuse it of being boring. "Aren't you worried your aunt will tattle to your grandmother?"

Aunt Liz snorted, a very unladylike move for the put-together elemental. "No, Aunt Sophia detests her."

I pressed the call button and put the phone to my ear. Here goes nothing. The phone rang for a whole minute, and the hope inside of me grew that Aunt Sophia wouldn't answer.

I was just about to kill the call when it stopped ringing. "Ayaulym," my aunt answered in a thick accent, which given the proximity and history sounded Russian. "You missed our monthly phone call."

"I apologize, Aunt, my attention has been diverted. There is a situation I need your help with." The trick to dealing with Aunt Sophia was to inflate her ego. If she felt needed, like an integral part of the solution to a huge problem, then she would be more likely to help.

Hudson folded his arms and leaned back in the chair. *Yes, yes, you also diverted my attention.*

"Bah, we can discuss my sister's ridiculous ambitions later." I glanced at Aunt Liz, she held her hands up. "Liz, don't act innocent."

I blinked. My Aunt Sophia was blessed with unknown gifts, and one of them seemed to be the knowledge of who was listening in on the conversation. "Sorry, Aunt," Liz said.

"What is more interesting is why you have The Principal of the North American packs in the room."

Hudson's eyebrows shot up and he scanned the room like he would find my aunt lurking in a shadowy corner.

Aunt Sophia's chuckle was deep and a little husky. "Mated? To Hudson Abbot? Well, my girl, you certainly could have done worse for yourself, and very clever to avoid the curse with a species that would sooner cut off their own arm than cause pain to their mate."

I opened my mouth and was shushed down the phone. "Why am I the last to know?"

My mouth continued to gape open as she went on. "I need to see him for myself."

"I can put the video on," I offered with a wince.

"Don't be ridiculous, Cora, I cannot find the measure of a man through a video call. I will be there soon."

"Aunt, that is not the reason I called," I said.

"Well, it should have been."

I chewed my lip. That was a fair point, but I still needed to push on with the problem. "My grandmother has taken Eunice's grimoire from the third vault."

Sophia went quiet. That was more disconcerting. "Without the book I cannot help you."

I pulled my bottom lip between my teeth. "I have a replica."

My shoulders hunched as I braced for the tirade of displeasure across the Atlantic. Aunt Liz laid her hand over mine and gave it a quick squeeze.

"You made a copy of the most powerful grimoire in existence?" Aunt Sophia asked carefully.

"Technically," Aunt Liz interrupted. "She made a copy of the entire vault and put a magical signature trace on every item in there."

I glared at my aunt. "Stop helping me," I mouthed. Hudson tilted his head like he was considering the significance of what I'd revealed. Big clue, I was in deep shit with my family.

"That's my girl," Aunt Sophia gushed, and then launched into a monologue in her native language. "I'll be there shortly."

"No—wait," I tried. I did not need another meddling family member in my business.

"Don't you understand what's at stake?" Aunt Sophia snapped. Her turnabout of emotion was giving me whiplash.

"Clearly, that's why I'm calling you."

"Don't you take that tone with me, Cora Roberts, you aren't too old to go over my knee."

Hudson snorted. "Yes, Aunt," I whispered as my cheeks flushed. There was nothing like getting chastised by your family in front of your mate.

"What's the worst spell in there?" Aunt Liz asked.

A resigned chuckle came down the phone. "The worst thing in that book isn't the spells."

She'd lost it, surely the worst thing in a spell book, was a spell? It wasn't like it had recipes for cakes in there.

"What is the worst thing?" Aunt Liz asked.

I could hear shuffling and Aunt Sophia shouting at some poor person. I think I caught the word stew and customs.

"The worst thing by far in that book is the location of another book." Yup, utterly lost it.

"What book would that be?" I asked.

"The Grand Grimoire, of course. The Red Dragon."

Well fuck. That was so much worse.

# Chapter Eighteen

*Don't trust the unicorn or the mushrooms.*

The Red Dragon, or The Grand Grimoire, is essentially a black magic bible. It's widely believed that the grimoire derives from the Key of Solomon and the Lesser Key of Solomon. There are numerous editions, copies, and translations, but the original—supposedly written by a man possessed by the Devil—is said to be stored in the Vatican vaults.

I knew better. My uncle didn't sully himself with possession, and there was no spell powerful enough to summon him to earth. If he came, it was because he wanted to, not because some power-hungry human decided to try and harness his power. And if Lucifer appeared before you—you should run. Run far and run fast because if the Devil was on your tail, you were fucked.

"Apparently, you can buy The Red Dragon on Amazon for $18," Hudson said, glancing from his phone to me. Aunt Liz had been summoned upstairs by Dave, while Hudson and I had remained in my office while we researched the seriousness of what my grandmother was planning. There were a hundred things in the original book that would be a disaster.

"It's a poor imitation of the original, and it's purposefully missing essential elements, meaning whoever uses it will be unsuccessful in their endeavors. The original, however, is a masterpiece in the underworld. It can be used to summon demons."

"Lucifer?"

I shook my head. "No. Lucifer isn't a demon, he's an archangel. Just because he fell, doesn't alter his chemistry."

Hudson rubbed his chin as he thought that through. "There are too many links to the underworld."

That hadn't escaped my notice either. Even though Peach Tree was staged, it was an odd decision to attribute it to Satanic worship, and now with the possibility that my grandmother was searching for the ultimate black magic book, we couldn't ignore it. Perhaps that's not what she wanted. Ugh, who was I trying to kid? Lying to myself got us nowhere.

Footsteps pattered down the steps, and Hudson tensed as Sebastian appeared. The wards clanged in my head, signaling a visitor, someone I didn't recognize. Perhaps we had new guests?

"You are required in the kitchen," Sebastian said with a grimace. "Maggie has been cooking."

My stomach flipped. I'm not sure I could take an assault on my senses right now. Sebastian tensed, spun on his heel, and sped up the stairs. My gaze collided with Hudson.

"Why is everyone acting weird?" I asked.

Hudson shrugged. "This is the company you keep, I cannot be held responsible."

With a sigh, I stood and Hudson followed me to the stairs. I cast a glance over my shoulder, finding him ogling my ass.

The front door was open and Sebastian stood on the porch with his arms folded. I joined him on his left. Hudson stood next to me, sandwiching me between them.

A limousine inched up the driveway. I recognized the car and brushed my arm against Sebastian's in a show of support. The car stopped at the steps and the driver exited, rounded the car, and opened the rear door. Aira climbed out, looking as royal as ever. The driver closed the door, and I relaxed a little. Sebastian's mother I could deal with. She climbed the stairs and offered me a bundle of letters.

"The postman was just delivering these as we passed, I thought I would bring them to you."

I took the bundle. "Thank you."

"Principal," she greeted Hudson.

"Aira," his voice was cold, making me blink. Could I love this man anymore? He detested Sebastian, but was icing Aira out because she had hurt my best friend, who he loathed.

Sebastian's throat bobbed as he stared at his mother. "Can we go inside?" she asked. I nudged him with my arm. He relented and led the way through the front door and into the parlor. Hudson caught my gaze, and I shook my head.

He dropped a kiss on my head. "I'll be in the kitchen," he said before leaving us.

Aira sat in an armchair, while I took a position on the sofa next to Sebastian.

"Son," she started. "Are you okay?"

Sebastian's fists tightened and he sucked in a breath. "No, mother, I am not okay. My parents threw my confession back in my face because it doesn't suit their agenda."

Aira's smile fell. "I cannot speak for your father."

"Does he know you are here?" Sebastian snapped. "Or have you snuck out?"

"He knows."

"Have you come to welcome him back into your home?" I asked.

Aira's brow pinched in pain. "No, I believe for his mental health, it would be better if my son stayed with you. You have protected him for many years, I can't thank you enough for that and I hate to ask more of you."

"I'm not doing it for you. Sebastian is my best friend, I would do anything for him. My goodwill and hospitality don't expire because I love him."

A growl rumbled from the kitchen and I resisted the urge to roll my eyes. "As a friend," I clarified before a prehistoric tiger came to mark his territory.

Aira dragged a long breath in through her nose. "I love you, son. Your father will take some time to come to terms with your revelations."

"You knew?" I checked what I had suspected earlier.

Aira's lips tipped up in a sad smile. "I'm his mother, of course I knew."

Sebastian trembled at my side. "I don't want to ever see him again," he whispered.

Aira didn't seem surprised. "I understand, but I don't want to lose you. Perhaps I could continue to visit you here?"

Sebastian nodded once. "I would like that."

Aira's face relaxed. "I've brought you some clothing and personal items. I've also moved funds from your family related bank account to this one."

She pulled a bank card from her bag and some documents and placed them on the coffee table. "I've also paid for your room here for the next year."

A year? She expected it to take that long for her husband to grow up? Except this was Leon, it was highly unlikely he would ever grow up.

Maggie appeared from the kitchen. "Would you like to stay for lunch?" she asked Aira.

I sent a silent prayer to anyone with the power that Aira would refuse.

"It's mushroom soup," Maggie pushed.

Oh no, again with the mushrooms. The girl had a thing for the fungi and it never turned out well.

"Oh, my favorite," Aira said. "I would be honored to stay and share a meal."

Sebastian didn't say anything to intervene, perhaps this was part of his revenge on his mother?

Maggie clapped her hands, delighted to have a new person to torment with her food. The gang appeared from the kitchen, Hudson, Dave, and Aunt Liz carried two bowls each and set them on the dining table. Rebecca and Maggie joined us with their own suspicious bowls.

I took my seat and Sebastian pulled out the chair next to his usual seat for Aira to sit in. Her eyes widened at the bowl in front of her.

The soup was blue. I thought it over for a second. Typically, food isn't blue—blueberries the obvious exception—however, this was a luminous shade of blue, and I had no idea how you would even achieve it.

A gray lump floated in a slow circle around the edge of my bowl, like a dead body trying to find shore. Ugh.

"What's in the soup?" Aira asked.

Maggie eyeballed her own bowl. "Mushrooms," she said. *Yup, we got the mushrooms, kid, we just needed to know why the hell it was blue.*

A slight snarl came from Dave who considered anything vegetarian a slight on shifters. Aunt Liz lasered him with a look designed to cut diamonds. "Why is it blue?" he asked, ignoring my aunt.

"Oh, that's the red cabbage," Maggie said with a brilliant smile. "If you mix it with baking soda, it makes a natural food coloring."

I suppose we should be grateful it's natural. Here goes. I took a small sip from my spoon at the same time as Hudson. Huh, it wasn't actually that bad. If you ignored the color and concentrated on the soup, it was edible. That was progress.

"You like it?" Maggie asked as the rest of the supernaturals took a tentative sip.

"I think it's your best yet," I said with complete and utter honesty. The gang resolved to eat their bowls of soup without complaint, including Aira, who resisted asking any further questions. My opinion of her rose with every sip she took.

"What are your plans for the holidays?" Rebecca asked Aira.

Sebastian's face moved into the passive one I associated with his need to lock down his emotions. It was clear he wouldn't be spending it with his parents this year.

"We hold a Christmas Eve ball for our faction." She glanced at Sebastian. "Christmas day is reserved for family. What about yourself?" she asked Rebecca.

"I don't miss the formal pomp and circumstance of spending the holidays with people who only care for my station," Rebecca said. "But I've found that spending it with the family you choose, not the one you are born into, makes for a more genuine experience that cannot be compared. Here, you are among people who love you, who treasure your company, and will accept you just as you are."

Sebastian's head raised as he listened to Rebecca's explanation of what awaited him this year.

"Perhaps it is time for new traditions and new memories," Aira said as she swallowed the last of her soup and placed her spoon in the empty bowl. I glanced around, we'd all finished. Even Dave.

Maggie giggled. I frowned at her as her cheeks flushed. "I'm so happy you all enjoyed the soup. I know you hate my cooking."

I opened my mouth to argue. She waved her hand at me around another giggle. "Save it, Cora, I love that you try to hide it from me, but I'm not stupid."

"Then why do we continue to suffer through this?" Dave asked.

Maggie giggled again, and Dave joined her. Dave was giggling. What in the ever-loving fu—

Hudson snorted. My head snapped to him.

"The mushrooms looked like little pale turds," he said between his laughter.

Aira's lips twitched. "It's not the taste, it's the color, like a psychedelic party in my stomach."

A what? Aunt Liz went to sip her water and then blew it out at Aira's comment, covering Dave in the liquid.

He wiped a hand down his face, then leaned over and licked her cheek in retaliation. Oh, my god. I could never unsee that.

"Remember the slug lasagna?" Rebecca chuckled as she clutched her stomach.

A bubble of laughter began in my chest and erupted unbidden like it had a mind of its own.

Maggie waved her hand in front of her face and gazed at it like it was the second coming of Christ. Oh, for the love of all that is fungi.

"Maggie," I said while I still had the mind to. "Where did you get the mushrooms?"

Maggie stood and spun in a circle, grabbed Rebecca, and began to dance with her. "From the gardens, little toadstools of fun, some short and stubby, others long and skinny, an array of mushrooms for my soup."

Magic mushrooms. She'd cooked magic mushroom soup and we'd eaten it all.

I stood up, ready to declare our predicament, but my lips were a little numb. Not good. Harry drifted from the ceiling and landed in the middle of the table before spinning to take in the hysterical occupants. He floated toward me and I swung my arms out and around him. A warm burst of emotion drenched my worries.

"Harry, my bestest ghost friend in the whole wide world."

My arms passed through him, and he floated away from me with a frown. "Are you quite well, Miss Roberts?"

I bobbed my head. "Of course."

"Who is she talking to?" Aira asked with wide eyes. "Oh wait, no, I see it. So cute, a little magical unicorn."

I glanced around looking for said unicorn. If there was one here I wanted to ride it. Harry frowned and also looked for the unicorn. Bah, where was the little nugget of joyous mythicalism?

"I can't see it," Hudson grumbled.

"I'm not surprised," Sebastian answered. "You are hardly the epitome of imagination and acceptance. If there is a unicorn, it would hide from your growly tiger."

"You know nothing about my growly tiger, just keep your pointy teeth away from my mate."

Sebastian grinned. Oh boy, where was that shiny unicorn? We needed a distraction.

Sebastian wiggled his index finger at Hudson. "Come closer, let me tell you a secret."

Hudson's gaze narrowed and he leaned across the table, clearly curious about Sebastian's secret.

"If you are to be concerned about my teeth sinking into anybody, you should be thinking of yourself."

Hudson jerked back. Everyone else froze, including Rebecca and Maggie in their impromptu dance party.

Sebastian waved his arms in the air. "That's right, folks, I'm a gay royal vampire. Your princesses are safe, but clutch those pearls if you are a man."

Hudson's gaze swung to me. "Is he being serious?"

I nodded. A chuckle bubbled out of his lips, then he threw his head back and let a huge rumbling belly laugh free.

"I bet your father just loved hearing that," Dave said as he wiped tears from his eyes.

All gazes swung to Aira. She shrugged. "My husband is an asshole."

I blinked. It was the truth, but royals never badmouthed each other in front of outsiders. It simply wasn't done. Apparently, magic mushrooms made our tongues loose.

A knock rattled against the front door. My wards hadn't warned me of any newcomers.

Hudson jumped up. Apparently, proclaiming himself as my mate also made him the man of the house. Oh good, we were all saved.

He swung the door open and snorted. "The Devil is here, now it's a party."

Uncle Lucifer swaggered into my house looking like a curious kitten.

"Just clarifying that we can all see the Devil? It's not another unicorn situation where only the blessed and crazy can see it, right?" Dave muttered, angling his chair in front of Aunt Liz. These alpha males needed to learn that Roberts women could protect themselves.

"I see him," Sebastian said, all laughter now gone from his tone and his features as he leveled Lucifer with a deadly stare. The effect of the mushrooms was being burned away by the seriousness of the situation.

"You shouldn't be able to get in here," I stated.

He shoved his hands in his pants pockets and smirked. "You think I wouldn't leave a little back door entrance to your home when I had the opportunity?"

Huh. Well no, I hadn't considered that. "What do you want?"

He scanned the people giving him death glares and smiled. I guess he was used to the evil eye.

"What I want is to speak to Cora Roberts, daughter of death, seer of spirits, doctor of supernaturals."

I held up my hand which made him pause. "Okay, okay I get it. I'm not Daenerys Targaryen, I don't need a list of titles declaring me to be the mother of dragons and breaker of chains."

"Lucifer?" Aira said with wide eyes as she scanned my uncle like he was a yummy treat.

I'm not even entertaining the idea of them together. "What are you talking about, mother?" Sebastian asked. "Can you still see the unicorn?"

Aira blinked and her mouth popped open. I jerked my head toward the stairs which lead down to my office. Hudson followed, hot on my heels, with Lucifer positioned between us. Once inside I closed the door and raised the wards to ensure our privacy.

I spun on my heel just as Lucifer made himself comfy in my chair. He was gazing around the room with apt interest. "What do you want?"

His gaze lasered onto me and his grin fell as he steepled his hands together. I half expected him to drawl, 'excellent'.

"What I want, sweet niece, is for you to use your gifts to tell me why my demons are dying."

"Demons die, it's hardly a mystery. They aren't normally leading wholesome lives."

Lucifer leaned forward. "My demons aren't just dead, they are husks of themselves, drained of their power and energy. This isn't a demon slayer who got lucky. This is an organized and sustained attack on my own. This is a declaration of war, and I want to be absolutely clear when I retaliate that I have the right person. So I will ask you again, because if you can't tell me, then I will need to draw my own conclusions, and nobody will be safe."

I glanced at Hudson. It felt like I was caught in a noose and it was tightening inch by inch. Satanic worship, the Red

Dragon, and now a pissed off King of Hell. *What have you done, grandmother?*

# CHAPTER NINETEEN

*When visiting Hell, keep your arms and legs inside the cart and don't mind the talking heads stored in refrigerators.*

If the Devil himself comes knocking, you know for sure you are in trouble. That's what my grandmother used to tell me, and while I'm not certain she knows of my familial ties to Lucifer, it does seem to have been a prophetic saying.

"Where are these demons?" Hudson asked, folding his arms and steadying his gaze on my uncle. It seemed his laughing trip was over too.

My uncle spread his arms wide. "Where all demons are, whether dead or alive."

My face fell, because this was not a trip I wanted to take.

Hudson glanced at me and must have read the dread on my face. "What is he talking about?"

"Hell, that's where the demons are."

Hudson sliced his hand through the air. "No."

I grimaced, it wasn't like Hell was on my bucket list. "We cannot ignore this," I snapped.

"We can and we will. We have enough going on without adding the Devil's issues to the mix."

Lucifer tilted his head. That's right, collect my secrets. I massaged my right temple, ugh, a migraine was coming.

"Remember what I said," I reminded Hudson.

His eyes narrowed as he thought over the hundred and one things I'd landed him with in the last twenty-four hours alone. I waited for him to put it together, and then I waited some more.

"This is a time-sensitive matter, Cora, I must insist you come now while your cat figures out the meaning of life."

"Give us a minute," I told my uncle.

Lucifer rolled his eyes and then disappeared. "He's gone?" Hudson checked.

I nodded once and stepped between his legs. "Remember I said magic can't be made or destroyed?"

"Yes," he replied carefully.

"So if my grandmother is delivering magic on the Datura—for what purpose we don't know—she must be fueling it from somewhere, stealing it from another source."

"Right," Hudson said as the light dawned in his eyes. "And she can't steal it from the factions, we would notice."

"Exactly, and demons aren't of this world. They pack a huge punch in magical energy."

"You believe she's draining demons?"

"There's only one way to find out."

My uncle reappeared back in my chair. "What do you mean, your grandmother is stealing my demon's magic?"

Ugh, I thought he'd left, tricky Devil. I spun toward him, and Hudson gripped my hips like he could stop me from escaping. "There was an incident in the town of Peach Tree. Everyone is dead and it was staged to look like a Satanic ritual."

Lucifer rolled his eyes. "Please, if these folks knew how to worship me they'd already be in Hell at my feet."

"I did say staged," I pointed out. If the demons were being summoned, then I needed to get Lucifer on my side, and hiding the facts from him wouldn't warm him to me—particularly if he found out I'd hidden facts from him later on. "The clues led us to a field of Datura and my grandmother's favorite elementals defending the crop."

Lucifer went preternaturally still. "Your grandmother is behind this?" he finally drawled. It was a quiet sound that made the hairs on my arms stand on end.

"That's yet to be determined, but there was a strong source of magic on the Datura bloom I found in Peach Tree, and that power has to come from somewhere."

"Is there anything else that is leading you to this conclusion?"

Yeah, she had access to a book which would lead her to the one grimoire which might bring him to his knees. I decided that was a step too far. "Nothing concrete," I ventured.

Hudson's grip tightened. Yeah, I know, messing with the truth was a bad thing. But I didn't need the Devil on a warpath—having one homicidal relative was enough. The world wouldn't survive two narcissists barreling through humanity.

"I see," Lucifer said. His gaze would draw most people to their knees. Good thing my grandmother had trained me. Show no weakness.

"Let's get this over with," he eventually said as he stood.

"I'm coming," Hudson growled.

"You cannot," Lucifer said as he moved around the desk.

"She's my mate. Where she goes, I go."

Lucifer's eyebrows rose. "Did my invite get lost?"

Ugh. "There's not been any ceremony as of yet. No plans, no invites."

"I shall await my invitation with bated breath then."

"Why don't you hold your breath permanently, that would be more preferable," Hudson muttered.

Lucifer ignored him, which was probably for the best. "You can't come to Hell with Cora unless you plan on staying there."

"What does he mean?" Hudson snapped as he stood and towered over me. "You aren't staying in Hell."

"No, I won't need to. But your soul, should it breach Heaven or Hell, will remain there. It's the law of the universe."

"And the laws don't apply to you?"

"Of course they apply," Lucifer stated. "But being part angel means she can travel into different dimensions without being bound by them."

Hudson folded his arms. "I don't like it."

"You don't have to like it, Principal."

Hudson seemed to grow a little larger. *Please don't get furry right now.* "I am holding you personally responsible for Cora's safety. If one hair on her head is damaged, I will come for you."

"Of course, I would expect no less," Lucifer said with a smirk.

"Let me get changed," I mumbled.

"Wear something warm," Lucifer advised as I strode out of the room.

"Isn't Hell hot?" Hudson commented.

Lucifer laughed. "On the contrary, Hell is a frozen wasteland of despair. Nothing says torment like an icy landscape."

Oh, I can think of a hundred things that say torment more than a little cold weather. Good thing this isn't a competition.

"For the record, I don't support this adventure," Aunt Liz grumped.

My family and friends had shaken off the effects of the mushrooms, and Maggie was nowhere to be seen. Aira had left, stating she needed to lie down after having so much fun. Leaving me with Hudson, Dave, Aunt Liz, Rebecca, Sebastian, and Harry, all shooting scowls of disapproval at my Uncle.

I sighed as I wrapped a wooly scarf around my neck and checked that my bag of tricks had everything I needed. Salt, gloves, nulling potion, cheese…wait, why did I have cheese? Oh right, I remembered now.

"Here," Sebastian said, handing me three juice boxes. He glared at Lucifer. "She'll need the sugar if she successfully performs a read and she might—"

"Why wouldn't you be successful?" Lucifer interrupted.

I lasered Sebastian with a look that promised retribution. He had the common sense to look away. "Someone had blocked me from figuring out how the residents of Peach Tree died."

Lucifer tilted his head. "Are you certain it was a block and not an issue with your gift?"

"No, but I guess we are about to find out."

Lucifer offered me his hand. A growl rumbled from Hudson. He was a second away from exploding into his cat form and disappearing with me into the horizon. I offered a smile. "I'll be fine, back before you know it."

"Technically, if you are gone for an hour in Hell, it will be the next day here. So try not to panic and launch into a suicide mission," Lucifer explained. That's right, time moves differently.

"One day, hell spawn, then I'm coming for you," Hudson growled.

Lucifer smirked and grabbed my hand. The world tilted, and my molecules began rearranging themselves in preparation. Indigo pushed against my spine, wanting to see what was happening.

*"It's fine, we are taking a little trip to Hell,"* I told her. *"The souls there have already been claimed, so settle down."*

*"I don't like it."*

*"Nobody likes Hell, that's the point."*

Darkness blanketed my vision and bile rushed up my throat as we traveled across dimensions the human mind struggled to comprehend. Perhaps one day they would know the truth definitively.

The temperature around me plummeted, sending a shiver up my spine. The echoes of the tormented wrapped around me and tugged at my soul. I had to remember you didn't make it to Hell because you'd lived a good life. Lucifer might be the Devil, but he also had rules to follow, and the condition of the souls he claimed had firm boundaries. It didn't make it any easier listening to their pleas for mercy. It was the human condition to offer comfort to those in pain.

My body rearranged itself and my vision came into focus. Lucifer released my hand and I spun in a circle. My eyes were wide as I surveyed the room we'd materialized in.

It was a huge cavern, with floor-to-ceiling arched openings giving me a view of the barren landscape outside. A freezing wind whipped through the room, and a growling three-headed dog snapped at me and jerked in his chains. This wasn't my first rodeo in Hell—albeit, last time I'd been a child, but that was a tale for another day.

"Play nice," Lucifer instructed the mythical beast.

I dug in my bag and extracted the large cubes of cheese. I raised a brow as the monster eyeballed the treat in my hand.

"Sit," I commanded. The huge dog plonked its ass on the floor and growled at me. "Now that's no way to greet a guest."

Cerberus tilted all three of its heads and their tongues lolled out in perfect synchronization, drool pooling on the floor.

I took a step closer as my Uncle watched with amusement. I threw the first cube at the middle head. He caught it just as the other two heads snapped and snarled at him.

"There's enough for everyone," I uttered quickly, giving the other two equal amounts of cheese.

The huge monster lay on the floor and gazed up at me with adoration. Look at me, I'd made friends with a hell dog. Bella would be appalled.

"This way," Lucifer said with a jerk of his head. He began walking down a set of stone steps sunken into the middle of an uneven floor. I hurried to keep up with him, not wanting to get lost in Hell.

Thankfully, the icy wind didn't follow us down the stairs. Flames erupted along the torches as if responding to the Devil's presence. It was his domain, after all.

"Show off," I muttered as we trotted down the thin set of steep steps. He glanced over his shoulder and grinned.

"Here I am the king, Cora, you would do well to remember that fact."

"You might be a king, but you are not my king."

"I suppose that crown goes to the cat?"

"Hudson doesn't need me to worship at his feet."

"You really believe that?"

"Yes."

"Then you are a fool. All men need their woman to bow down to them, it is their nature."

"Clearly, you are stuck in the previous century. Since then, women have burned their bras, gone into space, and fought for equal rights."

We spilled out into a throne room, complete with hundreds of candles and a red carpet leading down the center to his dark and twisted throne. He probably built it with bones of the damned. Ugh, please don't let it be a bone throne.

"It isn't about society's progress," he continued. "It's about the fundamental nature of a man needing to control a beautiful woman. It's a greater symbol of power than any amount of money or status."

A tremble of apprehension rippled through me. "Well, he's shit out of luck if that's what he expects." The words flew out of my mouth before I could stop them.

The seed of doubt wiggled in my soul. If Hudson needed that kind of worship, I couldn't give him it. We were doomed.

I shook my head. This is what the Devil did, he made you question what you knew in your heart to be true. Hudson didn't want a simpering female, there were a hundred of them begging for his attention in the pack. He wanted me. He wanted my darkness, my secrets, he took my ugly along with my beauty and made anything seem possible. With him I am complete, not oppressed. The Devil was wrong.

Lucifer's smile widened as I raised my head and squared my shoulders. "Nice try, Uncle."

He shrugged. "Just testing the strength of your connection and conviction, making sure he is a worthy partner for my niece."

We passed through the empty throne room and out a door on the right. Another cold empty corridor. Where were all the demons?

"I had the castle cleared of all my servants for your arrival. I didn't want any of them getting ideas about the purity of the angelic soul in their midst, as it is, you will be difficult to conceal."

"Thank you, I think."

He pushed open a set of double doors and I came screeching to a halt. Gone was the medieval castle with stone floors and cold drafty corridors. Now we'd stepped inside a modern room with a white marble floor. Gold accented furniture littered the space, and it was warmed by a roaring fire.

I blinked.

"You think I command the legions of Hell and sit in that barbaric atmosphere?"

"Well, yes."

He snorted as he shook his head and shed his suit jacket, placing it on the back of a huge overfilled cream sofa. Not exactly the color to cover blood stains.

"The rest of the castle is for show, it's the posturing needed to lord over the worst of humanity. Here is where I live and conduct much of my business, in warmth and comfort. Out there, you'll catch your death."

"Literally," I mumbled, not enjoying this very domesticated and ordinary peek behind the curtain.

I clutched my bag to my chest tighter, using it as a barrier to stop me seeing him as an actual person. It's easier to think of him as the embodiment of evil.

"I have two of the victims in the kitchen," he said. Oh, well *now* it was easier. Who kept bodies in the kitchen? Any self-respecting person would at least keep them in the basement. That's what I did.

He opened a white painted door with a pretty gold pattern embossed on it. And once again, my mouth popped open as we entered a huge kitchen full of shiny chrome appliances.

"What?" he asked.

"It's just so well-equipped."

He winked. "That's what she said."

I rolled my eyes and looked for the demon bodies I'd been promised. Unless he'd stored them in the freezer, he'd lied. I should stop being surprised when the Devil lied. Indigo squirmed inside of me, like she was itching to break free.

"Where are the bodies?" I asked. I needed to get this over with, Hell didn't agree with me or my alter ego.

He pulled open the refrigerator door which let free a small hiss. "I didn't say bodies. I said victims."

He peeled the door fully open and if I had a weaker stomach, I may have lost the mushroom soup all over his sparkly white tiled floor. Two white eyes popped open and stared at me from a head covered in deep purple flesh, like the color of bruises.

"He's not dead," I uttered. "For this to work, he has to be dead."

The eyes, while totally white, seemed to focus on me. His mouth parted, revealing short, sharp sparkly white teeth. "That's not a pleasant greeting," he declared. His voice was raspy, not a surprise given he was missing his body.

Of course, my Southern upbringing came out in full force, even when in Hell. "I apologize for my rudeness," I said. "I was asked to investigate a death, but one has not occurred."

I glared at Lucifer. The head in the fridge jerked a little on the glass shelf. "Oh no, there's been a number of deaths. I survived, but Bill and Wendy didn't. They are on the bottom shelf under the fruit and vegetables." I blinked. Well, I couldn't fault Lucifer for his correct storage knowledge. Always keep the meat below the veggies.

My gaze traveled lower while Lucifer pulled out a glass mixing bowl, placing it on the large island between us. The rancid red meat inside made me wrinkle my nose. Okay, now whomever that was, was dead.

I took a step toward it. "What are you doing?" Lucifer asked as he held a foil-covered tray in his hands.

"I'm assuming this is the dead demon? Bill or Wendy?"

Lucifer looked at the bowl then back at me. "No, that's the beef steak being marinated in red wine vinegar for my dinner."

I blinked as he pushed the tray onto the counter and peeled back the foil, revealing a red, sopping, chunky, mess.

Hopefully, this wasn't also part of his dinner, because I was one hundred percent sure that it had not come from an animal.

I stepped closer and placed my bag on the side next to the tray. It wasn't necessary to do a physical examination, that would tell me nothing about how they had ended up like this.

"Poor Bill," the head in the fridge said on a sigh. Lucifer slammed the door closed.

"Do I want to know why you have a severed head in your fridge?"

Lucifer raised a brow and then rolled up his sleeves. Clearly, he didn't want to get demon guts on his dress shirt.

"No, he's in there to think about his actions."

"You put him in a timeout in your refrigerator?"

"Yes."

I shook my head and handed him a few of the juice boxes. "When I come around, I'm going to need those." I shoved a straw into an apple one and drank it quickly.

I sucked in a breath and stuck my hand in the chilled guts and closed my eyes. My vision went black and then I was sucked into the death memory.

*My view crisped and I was lounging on a sofa while watching a baseball game on a huge flat screen TV attached to the wall. I took a sip of beer as my buddy next to me cheered. I glanced at him, grinned, and took another gulp of the beer.*

*Who knew demons enjoyed baseball and beer?*

*A trembling ran through my body and I shifted to get rid of the unsettling feeling. My flesh heated and then a circle of flames erupted around my sofa, the criss cross pattern of a pentagram burned into the floor. I shot to my feet, as did my friend. While he made it out of the circle unscathed, I bounced off the edge and flew to the floor.*

*"Bill?" he said with wide eyes. "What is happening?"*

*I gritted my teeth. "I'm being summoned."*

*My body locked and pain exploded in my chest as my essence was dragged from Hell. I would murder whomever was performing this ritual. Humans understood very little when it came to my kind. They couldn't control us, and their failure meant their death.*

*My body materialized in a room, each side was boxed in with a panel of glass etched with runes meant to contain me. Outside, people scurried to close down the energy stream linking me to Hell. They meant to trap me here.*

*I slammed my fists against the glass, the blood bursting from my knuckles leaving a crimson streak on the clear pane. A silver-haired woman stepped forward out of the shadows and narrowed her gaze at me.*

*"Calm down, Beleth, I have summoned you, and now you are mine to command."*

*I threw my head back and laughed. The woman thought she had me trapped? How foolish. I calmly sat on the floor and let my power stream out of me as I leveled the bitch with my gaze. I will give her her due, she didn't flinch or retreat. Perhaps she was more of an adversary than I thought.*

*Let's see how confident she is once I'm free. Will she continue to hold her ground? A burst of power meant to break the walls erupted from me. The runes flared a bright blue and sucked my power from my body. I did it again, and like an eager leech, it lapped up every bit of magic I was expelling. The walls didn't even flex. That was concerning.*

*The woman smiled and folded her arms as she watched me struggle. I stopped trying to escape and conserved my energy. I glanced down, noticing the same circle and pentagram were etched onto the floor. My name was written in the dead language in the center, but she'd missed an essential ingredient. It was only a matter of time before I returned to my own dimension.*

*The woman tilted her head as I waited her out.* That's right witch, I'm not giving you any more of my power.

*She narrowed her gaze as we spent silent minutes glaring at each other.*

*A man whispered something in her ear. She jerked her head once and a malice most demons didn't contain entered her eyes.*

*"I need your magic," she said. "So you have a choice—you can either expel it yourself for me to collect, or we can do this the hard way."*

*I shook my head, a small smile pulling at my lips. She huffed and snapped her fingers.*

*Electricity erupted from the metal floor and caused my body to lock and jerk. My power splashed out and coated the room as it tried to defend me. The circle flared as it struggled to hold me here in this dimension.*

*She raised her hand and the pain locked my muscles tight, forcing more power to flood the room and be gobbled up by the runes. Her gaze studied the pentagram and she blinked as she realized I was about to disappear. I had just enough magic to survive my trip home.*

*"Full power," she shouted. I wasn't quick enough. The surge of electricity exploded through every molecule just as the spell broke and I began my transport home. Darkness claimed my vision, and my last thought was being thankful that while I wouldn't survive, my remains wouldn't be wasting away on Earth with a woman who had evil shining in her eyes and violence in her soul.*

When I woke, I was lying on Lucifer's plush sofa and he was holding out a juice box to me. I snatched it with shaky hands, gulping it down in twenty seconds flat. Lucifer raised an amused brow before handing me a second one, which I sipped more slowly as I pushed myself into a sitting position.

"You were successful?" he asked after a couple of minutes.

I jerked my head knowing if I told him the truth, it may start a war between Hell and Earth.

He raised a brow. "Are you going to tell me?"

I grimaced. "I need your reassurance that you won't react. I am dealing with the threat."

He leaned back and his gaze narrowed. "Just spit it out, Cora."

"No, not without the promise I'm after. I know it's a leap of faith, but these crimes will not go unanswered, I just need time."

"Fine."

"Say it."

"I will not react immediately to what you tell me. I will give you time to explain and share with me your plan."

Ugh, good enough I guess. "Bill was summoned to earth and trapped inside a glass room where he was provoked into expending his power which was collected by a complex set of runes."

"Who?"

My jaw ticked. "The summoner was my grandmother."

He shot to his feet and a growl rumbled from him as he paced in front of the fire which was now roaring. "Your grandmother is murdering my demons and stealing their magic?"

"I believe so, yes."

"Why?"

"I've yet to determine that."

"What aren't you telling me?"

"She tried to do something in Peach Tree, to the residents there, and it backfired."

"She is screwing with the natural order, Cora. Stealing magic is the ultimate crime, no matter your species. There's a reason this is termed black magic, and it has nothing to do with its apparent attachment to my realm."

"I'm not sure she has the spells correct, that's why Bill's remains reappeared in Hell. She was trying to stop him from returning."

"Demon bindings are rarely successful," Lucifer agreed. "And magic transfer is almost unheard of, it's a crime against the supernatural community that will not be forgiven. I don't even know how she's attempting it, the only book that would contain that knowledge is—"

"The Red Dragon," I finished for him with a grimace.

"But that's impossible, the location is a closely-guarded secret. Nobody has all the pieces to find it. It's too dangerous."

I lifted my gaze to his and let out a long sigh. "My grandmother has Eunice's grimoire."

"Fuck," he shouted. Indeed, the evidence was stacking up against my own flesh and blood, and I could no longer ignore the crimes she was committing. Whether vampire, shifter, elemental, or demon, the world has rules—and my grandmother had broken them. I couldn't stop the shitstorm coming her way, no more than I could prevent Lucifer from seeking her out and slaughtering her.

Lucifer turned to me. "You have one week, niece, then I will take matters into my own hands."

# CHAPTER TWENTY

*Don't fret, my crazy aunt with scarves had arrived.*

The sky was streaked with lilacs and pinks by the time we arrived on the edge of my property.

"That took less time than I expected," I muttered to a frowning Lucifer.

"It's not the same day," he explains as we begin the walk up to my house. I'd asked him to teleport us to the property border so I had a minute to collect my thoughts before my friends and family descended upon me demanding answers. "It's been over twenty-four hours."

I grimaced. That wouldn't go down well. As if my thoughts had summoned him, Hudson threw open the door and took the steps two at a time to reach me. His arms banded around me and he picked me up off my feet to squeeze me to him and I got a unique look into what a nut felt like. His body trembled against mine.

"I'll see you inside," Lucifer said, disappearing through the open door.

I tapped Hudson's back. "Delicate female here," I grumbled.

His grip loosened, allowing me to lean back. I took his face between my hands and placed a kiss on his lips. It was meant to be a chaste touching of our lips in greeting. Hudson's hand twisted in my hair and he ravished my mouth like he was starving and only I could relieve the ache.

He pulled away before I could pass out and leaned his forehead against mine. "You were gone."

My hands tightened in his shirt. "You knew that."

His eyes flipped open and green rolled over them. "No, you don't understand. I can sense you in the world. You could be a thousand miles away and I would still feel the beat of your heart against mine, but you were gone."

"Is that a mate thing?"

Hudson shrugged. "I don't believe it's a typical mate thing. But what about us is typical?"

Indigo snickered in my mind. Right, I had an insane, murderous, soul-sucking angel hiding inside me, and Hudson had a prehistoric tiger inside of him. We were the opposite of typical.

"Please don't have wild monkey sex on the lawn again, unless you want a bill for my therapy," Dave grumbled as he appeared on the porch with Sebastian.

"No, please do," Rebecca said as she joined them.

I rolled my eyes and gave Hudson a final squeeze. For a moment, I thought he wasn't going to release me, but he sighed and let me go.

I threaded my fingers through his. "Come on, I have stuff to tell you all."

We spilled into the parlor, Lucifer was eyeballing a plate of cookies that Maggie had laid on the table with tea. "Are they safe?" he asked.

"I don't believe they contain any illicit substances, unless you consider chocolate a drug."

Hudson sat so close to me on the sofa that his heat was blazing a warmth along my side. After the icy winds of Hell, I welcomed it.

Rebecca, Dave, Sebastian, and Aunt Liz joined us. Aunt Liz threw her hand in the air and a shimmer of magic coated the room, making sure we had privacy for this conversation.

"Tell us everything," Dave demanded.

"Yes, everything," Lucifer added. He was apparently here to ensure I told people the truth, the whole truth, and nothing but the truth about what I'd seen.

"My grandmother is summoning demons and siphoning their magic."

Wow, who knew I could wrap that up in a single sentence?

"For what purpose?" Sebastian asked as he leaned forward and snagged a cookie. I mirrored him.

"I have no idea."

Aunt Liz tilted her head and caught Dave's gaze. Ah, clearly they had been discussing this. "My mother is responsible for the death of an entire town and the magic depletion of demons. She's also collected a powerful family grimoire. How does this all fit together?"

"The key would be figuring out what she was trying to do in Peach Tree, because there's no way she meant to just murder a town."

"Eloise is a cruel, ruthless, cold woman. What makes you think she didn't mean to kill everyone?" Dave asked.

"My grandmother is all of those things, yes," I conceded. "But she isn't a psychopath. She might have no rules when it comes to getting what she wants, but senseless murder isn't her style."

"I agree," Hudson added. "To uncover her motivation, we need to consider her goals."

"World domination," Lucifer growled.

I blinked. "But the treaty failed. She might have wanted to climb to the top of the ladder, but she needed the backing of the packs and vampires to make that work."

Lucifer placed his booted foot over his opposite knee. "You think she has given up on her dreams because of a lack of signatures?"

My eyebrows slammed down. Well, when he put it like that, it seemed a foolish belief. "I still don't understand the link to Peach Tree, we are missing something."

Lucifer stood and straightened his tie. "I'm needed elsewhere, contact me if you discover anything new."

"How would I contact you? Call 666?"

He smirked and handed me a black business card. Scrawled in elegant gold was his name and underneath, lucifer666@hell.com.

Wow.

I stood just as my wards clanged in my head, making me grimace. Who was here now? I strode over to the door and flung it open. A short woman with a mass of dark curls threaded with silver and icy blue eyes that looked like they'd been cut from glaciers stood on my porch.

"Why do you smell of brimstone and sulfur?" she asked just as Lucifer stepped beside me. She glared at him. Oh boy. She bent, opened her knitting bag which had cute kittens printed on the side, and grabbed a long bright purple scarf. She took out the crochet hook from one end, knotted the wool, and handed it to Lucifer.

"Here, Lucifer, you'll be needing this where you are going. I certainly won't require it in this sweltering heat."

The *sweltering heat* was barely above fifty-seven degrees. "Aunt Sophia, you are here."

Lucifer took the scarf and wrapped it around his neck with a wink at Sophia. "Thank you for your kindness," he said and then trotted down the steps and off my property.

Aunt Sophia blushed like a virgin schoolgirl. What was happening?

She gazed at me. "Are you going to let me in, or should I make my bed on the porch swing?"

I stepped back and allowed her entry. Aunt Liz was already out of her seat and rushing toward us. "Aunty," she said, wrapping her in a hug.

Aunt Sophia squeezed her and then pushed her back. She poked me in my ribs and grunted.

"Ow," I mumbled.

She eyeballed me and then Aunt Liz. "What have you been eating, you are both skin and bones?"

I assumed she meant we were underweight, which we weren't, but Aunt Sophia solved problems with food, and I could get behind that strategy. My stomach rumbled in agreement.

She tutted. "Cabbage rolls."

Dave groaned from farther in the room. "That sounds like my worst nightmare."

Aunt Sophia poked her head around us and eyeballed the supernaturals in the parlor.

"My cabbage rolls are glorious."

Dave didn't look convinced. Hudson stood, and Aunt Sophia's eyes widened as she took in the size of him.

"Is this him?" she asked, bumbling into the parlor.

She circled the sofa, eyeballing him from head to toe. "You could do better, but I see the appeal," she said, eyes glued to his ass.

I pinched the bridge of my nose. Aunt Sophia had no filter.

Hudson huffed a laugh.

Aunt Sophia turned to Rebecca. "Lovely to see you again, my dear."

Rebecca offered her a smile and Aunt Sophia regarded Dave next. "You think you are good enough for my niece?"

He shook his head. "No, actually, I don't, but I'm too selfish to let her go."

She harrumphed. That was a positive noise, he might yet live to see another day. Lastly, she regarded Sebastian. She stepped toward him and squeezed his shoulder.

"All will be well, stay the course."

My aunt was a powerful empath, and a little psychic. It was an erratic gift though, we couldn't count on it to warn us of impending doom.

Sebastian's composure slipped as she hit the mark. "Get my bags for me, dear," she said to Dave.

Aunt Liz smothered a laugh behind her hand as Dave got up in a daze and went to retrieve her bags.

Maggie bounced into the room and offered him a key. "Room thirteen," she said. Dave took the key and shoved it into his pocket before trudging up the stairs with a heavy suitcase and her knitting bag. Maggie then handed me the post. "For you."

I flicked through the bills and groaned. Saving the world from my grandmother's quest for domination was draining my time when I should be paying bills and doing my taxes. Another black card fell out from between the white and brown envelopes. I flicked it around. Still no address, no indication of who had delivered it, either. The words 'Are you strong enough?' sat in elegant scrawl on one side, and on the other, another line going in the opposite direction of the last, still at a forty-five degree angle. The magic felt a little stronger, and when I ran my thumb over the gold line, it shimmered.

"What's that?" Aunt Liz asked.

I blinked and shoved the card in my jeans pocket. "Nothing, just a weird promotional thing."

Aunt Liz's gaze cut through me at the obvious lie I'd told. Something was wrong with these cards, but if I didn't have enough time to sort through my bills, I definitely didn't have enough time to figure out what these little mysterious cards meant.

I turned to Aunt Sophia and caught the look between my aunts. Yes, I was lying, deal with it. "Would you like to see the book?" I asked Aunt Sophia, I needed them to focus on the urgent matters.

She shook her head. "No. First, I'm making cabbage rolls."

Dave groaned from the next floor up.

Bella slunk down the stairs and eyed the newcomer with a wary expression. She stuck her tail in the air and showed us her ass as she padded toward the still open front door.

"That's a strange cat you have," Aunt Sophia noted as Rebecca disappeared up the stairs, Hudson following her. Where was everyone going?

"She has a thing for the males," I explained.

Aunt Sophia tilted her head. "No, that's not what I mean, but you already know she's not an ordinary cat."

I did know that, but it wasn't like I could ask her to explain why she turned into a beast in the face of danger. She wasn't a shifter, because she had no human form, and no amount of searching through the records had shed any light on Bella. She'd protected Rebecca, and that meant she had a place in my home for as long as she wanted.

"I can't translate on an empty stomach," Aunt Sophia said. "And the meal they served on the plane?" She shuddered.

Aunt Liz gave me a small smile and began ushering Sophia toward the kitchen. "You'll not be here for cabbage rolls," she said to me over her shoulder just as Dave came down the stairs.

"Lucky you," Dave grumbled.

"Why, where am I going?"

Rebecca reappeared with a dress bag in her hand. Hudson came down the stairs behind her with a large overnight bag which looked to be bursting at the seams. My overnight bag.

Hudson grinned. "We are going on a date."

My mouth popped open and Aunt Sophia paused just outside the kitchen. "I can't go on a date, we have shit to solve."

"Language," Aunt Sophia chastised. "It will take me all night to translate even a few parts of the book. Eunice didn't write in just one language, she had many, and enjoyed mixing them up to protect her spells. Go enjoy yourself, treasure the stolen moments of peace and pleasure. I don't see many of them in your future, so when presented with an opportunity, grab it with both hands and don't let go."

Hudson's hand grasped mine and he pulled me out of the door and into the night to steal that moment. My heart raced with anticipation and a flush of excitement tingled my skin. Steal the moment, I could do that.

# Chapter Twenty One

*I share everything but dessert.*

Dashing along the road in my Bugatti, Hudson drove like he was trying to beat the sundown.

"Where are we going?" I asked.

He darted a look my way. "It's a surprise, we have another hour of driving, get some sleep."

"I don't need sleep."

He smirked. "You will."

Oh, aren't we confident? "Perhaps I should drive and you sleep?"

He huffed a laugh and put his foot down. I turned in my seat and just stared at him. I was too wound up to sleep.

He side-eyed me. "What are you doing?"

My lips twitched. "Staring."

"Why?"

"Because when I complained that we hadn't had a date, you organized one in the middle of a crisis."

"It's not just what you said, we haven't caught our breath in days. To face what's coming you need to be rested."

I quirked a brow. "I'm going to get some rest on this trip?"

He grinned. "Rest? No, probably not. But a break from the crazy? That I can do."

The rest of the drive I just looked at him. It might be classed as creepy stalker territory, but I couldn't care less. I wanted to bask in his strength and allow it to curl around me, making me feel safe and protected.

He indicated to pull off the freeway, and a few minutes later we pulled into a long driveway leading to a mansion that was lit from within by candlelight.

I sat up straighter as a man in a penguin suit exited the front door and moved to greet us as Hudson stopped the car. The man opened Hudson's door, and then Hudson was rounding the car to help me out.

"Principal, Miss Roberts, welcome to The Mews. I'm Philip, your concierge this evening," he said as we followed him into the beautiful red brick building. So this was a supernatural-friendly place? I'd never heard of it. A younger man stepped forward, possibly still in his late teens. "Jack will retrieve your luggage and will park your car safely if you leave him the key." My eyes widened as I took in the understated luxury of the interior. It was decorated in a dark, moody palette of grays and blacks with splashes of gold and cream. "Your dinner is booked at nine, your turndown at eleven, and breakfast will be served in your room at eight. Allow me show you where dinner will be served," he said as Hudson handed the keys to Jack.

"Be careful with her," I instructed. Jack nodded and dashed out the door before Philip began a short tour. The decor continued throughout the house. We saw a few couples cozied up in different rooms, talking in hushed tones and gazing at each other with adoration. The supernaturals varied across all three factions, but it was clear we'd left the drama at the door and that was priceless. My gaze flicked to Hudson, he was staring at me like I hung the moon and stars in his darkness. I hope I reflected that. A wide grin broke out on his face, making it clear it wasn't romantic thoughts spinning through his mind right now.

"Your dinner will be served here," Philip said as we entered an intimate dining room, with just one small round table.

"Perfect," Hudson growled, as he gazed at me.

"I'll show you to your suite," Philip said, taking the hint that we needed to be alone before Hudson caused a scene in this posh establishment. Philip led the way back through the mansion and took us through a door on the left, in the opposite direction of the public rooms. We walked down a wide hallway, my feet sinking into the gray carpet, and then he swung open the door at the end.

"If you need me, please dial 0," Philip said.

"We won't need you," Hudson said as he crowded my back and all but pushed me inside the room.

He slammed the door closed, and I spun in a circle. Oh. My. God. I'd never seen a bed that big or lush. How did they get a plunge pool into the floor? This place was insane.

"You like it?" he asked.

I nodded and then squealed as he lifted me off the floor and threw me on the bed. Seconds later, my clothes were torn from my body and he was naked, crawling over me.

He gazed down at me with such stark longing it was impossible to break eye contact. His lips came down on mine, and he explored them in teasing nips and licks that lit a fire inside my body.

His tongue trailed a hot delicious path across my jaw, down my neck, and then he pulled a nipple into his scorching mouth. I arched my back and clutched his head. My legs wrapped around his back as he settled his hard length against me.

"Shit," he growled.

"What?"

"I forgot condoms." I laughed hard. "Why are you laughing?" he asked.

"Well, two reasons. One, you didn't seem so fussed when you powered into me on my lawn a few nights ago."

Hudson's face fell. "I'm sorry."

"And two, I've been taking oral contraception since our first time."

He blinked. "You never stopped even when you were angry with me?"

"Correct." The wicked grin he let loose was full of carnal promise. "Don't get cocky," I warned.

He glanced down between our bodies. "Too late."

The next second, my legs were thrown up and over his shoulders while his tongue swept between my thighs, making me groan. If the man was on a mission to make my head spin and heart race—he'd achieved it. He zoned in exactly where I needed and with the perfect amount of pressure. My thighs tensed and squeezed his head.

A growl rumbled from him, and I swear I felt it inside as my toes curled.

I exploded in a scream that may make me blush later at dinner. I was still screaming when he curled my leg over his arm and thrust inside of me. Our lips collided in a messy show of passion. There was nothing practiced about this, nothing slick or intentional. This was us—raw, captivating, all encompassing.

He moved faster and I arched to meet him, driving him deeper. His hand snaked between us and he rubbed my clit, careening me toward that precipice. Everything inside me snapped tight and then I was flying. He jerked above me and then followed me into bliss. The roar he released made my ears ring.

Okay, now I wasn't as embarrassed about my scream. If they were going to be talking about anything, it would be that roar.

He rolled to the side and pulled me on top of him as we both caught our breath.

"That was…" I sucked in another lungful of air.

"Amazing? Fabulous? The best sex you've ever had?" Hudson said.

I smacked his chest. "Maybe." He stood with me in his arms. "What are you doing?"

He suddenly dropped and then we were submerged in water. He rose and I gasped for breath, splashing him. He chuckled, then backed me against the wall of the pool. "Now let's see if we can change that maybe into a definitely," he growled as he lifted my ass to the surface. Oh boy.

When we emerged an hour later, Hudson wore the self-satisfied smirk of a cat who had got the cream, and he'd earned it. Many times.

Philip greeted us with the practiced smile of a professional host that hadn't heard any screaming, growling, or roaring. Hudson's warm hand skimmed my naked lower back. Rebecca had clearly packed for me. My underwear was a choice of scraps of lace or satin. Hudson's gaze went molten when he spied the satin, so that's what I was wearing under the black, knee-length, halter-neck dress. My long copper hair was pulled over one of my shoulders and paired with stiletto heels, and I was feeling rather tall and sexy.

Hudson kept it simple with black slacks and a white dress shirt. He wore them with the confidence of a king. He pulled my chair out and I sat, taking in the room which was lit by an array of candles scattered throughout.

"Would you care for the wine menu?" Philip asked.

"You choose," Hudson said as his gaze landed on me. I blinked. I knew nothing about wine. He glanced at Philip. "Not red, I'm not a fan, but other than that I trust your judgment."

"Excellent," Philip said and disappeared from the room.

"Living on the dangerous side letting a stranger pick your drink."

"I don't want to take my eyes off you for one second."

"How will you order?"

"You can pick for me."

I grinned and opened the menu in front of me. Hudson didn't even flinch as I surveyed the choices. I could torture him with salads and fruit, but the man had worked up an appetite, he deserved his belly to be full.

Philip returned with a bottle of chilled wine and served Hudson a drop. He never took his eyes off me as he drank the wine. He nodded. "Delicious."

"Would you like some more time to view the menu?" Philip asked.

Hudson raised a brow. I felt like this was one of those how well do you know your partner quizzes and I was about to fail.

"We'll have the venison carpaccio to start, the roast duck breast for the main, one chocolate and chili tart, and one white chocolate mousse with strawberries, please."

Philip nodded. "Good choice, Miss Roberts." He collected the menus from our table, and returned with a basket of freshly baked bread and a tray with melted butter, balsamic vinegar, and herby oil. My mouth watered as I tore off a chunk of the still warm bread and dipped it in the balsamic vinegar.

I groaned as I chewed and Hudson's lips twitched as he joined me in delicious yeasty bliss. "Why two different desserts?"

"The romantic thing would be for us to share the dessert, but since I'm starving, us sharing one would have been pointless. I ordered two different desserts so that we can both share."

Hudson grinned. "You are a romantic."

I shrugged. "It's hard not to be here."

"So you like it here?"

"I love it."

His smile stretched super wide and if I wasn't so hungry, I'd have dragged him back to our room. But we had the whole night, and the incredible food would give me the energy I needed to ensure it was memorable. Of course, in the delicate laws of the universe, my peace and happiness had an expiration date. The shit show of my life was waiting for me at dawn, but until then, I could bask in this moment of perfection with the man I love.

# Chapter Twenty Two

*The aliens did it.*

All too soon, the sun came up and my stomach was full of yummy bacon, eggs, and sausage. My body ached in a delicious way, and when I thought of everything we'd done last night, I blushed.

Hudson kept giving me knowing looks as we sped back to White Castle and the weight of responsibility began pushing down on my shoulders.

"At the risk of ruining our date, do you want to talk about your grandmother before we arrive back at the house?"

I squeezed my eyes closed and dragged in a steadying breath. "She's undoubtedly at the center of these crimes."

"Do you have any idea why she is doing this?"

My eyes flipped open. "I have theories."

"Would you like to share?"

I nibbled my bottom lip. Sharing your worries was what a partnership was about, but what if that worry could start a war? That if it transformed into truth, could mean the end of the tenuous peace between the factions?

"Her original plan was to unite the factions and then out us to the world. Together, we would be able to overpower the humans if they retaliated."

"Okay." His tone was calm as this wasn't new information, and thankfully, that treaty had never come to pass, leaving the packs and the vampires free of my grandmother's plan for domination. However, that didn't mean she'd given up.

"But that plan is in ruins, and she still wants to rule. I think she's figuring out a way to kill humans en masse, so it will terrify them into compliance."

Hudson's expression didn't change. He simply nodded. "I can see why you would think that, but isn't there a more simplistic way than whatever this is? Demon summoning, poisonous flowers, magic transfer? It seems overkill, excuse the pun."

"Fear of the unknown is the easiest way to create panic, chaos, and terror. Something they don't understand."

"You think she's faking a demon takeover so she can save everyone? Become their savior?" I nodded. "It's a solid theory," Hudson said as he indicated to come off the freeway.

"Lucifer won't stand for it."

"By the time he gathers his forces, it may be too late."

Lucifer didn't need *forces*. He was a tsunami of power, an archangel, blessed with the power of the Almighty.

We pulled into my driveway and nobody came out to greet us on the porch. That was positive, normally there was someone greeting me with today's problems.

I jumped out of the car and Hudson's hand tangled with mine as we approached the door. He yanked me to a stop and my eyes widened.

"What's wrong?" I whispered.

He tilted my chin up and his mouth descended onto mine. My body reacted by squashing itself against his. He pulled back with one final kiss.

"Nothing's wrong, I just wanted to do that before we launch into whatever awaits us today."

I smirked at him and then pushed open the door. Aunt Liz poked her head out from the kitchen. "Did you have a good time?"

I blinked, remembering just how good a time we'd had. "Yes."

She nodded. "Good, your Aunt Sophia made herself at home in your office and has some news which she wouldn't share until you got home."

"I'll take the bags up to our rooms," Hudson said, moving past me.

I trudged down the stairs, hearing voices floating from my office, making me wonder who my aunt had in there.

I spilled into the room and came to a halt. Dangerous Dave was sitting cross-legged on the floor, winding rainbow-colored wool around his hands. Aunt Sophia sat in my seat with a pencil in one hand and a mug in the other. Her mouth was moving as she read from the book and made notes on a pad.

Rebecca was in the visitor's chair with a laptop in front of her. Aunt Sophia tore a piece of the pad off and handed it to Rebecca. Sebastian was in the other chair, and had a pile of books open in front of him. It was like a supernatural book club, although I was a little lost as to what Dave was doing, and why.

Aunt Sophia's head snapped up. "Cora, you're back. Did you enjoy the duck?"

Clearly, she'd had a premonition about my meal.

"I did enjoy my duck."

"Excellent, because you are going to need your energy to go on this treasure hunt."

Hudson strode into the room, eyeballed his chief of security on the floor, and then leaned against the wall with his arms folded. "What are we going to find?" I asked as I circled the desk and peered over Aunt Sophia's shoulder.

She tapped her fingers on a page in the grimoire. "There are many dangerous things in this book, but none more so than the location of the Red Dragon. With what you've told me, I believe my sister," she spat the word like it was poison, "is after the summoning spells held within that book. She's tried and failed to recreate them, they don't hold the demons long enough. Also, there is forbidden magic that shouldn't exist, but cannot be destroyed."

"How can it not be destroyed?" Hudson asked.

"The Red Dragon is not simply a book, it is black magic in written form. The book isn't just a set of spells and summonings. It's the definitive bible of evil. It's impervious to our forces. The Vatican believes they have the original, but they are mistaken."

Rebecca wrote something on the paper Aunt Sophia had passed her and then gave it back to her. Aunt Sophia nodded and smiled. "We have the location."

"Excellent, where?"

"Have you ever been to Egypt?" Aunt Sophia asked.

Hudson grimaced. "I'm not a fan of airplanes."

I raised a brow. "Why?"

"I can survive most things—"

"But not a plane crash." I finished for him. "Just think, you'll be in the land where your alien show centers."

A smile lit up his face. Apparently, the lure of aliens was enough to squash his fears about flying thousands of feet in the air.

"I'm coming," Sebastian declared, snapping the book closed.

"No," Hudson snapped.

"Yes," my aunt agreed. "You'll need the combined power of the three factions to retrieve the book. Let's just hope that you beat Eloise, because once she has the Red Dragon, there will be no stopping her."

A witch, a shifter, and a vampire walk into an airport. The witch is the buffer between the animosity brewing between the two. Despite Sebastian's revelation that he would be more attracted to Hudson than me, my shifter lover still eyed my vampire bestie with all the distrust reserved for your worst enemy.

Ugh. After many hours on a plane squashed between them and two changeovers, I could report that we had arrived safely, but I may yet murder them both if they continued with their sniping.

Bringing only a carry-on each meant we were out of the airport in Cairo less than thirty minutes after landing. The sun drenched my skin and I was glad for the linen trousers and matching top Aunt Sophia had made me wear.

A dark blue sedan was idling at the curb, and a tall middle-aged Egyptian man was leaning against it with a cardboard sign reading C Roberts. Guess that was the ride my aunt had mentioned she would organize.

I moved toward him and held my hand out. "Cora," I announced.

He shook my hand and eyeballed the tall supernaturals at my back. "You're Sophia's niece?" he asked in a thick accent.

"I am, and this is Hudson and Sebastian."

"Babu." He nodded once and moved to pop the trunk of the car. Hudson placed mine and his carry-ons in there, leaving Sebastian to do his own. I slid into the back seat, the worn leather creaking under me, and Hudson followed, closing the door behind him. Sebastian huffed and climbed into the passenger seat just as Babu spun the steering wheel and peeled out into traffic like the hounds of Hell were on his tail.

"We headed to the new museum?" I checked the location my aunt had given me.

"No, the old museum," Babu answered.

Hudson leaned forward between the seats. "I thought it was destroyed?"

"Damaged during the riots, but not destroyed. What you need isn't in the main building anyway."

"Don't say basement," Sebastian groaned. "Nothing good ever came out of sneaking around in a basement for a book of evil."

"I can call it the underground," Babu said with a smirk. "Didn't take the vampire crown prince of North America to be a pussy."

Sebastian jabbed his thumb over his shoulder as Hudson sat back. "He's the pussy. I just have a high regard for life and know not to meddle in things I don't understand."

"Right, self-preservation," Hudson drawled. "That's the story we shall tell when we explain why you sat in the car and left us to face the danger alone."

"No can do. The seal needs the bloodlines of all four factions."

"Four?" Hudson asked.

"Elemental, shifter, vampire, and demon."

"Who's the demon?" Babu's face shifted into a cracked black mass with red eyes. "Got it."

What the hell had Aunt Sophia got us embroiled in?

"Don't worry, I'm friendly," Babu said as he tapped his thumbs on the steering wheel to the tune coming from the radio. "Plus, we have very specific orders from the big boss to help you." He caught my eyes in the rear view mirror.

Wonderful, my uncle was lending me a hand. I guess it was one less species to be battling, for now at least.

In no time, Babu pulled the car to the side of the road, earning him a chorus of beeps from the traffic he'd cut off.

We spilled out of the car and Babu jerked his head toward an area cordoned off by yellow tape. The construction guys must be taking a break, because no one was working as we ducked under the tape and sped through some rubble. Instead of going inside of the building, we trotted down a set of dusty steps, and found relief from the blistering sun in the shadows. Babu pushed open a bright blue door, it creaked as he gave it a final shove.

He looked at me over his shoulder. "The vault is just down here."

Sebastian closed the door behind us. "So far, so good," I muttered as I cast a look around the room filled with hundreds of shelves packed with artifacts. Hudson paused and picked up a hand sized statue.

"Do you know what this is?" he whispered.

My hand closed over his and I guided it back to the shelf. "We can do your alien show-and-tell another time. You know, when the world isn't in danger."

Sebastian snickered. "Let me know when you predict that so I can block out the date in my diary."

"Don't be so dramatic, the world isn't always in danger."

"Hurry up," Babu said. "We only have an hour before the staff return from lunch."

"An hour will be plenty of time," I muttered. I wasn't planning on hanging around with a priceless powerful book. We hurried to join Babu at the end of the room. He withdrew a dagger from a sheath on his belt. Hudson growled and elbowed in front of me. I groaned and rolled my eyes up to the heavens.

"The ritual needs blood," Babu said carefully. "Didn't Sophia go through this with you?"

I side-stepped my overgrown cat and nodded. "She did, he's just a little protective."

Babu nodded and scored his palm. I stepped back and watched as the blood sunk into the dusty floor.

"We have to go down?" Hudson asked.

"Yes," Babu said. "I thought we cleared this up already?"

"We already went down. Are you telling me there's a basement in the basement?" Sebastian grumbled.

Babu blinked and handed Hudson the blade. Hudson wiped it on his shirt and then held out a hand for mine. Aww, he was letting me go first.

I ran the blade over my palm and let my blood fall to the floor and Hudson followed. Sebastian, being all about the drama, bit his wrist and let his blood mix with the rest. Hudson rolled his eyes and handed Babu the blade back.

Babu began to utter some words in a foreign language and the floor shifted beneath us.

"Do you think—" My words were cut off as the floor fell away and we dropped down into a hole. I landed with a jolt while Hudson huffed and Sebastian grumbled. Babu looked down at us from the edge of the hole.

"The book you seek is in the cavern to your left," he said.

"If there are snakes, I'll murder him," Hudson growled as he leapt to his feet and offered me his hand.

"Why would you say that?" I asked.

"He's been watching too much *Indiana Jones*," Sebastian quipped.

"Hurry," Babu said. "I don't want to be caught here once they get back from lunch."

I pulled out my phone from my bag and switched on the flashlight. Not all of us had supernatural eyesight.

We were in a cave where four tunnels converged. I pointed at the tunnel to our left and we started trudging down it, Hudson in the lead, me in the middle, and Sebastian at the rear who was muttering about giant spiders and snakes.

The tunnel opened into a small room and in the center sat a large book on a tall stone pedestal. We surrounded it, but none of us made a move to remove the book.

"Is this feeling a little too easy for anybody else?" Sebastian asked.

I spun in a circle, taking in the room. There was nothing to suggest the room was booby trapped, but that didn't mean it wasn't. I nibbled my bottom lip and sucked in a breath.

"No amount of standing here is going to reveal what, if anything, awaits us. So be on your guard and if something other than us moves, kill it."

Indigo stirred in my chest and surveyed the room. *"Something is here,"* she told me.

Hudson reached out for the book, I slapped his hand away. "Um, Indigo can sense something."

"Who?" Sebastian asked.

Hudson smirked, clearly he felt smug that he knew something Sebastian did not.

"My creature."

"Your what?"

"Creature. It's a long story, let's take her word for it."

Sebastian blinked as Indigo's power rippled along my spine. *"Let me show the vampire our power."*

"Now is not the time to be showing off," I chastised her.

"She's inside of you, speaking?" Sebastian checked. Shit, I must have spoken aloud.

"Can we discuss this later?"

"Fine. You have hours on the flight home to share whatever you've been hiding."

Damn it, I could hardly run from him on a flight. Maybe I could get an upgrade and leave the men to figure out their differences.

I licked my lips and grasped the book. Power leached from it. Oily, heavy, seductive. It whispered of untold magic, promised that all my desires would come true. Wow. I'd never felt anything like it. Indigo rose inside me to gaze at the tomb.

"It lies," she said. Her voice escaped my mouth, coming out in the multilayered cadence that sounded terrifying.

Sebastian took a step back. Hudson's gaze narrowed as I lifted the book and gritted my teeth.

My shoulders relaxed as I drew the heavy book to my chest and I let out a steady breath. I grinned and spun to exit the cave. In the tunnel, a shadow moved, jerky and uncoordinated.

I squinted and lifted my phone to shine a light down the dark passage. Dirt crumbled from the wall as something broke away from it.

"Is that a skeleton?" Sebastian whispered.

"For a vampire, you're awfully skittish," Hudson mused.

"Skeletons aren't meant to move, Principal."

The skeletons formed a barrier between us and the outside world. "I guess when stealing a book of evil, you should expect the unexpected," I said. "How hard can it be to beat a bunch of bones?"

"Have you seen *Jason and the Argonauts*?" Hudson asked.

"Of course," I said. "But I am starting to get concerned with your obsession with aliens and mythology."

"It's only a myth if it doesn't exist," Hudson said with a nod at the cluster of skeletons. "And they most certainly do exist."

Pulling the satchel open that was slung over my body, I shoved the book inside it and fastened the buckles.

A skeleton broke free from his buddies and launched an attack, coming straight for me. They were probably keyed into the book, and since I had it, that meant they were going to focus on me. Hudson smashed his fist inside the skull. The skeleton gripped his arm and Hudson let out a surprised yelp as he jerked away, a scorch mark burned into his forearm. Of course, they couldn't just be normal skeletons—they had to be burning ones, because my life wasn't hard enough.

"Now what?" Sebastian said. His features had sharpened as he released his own inner monster to deal with the danger ahead.

We were trapped. Hudson could possibly barrel through them with sheer strength, and if we were quick enough, we could follow behind him and trap the skeletons inside the tunnel. But that would hurt him. Indigo pushed against my flesh. Clearly that plan wasn't acceptable.

*"Let me out,"* she roared. *"I will protect us all."*

I closed my eyes and sank inside my own mind, letting her free. I just hoped I could dial her back before she exposed us to the world. My flesh tore at my back and I cried out as my wings erupted from my spine. I grew taller, making the linen trousers rise, and my teeth sharpened into terrifying points. Indigo narrowed her eyes at Sebastian as he swallowed and held her gaze.

"This is your creature?" he asked as his hand reached out to touch one of my hundreds of feathers.

Indigo snapped them to her back out of his reach. "I'm Indigo, vampire, Cora isn't here right now. I will protect my mate and you because Cora cares if you live, but only my mate touches my wings." Huh, she was fussy about who touched her wings. Interesting.

"Good to know," he grumbled.

Indigo crouched and dug for the element she was attached to. Fire licked up our arms, but it didn't burn us. She pushed it out along the tunnel and the skeletons froze, their mouths opened in a silent scream as they burst into ashes.

"There are no souls," Indigo complained. I guess it was good to know those skeletons were mindless machines and not souls trapped in a nightmare. "And that was far too easy."

She led the way out of the tunnel, finding a ladder had been dropped from the hole to help us up. Indigo tensed then pushed off the ground with her wings, flying up to join

Babu. He fell back from her, landing on his ass as his eyes widened. Sebastian and Hudson used the ladder to join us.

"He has a soul," she said, causing Babu's mouth to fall open.

*"You can't have him,"* I instructed her. Her eyes rolled so hard, I felt them looking at me inside my mind.

We moved between the shelves and up the stairs, spilling out into the blistering sunshine and straight into a group of elementals waiting for us. They were spaced out amongst the rubble. People milled around, side-eyeing the elementals with suspicion. My grandmother's army had waited for us to retrieve the book and were now planning on taking it from us. They remained clueless about the creature they faced, if they held the knowledge of the horror coming for them, they wouldn't be here.

Hudson and Sebastian spanned out around me, just as Michael Glaister stepped forward. His long sweeping leather coat went with him whether he was braving the icy wings of Hell or the fiery temperament of the Middle East. Damn it, my grandmother had sent The Hound. This was going to be tricky.

"*He's dangerous?*" Indigo asked with a tilt of her head.

*"Yes, but don't kill him, my grandmother would not stop until she'd sacrificed us all on her altar of self-proclaimed righteous ruler ship."*

*"His soul is as black as the void."* That didn't sound healthy. *"But I'll still eat him."*

*"No."*

*"Spoil sport."*

Michael's cold eyes clamped on to Indigo's position. It wasn't like she was trying to hide. The crazy bitch was just standing proud as punch in the sunshine. Onlookers' steps faltered as they gazed at Indigo. She refused to withdraw until the danger had passed. Michael tilted his head to the right and narrowed his gaze. I still looked enough like me to be recognizable, but his mind would be turning over what creature faced him.

"Your grandmother wants the book, Cora, nobody has to get hurt if you hand it over."

He didn't look surprised to see us here, making me wonder if they'd been waiting for us. "Your terms are unacceptable," Indigo drawled. The cadence of her voice was otherworldly, and the two elementals at Michael's back took a step back. Michael, the idiot, took a step forward. I felt indigo's mouth stretch into a grin, he matched it. What happens when you get two psychos in a room? Nothing good is the answer.

Shadows moved in her periphery as Hudson and Sebastian widened their gap between us. They were closing in on the elementals refusing to let us go. Babu was behind us, giving Indigo the space she needed with those stupid giant wings.

Indigo ran her hand through the air and summoned a fireball in her hand, which she played with like a child's toy—if that toy was a burning lump of destruction. Gasps surrounded us and people no longer side-eyed us, they had their phones out and a small crowd was gathering to watch us. What I'd give for a time when people fled from danger, not whipped their phones out to video the carnage.

"I will give you to the count of five to remove yourselves from our path," Indigo said.

Michael laughed. The sound was as cold as his eyes, and as joyless as his life.

"One," she started.

Michael snapped his fingers and another female elemental emerged from the crowd with a struggling woman in her arms who was clearly cursing. She dropped her at Michael's feet and stepped back. Michael gripped her arm and yanked her up in front of him. She was a beautiful Egyptian woman and tears streamed down her face.

Babu pushed past Indigo. "Layla?" he shouted.

*"Stop him,"* I instructed.

Indigo snapped out her wing and prevented Babu from running into Michael's trap. The crowd murmured at the sight of Indigo's wings stretching. "Let go of my wife," Babu shouted, causing poor Layla to start a round of sobbing. How long had they been here to kidnap Babu's wife? A sickening lurch flipped my stomach into a knot.

"Last chance, Cora, give me the book and everyone lives," Michael said. The gleam in his eyes was of wicked anticipation. He didn't want me to give in, because then he couldn't cause the destruction he was known for.

"Give him the book," Babu snapped. He pulled at the satchel strapped across our chest. Indigo grabbed his wrist and let the power flow from her gaze.

"Be still," she ordered. Babu froze, the weight of the words forcing his body to obey.

"Two," Indigo snarled at Michael.

*"I hope you know what you are doing,"* I uttered.

Michael whispered something in Layla's ear then shoved her forward as resignation seeped into her features. Indigo's gaze lasered in on the woman as Babu made noises of distress.

"Three."

The corner of Michael's mouth lifted. When The Hound smirked, you ran. You didn't stop even if there was a hundred dollar bill on the floor. That man only smiled when something utterly evil was about to occur and he was the cause of it.

Layla lifted her trembling hand to her throat. Michael had passed her a dagger. He raised a brow, daring Indigo to continue counting and defying him.

*"You have to trust me,"* Indigo said in my mind.

"Four."

Michael made a motion across his own throat with his hand and Layla followed. Blood spilled down her simple pale blue dress, the contrast was startling. Michael took his time in slicing open her neck, making sure the horror of what was taking place fully sank into our veins. The crowd collectively took a step back and the mumblings paused as they watched the atrocity unfolding in front of them. Why weren't they running and screaming? Was society this numb?

"Five," Indigo shouted. She moved so fast, the world was a blur. Hudson and Sebastian launched at the surrounding elementals. Hudson's claws ripped free and tore at the chest of the male in front him. Sebastian lunged for the female and snapped her neck. Indigo set her sights on Michael, stepping over Layla's crumpled body to reach him. Michael looked shocked for a moment, clearly not heeding the warning that Cora Roberts was not in control, and no amount of threats would deter her. She didn't weigh the value of human life like a normal person, and wasn't bound by the emotional attachment most of us felt, and in that matter he had met his match.

Her claws extended and she wrapped her hand around his throat, while her free hand held something hot that I couldn't see. It couldn't be the fireball, Indigo was impervious to the effects of her own power. "I'm going to enjoy this," she said with a tilt of her head.

"Cora, stop," a familiar voice boomed from the crowd. Indigo squeezed Michael's throat.

*"Wait,"* I pleaded.

My grandmother emerged into the clearing and paused to inspect the carnage on the ground. She showed zero emotion as she stepped over her dead elementals and headed toward us.

"Well, aren't you quite remarkable? I always knew you had something special hiding inside you, Cora, but this is something entirely out of this world."

So she knew I was something, but not what? Meaning she had no clue who my father is. "I am Eloise Roberts, Head of The Order."

"A pauper posing as a president," Indigo snarled. My grandmother's throat bobbed as she locked eyes with the daughter of death. At least she had the common sense to be a little scared, Michael was still glaring at Indigo like he was going to dissect her and eat her entrails with a good chianti. Hannibal had nothing on this guy.

"Perhaps, but what are you posing as?" she asked, stopping a few yards away from us, just out of the danger zone. Hudson and Sebastian flanked Indigo's sides.

My grandmother's lips lifted as she took in three powerful representations of the factions. "I'd like to speak to my granddaughter."

"No," Indigo snarled. "Cora is weak for family, I hold no such reservations."

"Cora is powerful because of such familial ties, you would do well to remember that she houses you, not the other way around."

Oh snap. Granny Eloise was getting all soppy on me, what next? Would the sun start rising in the west and setting in the east?

*"Keep our form, but let me out,"* I instructed Indigo. This needed diplomacy, not the swift justice of a crazy half angel.

*"Fine."* She shrank back, letting me take control.

My grandmother's eyes watched with keen interest. "Cora, perhaps we can get this resolved."

"I will not give you the Red Dragon, you cannot steal the demon magic and murder innocents to create the fear you need to take control."

She threw her head back and laughed. "Child, you are being led around by your emotions and remain blind to the truth. You played right into my hands. Your duplicate vault is not the big secret you believe, and the walls you live in aren't as private as you wish. I knew Sophia wouldn't translate the grimoire for me, but she would do it to stop me, leading us to the location of the tomb you now hold." I blinked and my grip loosened around Michael, not freeing him completely but enough so he could breathe. "Your quest to save the weak humans is admirable, but my intention was never to murder them."

"What are you trying to do then?"

"Oh, you'll find out soon enough." That sounded ominous. "Now be a dutiful granddaughter and hand me the book."

"No."

She sighed like she used to when I'd failed to complete a spell as a child. She clapped her hands and the crowd parted to allow two men manhandling Aunt Dayna into the clearing. She glared at her mother and mumbled something behind the white cloth shoved in her mouth as she struggled between the assholes.

"Am I supposed to believe you'll kill your own daughter in pursuit of your power?" I said. She'd overplayed her hand. My grandmother was a tyrant, but she wouldn't kill her own flesh and blood, she would see it as a waste of magic.

"No," she said with a smile. "I won't kill her. But there are things worse than death that can be done to a woman, and once my men wear her out, I'll collect my next daughter, then the next." That was how ugly my grandmother was. She was promising a life of rape and torture to get what she wants.

*"She lies,"* Indigo reasoned.

*"I don't believe so. Eloise doesn't make idle threats."*

"Your Aunt Liz is currently shopping at the local supermarket with the young girl, Maggie. I believe my sister sent her for extra cabbage." I felt the tension rolling off Sebastian and Hudson next to me. They were staying silent, letting me take the lead. "I have a team ready to grab them if you refuse."

My hand cramped as I peeled it from Michael's neck. He stepped back and eyeballed me from head to toe, his slimy magic pushed at my flesh and I fought the violent urge to end him.

Aunt Dayna's protests loudened as I undid the satchel and pulled the book out. Michael lunged forward and snatched it from my hands with a wink. I grimaced.

"Good girl," Eloise said, eyeballing Hudson. "You were meant to control him, not marry him. That is a disappointment."

I glared at her. "I no longer yearn for your approval. That ended when you tried to use me to further your own power."

She rolled her eyes. "So dramatic, Cora. Don't burn the family bridge—it is irreplaceable."

"I have a family. You are no longer welcome in it. Don't call, don't visit, do not expect an invitation."

She shook her head sadly. "Soon you will see the future differently and long to be in my good graces."

With that, she spun and the deep crowd parted once more, followed by Michael and the remaining elementals. Sebastian reached Dayna first and undid her gag and bindings. "My psycho mother needs to be dealt with," she spat.

I gazed down at Layla and felt the moment Babu was released. He ran and collapsed over his dead wife. *"Not dead,"* Indigo muttered. She nudged me to look at what was in my hand. A white orb, with wisps of power flaring around it.

*"Her soul?"* I checked.

*"Yes, move the demon and I will bring her back."*

"Move him," I instructed Hudson.

"Let the man grieve," Hudson responded.

I snapped my gaze to his. "Principal, remove the man from his wife so I can concentrate on restoring her soul."

Babu was too distraught to hear me, but everyone else did.

"Move him," someone shouted from the crowd still, observing the scene. How the hell were we going to deal with this? I didn't own one of those little memory zapper things from *Men in Black*, but it sure would have been handy right now. My grandmother had purposefully caused a scene in broad daylight amongst the humans, then bailed to let me deal with the fall out. Hudson clutched Babu's arms and dragged him away. Indigo moved forward and took control. She pried open Layla's mouth and shoved the orb in before running her hand along her throat. With a satisfied hum, she jolted with power and Layla's body jerked like we'd shocked her. The crowd gasped. Indigo repeated it three times and then stood.

"Mind, body, and soul, returned."

Everyone's eyes were glued to the scene. Layla's chest suddenly moved and she gurgled before rolling and spitting blood out on the stone floor. Babu stopped crying and dived back to his wife, holding her in his arms and muttering something in Egyptian. The crowd cheered.

"You gave up the book," Hudson said, spinning me to face him. Indigo retreated but my body remained changed.

"Family is everything," I said, glancing at Dayna and Sebastian. "I'd be no less evil than my grandmother if I started weighing up the consequences of losing a life. That is a steep slippery slope."

He tucked a lock of my hair behind my ear and smiled. "It wasn't a criticism. You are stronger for those ties and beliefs, not weaker like Eloise believes."

*"I would have to disagree,"* Indigo complained.

*"Of course you would, you need to learn these are your family too, and we must protect them."*

*"I have a family?"*

The lost note in her voice almost broke me. My psychopathic creature was a lost soul looking for love.

*"Yes, Indigo, you have a huge family, and it's time they met you."*

"Are we going to talk about Cora's alter ego?" Dayna asked. "Anybody? Just me that saw the terrifying creature standing there a minute ago? The one that stuffed a soul back into a body? Okay, good to know I'm delusional. For the record, I think my mother needs to die."

*"I like her,"* Indigo said.

Oh no, I couldn't have the daughter of death and my most chaotic aunt loose on society. That is one shit storm it would not survive. Someone send help, any help, all help.

Hudson started clapping. "That's a wrap, people," he shouted. "Look out for this on the big screen next year."

Sebastian snorted. "They'll never believe that," he grumbled.

"What's the name of the movie?" someone shouted.

"Great effects on the girl," someone joined in.

"Can I get your autograph?"

I shook my head. Society couldn't recognize evil even when it slapped them in the face with blood and destruction.

# Chapter Twenty Three

*The angel of death enjoys diet soda.*

Dayna was uncharacteristically quiet all the way home. She ate, slept, and drank, but refused to discuss what her own mother had tried to do. She was shaken and with good reason.

Luckily, we'd brought Hudson's Escalade to the airport so we had plenty of room for an extra person.

Dayna seemed to come out of her haze as we pulled onto my property, her back straightening as she eyeballed the house. It was going to be a difficult conversation with Aunt

Liz, but first, I needed a shower to get rid of the two day grit and dirt that coated my skin.

Sebastian and Dayna opened the rear doors and spilled out. Hudson caught my hand. "You did the right thing," he told me again. He'd been repeating it nearly every hour, and while I appreciated the support, I didn't doubt my actions for one minute.

"I know. Why do you keep saying it?"

"Because you might know, but I can see the guilt shining in your eyes, and I'll keep saying it until you actually believe it."

I sighed as Sebastian and Dayna disappeared into the house. "We played right into her hands."

"Also not your fault. We agreed collectively to go get the book."

"I should have seen it coming."

His fingers wrapped around my chin and drew my gaze to his. "Are you a precog?"

"No."

"Do you have divine insight I'm unaware of?"

"No."

"Then why should you have seen it coming?"

My eyes fluttered closed for a second as I let his faith in me bolster my confidence. "Okay, I get it. Thank you."

"Anytime," he said as my eyes flipped open to find him smiling at me. After a soft, lingering kiss, he jumped out of the car and I followed.

Aunt Liz was already fussing over Aunt Dayna as we breached the house. She turned her stare on me and pointed to the parlor. "I need details."

"After I've showered," I told her. "I need to get the stench of The Hound off me."

Her eyes softened and she nodded.

Aunt Sophia's head appeared from the kitchen. "You need cabbage rolls." It wasn't a question, as far as she was concerned everything could be solved with cabbage rolls.

"Shower first," I gritted out.

"Fine, then food."

I nodded in acquiescence. Food, family feuds, and exposure. It was time to show those I love what I truly am and trust that they won't reject me. It was only a matter of time before everything was revealed, and it would be better coming from me.

Dave appeared down the stairs and swept his gaze over Hudson, then me. "What happened? Where's the evil book?"

Hudson met him on the stairs. "Come with me, and I'll tell you."

He sent a wink over his shoulder and I relaxed as I dragged my heavy limbs up the two flights of stairs.

Harry shot out of my room waving his arms in the air. "Pineapples, pineapples, pineapples, pineapples, pineapples."

A five pineapple situation was like DEFCON 1. My body sprang into motion as adrenaline shot through my limbs and I power walked the last few steps before flinging open my bedroom door. My body froze and my eyes widened. Well, fuck. This was not a five pineapple situation, it was more like a ten pineapple situation. Or perhaps a pineapple smoothie, it takes a lot of pineapples to make a smoothie. There was a fire-haired being with identical green eyes to my own lounging on my sofa with his giant wings spread out.

I carefully closed the door behind me. Harry stayed outside—probably a wise decision.

"Father," I said, aiming for nonchalance. Probably too late with the way I'd stumbled into the room. I made my wobbly legs move toward the kitchen and poured myself a drink of orange juice from the jug. "Drink?" I asked him over my shoulder as I tried to pull myself together.

"Do you have soda?"

I gazed in the fridge, spying a few cans. "Sure. Cola, Mountain Dew, or Fanta?"

"Is it diet?"

"The cola is."

"I'll have that."

Who knew the angel of death was sugar conscious and a soda lover?

I poured the soda into a glass, added some ice, and passed it to him as I stepped into the living area.

"Daughter, sit, we have much to discuss."

I did as I was told, taking residence in the oversized armchair by the French doors.

"To what do I owe the pleasure?" I asked. I thought I was all out of pleasantries, but when faced with the angel of death, one minded their p's and q's.

My father's cold gaze narrowed, and only years of dealing with Eloise prevented me from fidgeting or curling in on myself. "I gave you a task."

"You did."

A wave of power came from him before he clamped a lid on it. "What was that task?"

"To avoid exposure, and if I couldn't, then I should minimize the loss of life."

"How do you think that is going?"

Um, my grandmother is running around causing untold chaos and now has in her possession the ultimate guide to evil. "Fine."

He blinked. Then from somewhere in his black flowing pants, he produced the latest model of a popular phone. He tapped the screen with a frown marring his forehead, then spun it to face me. A jerky video of the scene in Egypt played. Everything from Indigo's snarling face with huge wings, to Layla's death and rebirth. The title at the top read. "What movie is this? I need it in my life." That movie was my life, and no, the owner of the video definitely didn't want it.

"There are hundreds of these circulating the web," my father ground out. "This is not being discreet."

I swallowed, noting he'd not spoken about the exchange between Indigo and Michael. Perhaps he hadn't noticed? *Cora Roberts - Master of Wishful Thinking.*

"The world cannot learn of our kind, Cora. If you threaten exposure, I must move to take you out."

And we'd come full circle to him threatening my life. It wasn't a parental visit without it.

I folded my arms. "Then who would do your bidding?"

"I could make a hundred more of you."

"Nephilim? Sure. But not a hundred more of me. A powerful elemental born of an original bloodline mixed with an archangel."

The phone in his hand disappeared and he leaned forward. Power swelled in the room, pushing against my flesh. Indigo shot forward to protect us, and my tired mind couldn't stop her from exploding through. She'd left her wings buried, but the rest of me had changed.

My father tilted his head. "Cora has accepted you, creature?"

"My name is Indigo, and I am her family. Of course, she accepts me."

"She chained you for years and was ashamed of you." Indigo's thoughts rippled with what he was saying.

What an asshole. *"That's not true, I was not ashamed, I was afraid. There's a world of difference."*

*"I know, but we will never know what he wants if we don't play the game."*

It should worry me that she was picking up how to manipulate people so quickly.

"Well I am here now, we made an agreement that I will never be chained again."

"Until she no longer needs you," my father said, trying to worm his way into her mind with seeds of doubt.

"What is your point?"

"I can free you from the confines of her mind. Once expelled of your humanity, you can return to Heaven with me."

Both myself and Indigo jerked away from him with shock. What game was he playing? "Why would I do that?"

"Aren't you tired of being called upon only when she needs you to protect her?"

"Cora is me, and I am her."

"You don't have to be."

Indigo shook her head but I could sense her hesitancy. Did she really resent me? I couldn't help that she was a creature within me.

"What would happen to Cora?"

My father leaned back on the sofa and smiled. "She would be no more."

"She would also go to Heaven?"

"No, she would not exist."

Wow, this asshole of a sperm donor was actually trying to wipe out my existence. I should feel honored he cared at all.

"Why not just kill us as we are?" Indigo asked.

"I long for a daughter in my own image. That would be you, Indigo."

Lies, lies, lies. Something was wrong with this whole situation.

"How would you separate us?"

His lips kicked up further. "There's a spell in the book Cora willingly traded for a few pitiful lives. She is a disappointment. You would have never taken such action."

So he did know about the book. His assertion about Indigo's thoughts wasn't incorrect. Indigo had said as much, but I hoped I was beginning to show her that family mattered. Well, most of it. What surprised me the most was my father's apparent willingness to deal with a book of evil. Wouldn't he burst into flames or something apocalyptic if he tried using it?

"The spell is in the Red Dragon?" she checked.

"It is. Also, Eloise cannot be allowed to carry out her plan." Why did that sound like a side note? Surely, he was here because a crazy woman was wielding a powerful book with undisclosed intentions? I was meant to be the side note.

"*He wants you dead,*" Indigo said.

"*Apparently, I'm a disappointment all around.*"

"*I could try to kill him?*"

I took a beat, because for a split second I contemplated ridding the earth of another supernatural force with a hidden agenda. My father's gaze flashed with blue fire.

"*Um, no, probably not a good idea.*"

"*Ending those that threaten us is essential for survival.*"

"*Killing everyone who threatens us is not a life plan.*"

"Are you communicating with my daughter right now?" Abaddon asked with his eyes narrowed.

"She is me, and I am her."

Okay, she was also channeling The Riddler. My head was a crowded space.

"I don't think I've ever met anything like you," he said.

I growled and Indigo echoed it out loud. I didn't like him referring to either of us as a thing. I was a person, and so was she. We were born together, we'd live together, and one day would die together. By some miracle I'd found our match in Hudson who harbored his own creature. Indigo's agreement warmed my chest.

*"Let me back to deal with our father,"* I told her.

*"I don't trust him."*

*"Neither do I, but for some reason, he's hesitant to act against us together. I think we are safe."*

She grumbled as she shrank back and allowed me to break free. My father's forehead crumpled as he eyeballed me.

"It's remarkable how you've trained her."

*"Give me a minute and I can train him also,"* Indigo growled. He clearly didn't realize we could hear him no matter who was in control. Meaning he was now trying to play me off against Indigo, even though we'd revealed we can communicate.

He finished the last of his soda and placed the empty glass on the table. "You must retrieve The Red Dragon from your grandmother, humanity's fate is in the balance."

"No more so than usual."

"Wrong. If Eloise succeeds, she will alter the fabric of civilization and will usher in a new and disastrous era. How much blood on your hands will it take for you to see the sacrifice of the few is for the good of the many? Ten? A hundred? A thousand?"

I shook my head. "That is not a path I'm willing to travel. All life is sacred."

"Your precious humans pray to a god who sacrificed his own son for the many."

I blinked. "Are you trying to draw parallels between Jesus Christ and this situation? Because you are purposefully omitting some very important details."

"Like?"

"Jesus was God's son."

"And you are my daughter."

"Are you chiding me for letting the book go to save a life, or saying I should be sacrificed? Because I'm one hundred percent sure my death will not help this situation. My grandmother might shed a tear for a missed opportunity to control something new and powerful, but it wouldn't prevent her from enacting her plans and crowning herself queen of all that lives."

"I was there when they nailed him to the cross. If I believed sacrificing you would stop what's coming, I would do it in a heartbeat."

"Then you've come full circle, admonishing me for protecting those I love. Is that not what Jesus did? Protect those he loved by dying?"

"As you've pointed out, you aren't sacrificing yourself, you are risking the sacrifice of the masses. Selfish in name, selfish in nature."

I'd been called many things, but selfish wasn't one of them. "You are trying to provoke me and I don't have the slightest clue what you hope to gain from it. But let me reassure you that after navigating Eloise Roberts all of my life, this is child's play."

He lurched forward and grabbed my arm, causing my breath to stutter in my chest. "You want to witness the end of civilizations? The utter decimation of life as you know it?"

The room spun around us and disintegrated, giving way to a dull landscape. My father released my arm as I twisted toward a billow of smoke in the sky. Rows and rows of people dressed in vertical striped clothing clung to the caged fence surrounding them. Screams echoed from a building and I slapped my hand over my mouth as ash rained down from the sky. War-torn Poland was a poignant place to start as a warning against tyrannical rulers intent on world domination. I squeezed my eyes closed.

"Of course, no greater evil has been committed than by those that do so in the name of the Lord."

I opened my eyes just in time to see the first fatal flight hit the tower and forever alter the Manhattan skyline. The world spun and a double decker bus passed me on a busy street before a deafening explosion rocked the world. Screams of terror surrounded me as tears leaked from my eyes.

"Enough," I whispered.

"Of course, crimes committed through religion aren't a new thing," he went on, ignoring the pain shattering my heart. "Open your eyes, daughter. Witness what evil walks the earth even between humans that worship the same God."

I did as he instructed because he would hold me here until he got his point across. A large field surrounded us on all sides. Thunder erupted from every direction and a minute later, men on horses clashed in a bloody and violent battle while terrified cries from the dying pulsed in the air.

"No more," I begged.

"Something less recent perhaps, committed not by one community onto another, but between themselves?" My father said through gritted teeth.

The landscape shifted again and we came to a stop among a deafening crowd that screamed with excitement. I looked over the heads in front of me, trying to see what everyone was excited about.

"Can't see, daughter? Let's get closer."

He snatched my hand and in a blink, we were on the dusty ground just as a spear drove through the chest of a gladiator and he hit the deck, blood spraying in an arc. All around us, carnage was ensuing for the entertainment of the masses, and in pride of place sat no other than Caesar himself.

"Enough," I whispered.

"No, not until I'm sure you will choose differently next time you are faced with a decision between a loved one and the future of all living beings."

The scene shifted again and we were among a sun-drenched forest. I froze, waiting for the horror to show itself. My father wrapped his hand around my chin and lifted my head to the sky.

Among the trees, hundreds of bodies hung. Children, women, men, nobody was spared. I wasn't sure what atrocity this was and where in time, but my stomach twisted with unease.

The change was longer this time and when we stopped, it was to a reddened sky littered with angels locked in battle. I recognized my Uncle Lucifer on one side and my father on the other. A single feather floated down in front of my face. I reached out and caught it between my fingers, the blood-soaked tip dripping onto my palm. My legs collapsed and I fell to the floor as a sob broke free.

He moved us once more and the world became quiet. There were no screams, no shouts, no pain or terror. His whispered words of horror had ceased.

"Child, open your eyes," someone new implored me. A warmth blanketed me and my head rose, finding myself at the edge of a still lake. My head shot up. A thick mist covered the water but a figure was in the center, seemingly floating on the surface.

"Come to me, Cora," he called.

I lurched to my feet, the water beneath me feeling solid as I began to walk toward him. I got a few steps in and looked down, panic piercing my chest at the deep water below. The surface bowed and then I was swallowed in the icy liquid. I clawed for the surface, but it wouldn't come.

"Faith lives inside you, Cora. You just have to reach for me and I will always be your guide. When you are ready to accept all that you truly are, you will know you are loved unconditionally without borders."

I flailed harder as I sank lower and my chest burned with the pressure. My vision darkened and then I hit a wooden floor with a harsh thump. I rolled over onto my side and coughed up the water with a heaving chest. A sob tore free of my throat as I grieved for all the life wasted, sacrificed, and for the faith I'd lost somewhere along the way without realizing it.

"Now do you understand? Perhaps it will give you pause when you forsake all others for the bonds of love and family."

He disappeared, leaving me alone in a wet puddle. My hand unclasped and in my palm was a feather of the purist white, free of the crimson stain.

The door burst open, hammering against the wall and Hudson ran in with Dave hot on his heels. He scooped me into his arms and squashed me so tightly my ribs creaked. "I couldn't feel you," he mumbled into my wet hair. "I'll kill Lucifer if he keeps taking you to Hell."

"Not Lucifer, my father," I whispered.

He leaned back and frowned. "Your father? Why couldn't I feel you?"

We needed to discuss that a little more closely, because I don't think sensing if your mate was still of this world was normal. Sure, people got feelings of dread, but Hudson wasn't simply going on his gut. He knew categorically that I was no longer in this space and time.

"He decided a little show and tell was in order, showcasing some of the worst atrocities known to humankind."

I neglected to tell him the part where I'd been asked to walk on water, and my faith had faltered. *Cora Roberts—queen of ignoring the bigger picture.*

# CHAPTER TWENTY FOUR

*Let's take off the mask.*

It's surprising how small my rooms feel when packed with family and friends. Every surface, from my sofas and chairs to the kitchen counter, was being utilized as sitting space. Even Bella was lying on the back of the armchair behind Hudson, her tail curled around his neck. I was left standing in front of everyone.

It was time, but I still felt nervous.

"My father just visited," I explained as I forced my hands to unclench at my sides. I was dry now, but no less shaken from the experience. Oh, what I would give to travel back to a simpler time when my father was absent from my life completely. Then again, that also meant a time when Hudson wasn't in my life and that was no longer acceptable.

Aunt Liz leaned toward me from her spot on the sofa between Aunt Dayna and Aunt Sophia. "Your father was here?" she checked.

I nodded.

Aunt Sophia paused in her crochet project, another scarf perhaps. This time with the rainbow wool she'd made Dave wind up for her. "Please tell me you aren't the spawn of Satan," she said.

I guess the only way was up from that statement. Dave tilted his head like he was enjoying the hell out of my uncomfortableness. Maybe I could get Aunt Liz to swear off meat for a month, that would annoy him.

"Cora, focus," Sebastian said from his place on the kitchen counter which held him, Maggie, and Rebecca.

"No, Lucifer isn't my father, he's my uncle."

And Liz jerked back in her seat like I'd slapped her. "Who is your father?"

Hudson gave me an encouraging smile. "Abaddon," I whispered, as soon the word was out I wanted to stuff it back inside my mouth.

"*The* Angel of Death?" Aunt Dayna checked.

I nodded once. "That's right."

"That's why you can see the dead and have access to their final moments," Aunt Sophia declared. "It all makes sense now."

"You are a Nephilim," Aunt Liz said carefully, like she was tiptoeing through a minefield.

"A what?" Maggie asked.

"Half angel, and in Cora's case, half elemental," Aunt Liz explained.

"Wow," Maggie whispered.

"They are normally slaughtered while still in the womb," Aunt Sophia added. You could always count on her to give it straight and cut through the shit. "For some reason your father has let you live."

Aunt Liz scowled at her, clearly unimpressed at Sophia's lack of tact.

I shrugged because if I was being honest, I wasn't entirely sure how I was still alive—but I'd decided not to look too closely at it. My life was a gift, and I would use it for good.

"Is that why you monstered out in Egypt?" Maggie asked.

"Shush," Rebecca said. "This is her big secret reveal and you are spoiling it."

"Apparently, the internet has already spoiled it," I muttered as I eyeballed my bedroom door and contemplated if I could chicken out and make my escape.

Hudson shook his head subtly. Damn cat knew everything I was thinking.

"Rockhard sent me the video, but we were giving you space to tell us in your own time," Rebecca explained.

"Actually, we had given that space a time limit," Dave added.

"Show us then," Aunt Sophia said with a wave of her hand. "The suspense is killing me."

"Didn't you watch the video?"

She huffed. "No, I don't like the web, it seems unsavory."

*"Time to shine,"* I told Indigo. *"Everyone here I love, so no eating of any souls."*

*"I need nourishment,"* she declared.

I rolled my eyes. *"Later. I'm sure whatever my grandmother is planning will send many evil souls our way."*

*"I want Michael."*

Of course she did. *"If you see an opportunity, take it."* I reasoned.

"What's happening?" Rebecca said.

"She's speaking with Indigo," Hudson told them.

Rebecca and Maggie looked around the room. "Who?" Rebecca asked.

Hudson tapped his temple with a finger. "Up here. She's probably reasoning with her, telling her she can't devour any of your souls."

Maggie shrank back and her mouth popped open while Aunt Sophia continued her rapid crocheting.

I'd worn a strappy sundress that crisscrossed down my back, saving any more clothing from being shredded. My back arched and my wings tore free from my spine as Indigo's form took over mine. I rose taller, my teeth sharpened and claws extended from my hands.

"Holy mother, Jesus Christ, God Almighty, and anyone else who is listening," Aunt Liz murmured.

Coming from her, that was a curse worthy of twenty dollars in the jar.

"I am Indigo." Her voice vibrated with power and rattled our chest.

"You live inside her?" Aunt Sophia asked. "Like a possession?"

Indigo bristled and her wings shot out, knocking over my vase. Hudson reached out and caught it, his cat reflexes coming in handy. "I am not a virus, I do not possess, Cora is me and I am her."

This all sounded so familiar, but she was right. The fact that I had the lion's share of control didn't make Indigo lesser, or even a stowaway in my body. We were one, and this was the first step in the acceptance she had been missing. The fact that she was lacking social skills and empathy for humankind was my doing—I'd locked her up tight and now I had the mammoth task of introducing her to the world, while hoping the world survived the transition.

"I've always been with Cora, from the time she first walked, to the torture that boy subjected her to."

Everyone in the room froze. Indigo caught Sebastian's eyes as we shared the memory of my pain and his rescue of me that solidified a lifelong friendship.

"I was there when her grandmother taught her fortitude and stole her childhood under the guise of making her stronger, when the truth is, she's always known Cora could be a weapon she needed to wield."

Indigo snapped her wings beneath our flesh as she moved closer to Hudson then dropped into his lap and hissed at Bella. Sensing the bigger predator, Bella shot off the chair and wound around Dave's legs. Hudson smirked at her show of possession.

"You mean she's always known that you exist?" Aunt Liz said with a frown.

"Specifically? No, but there are times I've shielded Cora from Eloise's cruelty, that's when she knew something other than elemental blood ran through our veins."

And the revelations kept on coming. "*You protected me?*" I asked.

"*I will always protect you, and just for the record, if I eat Eloise, it will be one less scourge on the earth. The things you remember at her hands are simply the tip of the iceberg.*"

"*You mean eat her soul?*" I clarified, ignoring the fact I had missing memories, so horrible my chained alter ego had emerged to protect me, and all of it was by the hand of my own flesh and blood.

A trickle of amusement filtered through my mind as Indigo left me with that disturbing image.

"What does Cora think about this?" Aunt Sophia asked as Bella decided to give up on her hussy ways with the men in the room and took to eyeballing the ball of wool at my aunt's feet with the focused gaze of a lion sighting a gazelle.

"Cora is in agreement that Eloise needs to be stopped at all costs."

"*Umm, yeah. Stopped, not eaten.*" No amount of therapy would get rid of that nightmare.

"*If I ate her, she would be stopped.*"

When the psycho soul-sucking half angel started making sense, you needed to get yourself checked out or checked in. Whichever worked.

"*We don't have time for dramatics. Pull your shit together, Cora.*"

And finally, when that being told you to pull yourself together, you knew you'd lost it. Oh well, may as well embrace the crazy.

*"That's more like it,"* Indigo mused. Harry floated into the room and froze as he took in my crowded living area and the creature before him.

"Pineapples, pineapples, pineapples, pineapples, pineapples, pineapples, pineapples, pine—"

"Why is the ghost shouting about fruit?" she asked the room. Look at that, my father got a five pineapple rating and my alter ego topped it.

Everyone glanced around the room, fully expecting to see a spirit. Why? Because seeing a divine being suddenly lifted the veil? I had to wonder who the crazy ones were.

Harry's arm raised and he pointed at Indigo. "She's eaten Miss Roberts. This is not acceptable. Why are you all just sitting there like she's welcome?"

He huffed and floated closer. Apparently, I warranted the extra courage. He flung his hand at Hudson. "The creature in your lap is not your mate."

Indigo leaned forward and Hudson's hands wrapped around her waist. "He is most certainly my mate, and I have not eaten your mistress, ghoul. Now be still." Harry froze.

*"Be nice, he's a friend who isn't certain of what's happening or who you are."*

*"You have the strangest collection of friends."*

Ignoring the possibility of a ghost in the room, Aunt Dayna folded her arms and squinted at Indigo. "Do you have an idea of what my mother is up to? Why she needs the Red Dragon?"

"And what the Datura are for," Aunt Liz added.

"And why an entire town was found dead," Sebastian chimed in.

Did they think Indigo suddenly had all the answers and that she'd been hiding them from me?

Indigo tilted her head. "I don't know these things." I sighed a breath of relief in our mind, I didn't want to look like an idiot who'd had these answers inside of her this whole time. "Ask yourselves, why now? Eloise has had these ambitions for a long time. The plant is hardly uncommon and the grimoire has been sitting in the vaults for years. These tools she's had at her disposal for many years, so what has changed?"

"You," Rebecca whispered, catching on to whatever Indigo was hinting at. "Up until a couple of months ago, Cora had you locked down tight."

I feel like we should have discussed these revelations before we shared with the group.

"Isn't it more likely a coincidence, given that Eloise tried a treaty not so long ago, and the failure of that led her down this path?" Sebastian asked.

Indigo nodded. "Unless the aim of that treaty was never to unite the factions."

Sebastian's eyebrows slammed down. "What else could it have been for?"

"Do you still have the treaty?" she asked.

"I have a copy," Hudson said. What? Why? His thumb rubbed soothing circles on Indigo's hip which I could feel. Clearly, he'd sensed my pissed off state.

"I'd need the original," Indigo said.

"The original was torn up by my father. But the copy Hudson has would be identical," Sebastian explained.

"It's not the words I need, it's the magic."

I saw where this was headed and tried to derail the train before it crashed. *"Don't say anything else."*

"You're saying Eloise spelled the treaty, to what end?" Dave said, breaking his excellent impression of a marble statue.

Bella dived on the ball of wool and proceeded to wrestle with it like it was her arch nemesis.

"She was uniting the factions under the guise of peace to build her an army of supernaturals for when she planned to expose us all to the humans," Sebastian said. None of that was news.

"You think Eloise Roberts wants the vampires and shifters at her side?" Indigo asked, then threw back her head and laughed.

*"You're making us look unhinged."*

The laughter stopped and she shook her head. "She wants your magic, your power, your numbers, but never for one instant did Eloise want to work alongside you. If I had the original treaty, I might be able to glean what she intended."

"But my idiot father destroyed it," Sebastian grumbled. Yet again, Leon's short-sighted idiocy burned us.

Hudson shifted under Indigo as he cleared his throat. "Actually, I have the original."

Nobody breathed as that sunk in. "You swapped them?" Aunt Dayna said with a delighted look on her face.

Dave didn't blink, clearly in on this fact. Everyone else in the room eyeballed Hudson with distrust.

"What?" he growled. "You expected me to just sign a piece of parchment that The President of The Order made, without having it examined first? I'm not stupid."

"We shall discuss that breach in trust another time," Sebastian answered with all the royal entitlement in his blood.

"Did you find anything unusual?" Aunt Liz asked.

Hudson shook his head. "No, but I couldn't use the most powerful elementals to check, because they would all report back to Eloise, or they are her family."

"And now that we stand united against her, you trust us?" Rebecca said.

"Yes," Hudson said.

"After we are done here, I'll retrieve it," Dave said.

"And in the meantime, I believe we should be working on a counter spell," Aunt Dayna said as she stood.

"To counteract what?" Hudson asked.

"Everything," she said with a grin before stepping over Bella who was still tumbling around on the floor with my aunt's ball of wool. Dayna skipped out of the room.

"Could you bring Cora back?" Hudson asked.

Indigo pouted. "I'm hungry." Oh boy.

Harry flung himself at Indigo with a warrior's cry and passed right through us, Hudson, and the chair. Hudson shivered.

"Stop that, you foolish spirit, you can't force me out of where I belong," Indigo muttered just as Aunt Sophia stood. She shooed Bella away and handed the wool to Sebastian.

"Roll that for me, dear," she demanded, patting his cheek.

Sebastian began winding the wool with an expression that seemed to be contemplating how he ended up here. Welcome to my life.

"Now, we can't have the growing girl go hungry," Sophia muttered, going to my kitchen and claiming something from the refrigerator. She popped the bowl in the microwave. Wait, when did I get a microwave?

The little light popped on and she hummed some tune I vaguely recalled from my childhood.

The scent of meat, spices, and cabbage flooded the room. "I'm out," Dave said, rushing out the door. Damn, I don't think I've ever seen him move that fast.

*"What is that?"* Indigo asked.

*"My aunt's famous cabbage rolls."*

*"Are they better than souls?"*

Umm, not exactly sure what eating a soul was akin to, so I felt unqualified to answer that. *"Sure,"* I decided on to protect the soul-burdened population.

Aunt Sophia approached us with a steaming plate in one hand and a fork in the other. I briefly worried Indigo would fling the plate at the wall and munch on my aunt instead.

Indigo accepted the plate and eyeballed the fork before grabbing a steaming ball with her hand and throwing it in her mouth. I braced myself, not entirely sure who would win in a battle between Indigo and Sophia.

Indigo hummed and grabbed another before popping it in her mouth. Two minutes later, the plate was empty she held it out to a smiling Aunt Sophia. "More."

Well, knock me down with a feather, Indigo liked to munch on something other than souls and bleeding hearts. "It is not the same, but a satisfactory, temporary, substitute."

I relaxed a little as Aunt Sophia marched back to the kitchen and heated up more cabbage rolls.

"You can stay permanently and feed us," Indigo said.

Wait, what? No.

"We shall see if I like you enough for that," Aunt Sophia said from the kitchen.

The supernaturals in the room were highly amused at the exchange, watching with rapt interest. They'd accepted Indigo like one of their own, and I was more than a little relieved to have my secrets out in the open for my family. At least, I believed it was all my secrets. How wrong I was would be revealed soon enough, because it's the secrets contained in your blood, the ones not even you knew of, that were the ones that could ruin you.

# Chapter Twenty Five

*How does one expel the thought of your aunt with some male strippers?*

My stomach gurgled and I cringed at the cabbage rolls that seemed to be endlessly repeating. Indigo had stopped eating when Aunt Sophia declared that she needed to go to the store for more ingredients. If I never saw another cabbage roll again, it would be too soon.

Finally showered and feeling a little more human, I dressed in a pair of jeans, a t-shirt, and a pair of biker boots that had seen better days but were just so comfy I couldn't bring myself to discard them. I think they'd become molded to my feet. I trudged down to the ground floor of the house and took in the sparkles, lights, and tinsel covering every available nook and surface. I didn't know I owned that many Christmas decorations.

Picking up the stack of mail on the reception desk, I miraculously didn't bump into anyone as I descended to my office. Time to pay the bills. Supernatural drama didn't excuse me in the gas company's eyes, which was a pity because at this rate, I would have free power for the next year.

I pulled my laptop out from my desk drawer alongside the previous bills and added the latest pile to them. I found a classic rock playlist courtesy of some kind soul on Spotify and proceeded to work my way through the endless demands.

I was on my second repeat of Guns N' Roses' greatest hits when my hand reached out for the next bill. Instead, I came up with another black card. This time, on one side there was a vertical line, and attached to the top, another line angling at a forty-five degree slope. On the reverse side, the same elegant writing read, 'Only the brave'. Again, another faint trace of magic hummed from the lines on the front. I pulled out the previous cards and laid them out on the desk next to each other. Someone was trying to communicate with me and it was missing the mark because I had no clue what they were saying. I searched for the phrases on the internet and other than some cleverly worded memes, I was drawing a blank. Whoever this was needed to start speaking clearly, I didn't have enough mental space to ponder the meaning of some mysterious calling cards. The wards clanged in my head, making me grit my teeth. I was feeling extra sensitive to pain and was wholeheartedly blaming it on the cabbage rolls. Two minutes later, footsteps echoed down the stairs. I gathered up the cards and stashed them in my drawer. Maggie burst through the door in a whirlwind of chestnut hair and a dress that had Rebecca's influence written all over it.

"What's wrong?" I asked as I closed my laptop and placed it back in the drawer.

"The sheriff is here."

My eyes closed briefly. Sheriff Robert Peterson no longer stalked my movements and scouted out my property because, as of a few months ago, he'd been welcomed into the inner circle of the few humans who knew that they weren't alone on the planet. So far, he hadn't crumbled from the knowledge, but we kept a close eye on him. The gag spell on him would prevent him from attempting to share what he knew, but someone's mental state needed to be monitored when their axis had shifted. I'd known Robert for a long time, since I was a little girl. He was a solid guy with no patience for dramatics.

"Did he say what he wanted?" I asked as I rubbed my temple. I couldn't handle any more chaos. Things were complicated enough, but the Sheriff didn't stop by for cookies and tea.

Maggie shrugged. "Yes, you." Someone save me from the teenage bobcat and her inability to read between the lines.

I sighed and followed her up the stairs. Everyone else was suspiciously absent, making me wonder what they were up to when for the last several weeks I hadn't been able to move without a shifter shadow. Perhaps accepting the mating meant Hudson was getting more comfortable with our connection and he didn't feel the obsessive need to stalk my every movement. I huffed a laugh at myself. Yeah, right.

Robert stood just inside the parlor, inspecting the result of the Christmas spirit vomiting throughout the house.

"Sheriff, how can I assist you today?" I asked.

Robert spun on his heel and I blinked at the terror lurking in the depths of his brown eyes. The unflappable sheriff had seen something recently that haunted him and it wasn't the Christmas decorations. Humans committed enough acts of horror to cause that look, but instinct told me this particular incident involved the unexplained and that is why he was here.

"I need your help," he said, taking a step toward me.

"Of course, anything I can do to assist local law enforcement."

"I need you to come with me."

I'm pretty sure running off with the Sheriff wouldn't go down well with my betrothed. I waved a hand at the sofa. "Explain what is happening first, then we can take it from there."

"There's no time, every second we stand here debating, the event will risk another life. I can fill you in on the way over. Bring your vampire and shifter friend—they are needed too."

Sebastian rounded the corner and tilted his head at the sheriff. "Hudson is at the pack house and Dave is out with Aunt Liz grocery shopping."

How very domesticated. Aunt Sophia appeared, clutching her knitting bag in one hand and a plate in the other. "So you are left with me," she said as she eyeballed Robert.

"Who are you?" he asked, running a hand over his clean-shaven head.

"You said this was urgent, we can do introductions on the way."

Sebastian rode with Sophia in the back of the police car, while I sat in the passenger seat. I gripped my phone and knocked out a message to Hudson.

**Cora:** With the sheriff, something has gone down in the next town, Chatsham.

Hudson: Stay at the house, I will be back in thirty minutes.

**Cora:** Already left.

I swear I felt the phantom growl that I'm sure just left his throat. Nobody else seemed to react so I'm sure it was just my overactive imagination.

**Hudson:** Text me your exact location once you arrive.

**Cora:** Okay.

**Hudson:** Who is with you?

**Cora:** Sebastian and Aunt Sophia.

**Hudson:** If the vampire bleeds, make sure it doesn't get in your mouth.

I rolled my eyes and stuffed my phone back in my pocket as we sailed through White Castle and out toward Chatsham.

I'd visited it a few times. It was a quaint little town with an abundance of swanky overpriced cafés and little bistros. Certainly, it beat The Pit. The population consisted of the trendier thirty-something crowd who didn't want to live in the cities, meaning the houses were well kept and the town center was always bustling with folks working remotely.

"Two hours ago, I received a call from one of my officers," Robert started. "Reports of spontaneous fire, mini tornados that dropped to the ground out of nowhere, giant wolves stalking the streets, and a wave that washed through the main street, bringing with it a cascade of flopping fish."

"That's concerning," I said carefully.

Robert's head snapped to me, his eyes wild. "It's not concerning, it's a fucking catastrophe, Cora, and I'm betting you have an inkling of what is happening, because you don't seem entirely surprised."

"Nothing surprises me these days," I grumbled.

"Because you are a Roberts woman," Aunt Sophia declared. I glanced over my shoulder, finding her three-quarters of the way done with her new scarf. Sebastian had been tasked with making sure the wool kept coming and didn't get snagged. "And we are always prepared for the unknown."

"You've failed to explain who you are," Robert said, glancing in the mirror at the short woman.

"She's my Great-aunt Sophia, visiting from Kazakhstan."

Robert's jaw ticked as he absorbed this information. It was clear something was going down in the supernatural world, and he had now been pulled into the middle of it.

We rode the final few miles in silence. As we entered the town, the sidewalks were covered in dead fish and a crack had opened up in the earth, splitting the road into two. My wide eyes met Sebastian's then my aunt's as they took in the destruction. The windows in multiple buildings had been blown out, and a bistro's front-facing wall had lost its battle with gravity, crumbling onto the sidewalk.

"Where is everyone?" I asked.

"We have the majority of the affected in the town hall, we are trying to keep them calm," Robert answered as he pulled in front of a tall building with two pillars, the engraving in the center declaring it as the town hall.

We spilled out of the car, Aunt Sophia abandoning her crochet before we ascended the few steps and entered through a set of double wooden doors. A faint smell hit me, chemicals and herbs in a potent mix, making me wrinkle my nose. Rows of pop-up tables and plastic chairs had been placed over the large floor. We walked down the center. Women, men, children, and the elderly—nobody had been spared. Their eyes tracked us with unease. I shot Hudson a message with our location and pocketed my phone.

We got to the back of the hall where a harassed-looking officer who looked like he'd just graduated from the police academy stood with a clipboard. His white-blond hair fell across his forehead in limp waves. He nodded at Robert and eyeballed the three strangers in his midst with unease.

"Logan, these are the experts I told you about," Robert said. "Cora, Sebastian, and Sophia."

He jerked his head for us to follow him. We stepped behind a huge navy curtain into a small space which was strewn with bits of a set from a past play. Cobwebs tickled my face, making me think that it had been a long time since the town hall had held such an event.

"We have forty-six locals in the hall who have exhibited unusual symptoms. Fire starters, earth controllers, wind summoners, and water raisers."

Damn, we should get him on the PR team for elementals—he made it sound even more majestic.

"There are three wolves locked in the kitchen and two lions in the basement. Casualty estimate is ten, three from animal attacks, and seven from being in the striking range."

Wow, I take it back, young Logan might be a fresh-faced cop, but he was efficient and had managed a difficult situation that no academy would have prepared him for. Color me impressed.

Logan flipped his notebook closed and slid it into his shirt pocket. He gazed at me with an expectant expression, like I could make sense of his world.

"Sophia and I will deal with the hall of people," I said. "Sebastian, you take the animals. Assess them, don't kill them."

Logan blinked, but that was the sum of his shock. I liked him more and more.

"They are abnormally large wolves, and the lions aren't quite the run of-the-mill cats you see in zoos either," Logan explained.

Sebastian's head dropped back and a long-suffering groan escaped his mouth. "Because these creatures don't roam in your zoos, they teach your kids, make your coffee, and style your hair."

"I'll show you the way," Logan said.

I raised a brow at Robert as Logan and Sebastian slipped out from behind the curtain. "He's awfully well put together," I observed.

"Yeah, he's a good kid. His family has a store in New Orleans, so I think he's seen his fair share of weird shit."

"Perhaps you should have stationed him in White Castle as your deputy? We could always use more steady law enforcement."

"I'll think about it. Now, explain to me what the hell happened here."

Aunt Sophia's head had been poking out from the curtain to study the room. She jerked back and huffed. "The depth of what has happened here is a long, long, conversation, Sheriff. Unless you have all night, you'll have to settle for the cliff notes' version."

He narrowed his eyes and folded his arms. "I've learned to not ask for the details. Just what threat I'm facing and how to help these folks would suffice."

"The initial threat has passed," my aunt said. "The biggest issue you have now is the forty new untrained and uneducated elementals with magic whipping through their systems. The wolves and lions don't fit the pattern, but I'd have to see them to understand." She froze and her eyes glazed over.

"Is she okay?" Robert asked.

"She's having a vision," I muttered. Knowing our luck, the vision would be how much traffic we might encounter on the way home.

Her eyes refocused. "I think your animals are newly turned shifters."

Wow, a helpful vision? Those didn't grace us often. "I thought shifters couldn't be turned?" Robert asked with a tilt of his head.

"They can't, usually," I reassured him.

"Unless," Aunt Sophia said. *Oh, boy.* "They had shifter blood in their lineage. Diluted enough to not take effect unless..." She tapped her finger against her lip and her brows crumpled.

"Unless what?" I asked.

She blinked. "Unless, someone cast a spell to infuse them with magic, forcing the change to come over them."

My grandmother was forcing people to change into animals. This sounded awfully familiar to the shitstorm that had taken place on my property not long ago. It couldn't be a coincidence. I no longer believed in them.

"But those people in the hall are just like you two," Robert said. "And they can't all have elemental blood in their lineage. That's everyone that was in town, there are no humans left."

"You're right, that theory doesn't fit for the elementals."

Aunt Sophia shook her head. "Actually, it does, but that is a tale for another time. Let's just say the human population has a more complex history than most realize. It's not secrets to be spilled right now, and I'm afraid, Sheriff, this isn't part of your remit." She glanced at me and promised me answers at a later date, but if my aunt had decreed that this made sense, then I had absolute trust that it did.

"Can we reverse it?" I wondered.

My aunt's mouth twisted to the side as she contemplated the best course of action. "The elementals, perhaps. The shifters, unlikely. For the elementals, we just need to dampen the magic in their blood, but the shifters have literally had their molecules rearranged. It's jarring on the psyche doing that change once, to repress it would likely sentence them to death."

"Do you have what you need to reverse it?" Robert asked.

My aunt raised a brow, rolled up the sleeves of her frumpy cardigan, and smirked at him. "I was born ready to fix my sister's fuck-ups, Sheriff."

Robert darted a look at me. Yup, she'd spilled the fact that my family was behind this particular fuck-up.

"Later," I muttered as we emerged from the curtains.

"They are remarkably calm," I said, noting the slightly sleepy look on everyone's faces.

Robert ran a hand over his head. "We might have hot boxed the room to stop them accidentally killing each other."

I blinked. Mr Right and Proper using illegal drugs? Wow. That must be the smell I'd picked up on when I first came in.

My aunt nodded. "Very smart, the drugs would likely have dulled their newly-formed connection. That's a good thing, it will be easier for us to suppress it."

"Us?" I wondered how I'd been roped into this.

"Of course. And the sheriff—I'll need to channel three of us."

"I've got about as much magic as Magic Mike," he grumbled.

"There's a lot of magic in those strapping young men. The way they gyrate—hot damn."

I choked on air, making Aunt Sophia roll her eyes. "I'm aging, not dead, grandniece."

I shook my head, trying to dislodge the image of my aunt and the cast of Magic Mike having a dance session. Nope, no, definitely not. Too late, the memory was burned in there now. Damn it. I would need therapy.

"Hold hands," she instructed as she held both of hers out, I grasped it and Robert's, he completed the circle and eyeballed me.

"I specifically said to keep me out of your supernatural shenanigans," he grumbled.

"You called me, remember?"

"Shush, I need to concentrate," my aunt commanded.

A yank on my magic made me bristle. "Don't fight it," she muttered.

I gritted my teeth and allowed her access, Robert flinched as she pulled from him too. The newly-emerged elementals in the room fell into a hush as they focused their attention on the three weirdos holding hands. My aunt began chanting in a language I wasn't sure of. Russian, perhaps?

She dragged our hands up in the air and we followed. A swell of power pulsed in the center of us and then exploded. Our hands broke apart and our asses hit the floor. I looked behind me, finding every other person in the room out cold, except me and Aunt Sophia.

"Please tell me they aren't dead," I whispered.

"Don't be ridiculous, I am not Eloise. My magic is more precise, I don't accidentally murder entire towns because I miscalculated."

Miscalculated? Peach Tree had been a failed test, and now that she had the Red Dragon, she'd decided to give it another shot. We'd scorched her crop of Datura, and she'd gotten creative, somehow delivering a powerful spell to these innocent folks. She'd made herself a mini army of elementals. They were untrained, which meant they'd be looking for guidance, leadership—and that's where Eloise would swoop in and gather them into the tender embrace of The Order. It was both brilliant and diabolical.

I rolled and got to my feet, then held out a hand for Aunt Sophia. She slapped it away and rose of her own accord.

"I'm old, not dead, we covered this."

And now my mind was back to Magic Mike. Thank you, universe.

# CHAPTER TWENTY-SIX

*Don't try to change me. I am who I am, and I make no excuses.*

When Robert woke, he pointed us in the direction of the kitchen as he began reassuring people that they'd been the victims of a prank by the local university frat houses. They looked skeptical, but the human condition meant they clung to any lie which helped them make sense of a supernatural occurrence.

Aunt Sophia followed me and I threw the door open. Sebastian stood in the middle of the room with his arms crossed and a pleased look on his handsome face. Off to the side lay a cast iron frying pan.

Three wolves were still on the floor, their tongues lolling out of their mouths. "They aren't dead, before you get on your high horse."

"How did you tame them?"

He arched a brow. "I didn't. I hit them over the head with a frying pan and knocked them out until your honey bun arrives and deals with them."

"Don't call him that."

A roar echoed from beneath my feet. A thud shook the floor, then another. I took a step back as Sebastian grabbed the frying pan. The floor exploded and a colossal furious ball of fur leapt into the room. It lunged for Sebastian, knocking him to the floor before he had a chance to even raise his frying pan. Claws as big as my hand tore through his shirt, spraying blood across the room.

My feet were moving before my brain. Aunt Sophia slammed an arm against my middle, preventing me from reaching Sebastian as he collapsed to the floor. The beast's jaw opened and he tore a chunk from Sebastian's throat with a thunderous roar of satisfaction. It was going to kill him.

No, no, no. I couldn't lose him. I needed him to survive the crazy show that had become my life. My chest tightened, like my heart was squeezing in distress. My throat constricted, making air difficult to drag in.

"Get a grip, Cora," I muttered to myself as I shook off the panic and forced myself to behave like the doctor I'm trained to be.

I threw my aunt's arm away and lurched into the fray. She flung her hand out and a spray of sand arced across the room, casting over the beast that was causing death and destruction. The beast sneezed, then its terrible black eyes rolled into the back of its head and it slumped forward, partially landing on the wolves. Whatever that was, it was not a typical shifter.

I reached Sebastian and dropped to my knees as I whipped my coat off and pushed it against the wound in his neck. Blood spurted between my shaky fingers, and a chill rocked through my body. Massive and sudden blood loss could kill a vampire. I needed to stop it.

"Hold on," I muttered.

His eyes fluttered open and he gave me a soft smile as his arm raised and he skimmed my cheek with his fingers. "No tears," he gurgled, choking on the blood bubbling from his mouth.

"He needs your blood, Cora," Aunt Sophia said from behind me. "If you want him to live."

Sebastian shook his head. "No."

"Yes," I uttered hoarsely.

I yanked my sleeve up and pushed my wrist over his mouth. His eyes flashed with defiance and he glared at me as I pushed my flesh harder against his lips. His eyes fell closed and he drew in a breath, but didn't expel it.

I stood, grabbed a butcher's knife from the block and slit my left wrist before moving behind him, lifting his head into my lap and forcing his mouth open so my blood spilled along his tongue. I massaged his throat, encouraging him to swallow. Splashes of hot tears mixed with my life force.

"Drink, damn you," I demanded. "I can't do this without you."

My aunt darted out of the door, leaving us alone. My head fell forward until our foreheads touched. A long sound of sorrow echoed around me as my heart broke for my best friend.

I hammered my fist on his chest as a flash of anger shot through me. "No, you don't get to leave me."

My fist thumped his chest once again and my vision danced with black spots. Cool lips suddenly moved against my wrist and he sucked weakly. I jerked my head back and my free hand cupped his pale cheek. "That's it, keep drinking."

The bleeding from the torn flesh on his neck began to slow, with each swallow of my blood it looked better. My rapidly beating heart began to slow, and a languid heat overcame me as two sharp points pierced my flesh. His vampire nature was taking over, forcing him to take what he needed to survive.

His eyes snapped open just as the door bounced against the wall and a furious Hudson stalked into the room. "No," he snarled.

I held my free hand up to stop him. "He was dying."

"I warned you," Hudson said, not slowing down as he approached me. He reached for my hand with the clear intention of yanking me away. Indigo heard my call and pushed out to growl at Hudson.

"Stop," she said. The sound was terrifying and made him pause. His eyes tightened and his jaw ticked. Dave followed into the room with Aunt Sophia. He surveyed the pile of shifters, before settling his gaze on me.

"This isn't good," he muttered, taking a slow step toward Hudson.

Indigo's gaze didn't falter. "You are *my* mate," Hudson roared. "You should not be nourishing another."

"He was dying," she snapped. "And your mate would have been distraught, heart broken, and in pain. Is that acceptable?"

Hudson pointed at Sebastian. "He has fed her his blood, and he is now receiving yours. The thrall bond is complete and can never be undone." He ran a hand through his hair and let loose a frustrated growl.

"Oh, Principal, you really haven't been paying attention if you believe for one moment that we can be bonded to anyone other than whom we choose, and we have already made it clear that we choose you. A vampire's thrall is not a match for the power in our blood."

I felt Sebastian's fangs slip from our flesh and Indigo diverted her attention to him. She patted his cheek in an awkward act of affection like she wasn't entirely sure how to process the emotion of affection and relief.

"You'll live," she said. "I'm glad."

That was almost gushing for her. Sebastian struggled to his feet, slipping twice on the pool of his own blood on the floor.

He swallowed and stared at the room of tense supernaturals, then glanced down at his shirt. "I'll go clean up before I terrify the locals," he uttered as he wobbled. Aunt Sophia looked like she was about to grab some popcorn and make herself comfortable for the show.

"Go and help the vampire," Indigo ordered. "He is healed but not healthy."

Aunt Sophia opened her mouth to argue. Dave grabbed her arm and pulled her from the room, leaving us alone with Hudson and a bunch of newly turned and unconscious shifters.

Hudson took a step toward her and offered her his hand.

*"Does he think me injured or incapable?"* she asked me.

*"No, that's more for him than you. Just accept the hand, it will help to ease the rift."*

She wrapped her hand in his and attempted a smile. I felt our cheeks stretch wide, but I'm sure the rows of sharp teeth negated the comforting effect she was aiming for. Hudson's eyes flashed green, Keverin was prowling close to the surface and didn't like what he saw.

*"Tag, you're it,"* Indigo said, sinking back into my mind.

*"I see, when the tough gets going, you hide behind your 'I'm the daughter of death' persona and leave me to deal with our homicidal mate."*

*"You're welcome,"* she said before disappearing altogether.

He gripped my chin and tilted it up to stare into my eyes. "Do I have you back?" he checked.

"Yes."

"Excellent, because I wouldn't want this to fall on deaf ears."

Oh boy.

"The bond between a vampire and another is a closely guarded secret and can only be complete if blood is shared both ways, completing the cycle of life."

I sucked my bottom lip between my teeth. He's right, that was a closely guarded secret, but one that I knew. "Okay."

His gaze narrowed. "You knew what would happen."

"Did you listen to what Indigo said?" I asked in as soothing a tone as I could manage, given I'd nearly lost my best friend as he bled out in front of me.

"I don't need your monster telling me pretty lies to appease me."

I sighed and wrapped my hands around his neck, dragging him close enough that our breaths mingled. "Look into my eyes, do I look the slightest bit enthralled?"

He squinted like he was looking for a tiny sign that read 'property of Sebastian'. "No."

"Can you still feel my heart beating in sync with yours?"

"Yes."

"Our bond is stronger and more complex than we even realize. I will only ever be bonded with someone I consciously choose, and just to be clear, I have chosen you. Every single part of me is yours, stop doubting that conviction. But, I won't change who I am, I will always come through for those I love, and that circle is bigger than just you and I. That doesn't mean I'm any less committed to you."

His chest expanded as my words penetrated, and his shoulders relaxed, leading me to believe I'd gotten through his thick skull.

"Just to be clear," he said with a low growl. "The only way to break a thrall is to kill the vampire responsible. If I even suspect for a second that you are under his influence, I won't hesitate to take him out."

I'd felt the call in my blood to Sebastian as he drank from me, the magic trying to entwine with mine, but Indigo had rebutted it, and it had recoiled from her. He might have my blood in his veins, but there was no link, and once it had cycled from his system, he would not have any connection to me other than the strong friendship we shared.

"I understand."

Dave reappeared through the door like he'd emerged from the shadows once it was safe from the domestic argument.

"What are we going to do about the shifters?" he asked.

"Sophia says it would be dangerous to reverse the magic for them," I warned. "So I guess you got some new pack members."

Dave wiped a hand down his face like he was exhausted. "This is not helpful."

"Why?" I wondered.

Hudson gave a subtle shake of his head at Dave. "There are issues with the pack," Hudson said with zero intention of giving me an explanation.

"Could you expand on that?"

"It's not important right now," Hudson said, brushing off my concern. A red-hot flush of anger swept through my veins.

"I see, so you get to know my deepest darkest secrets, lay claim to every part of my life, my home and my heart, but I get nothing in return from the things that trouble you? Some partnership."

I huffed just as one of the wolves raised their heads and caught Dave's steady gaze. "Change," he snapped. The lash of command echoed in the room and the wolf trembled. Please, don't be stuck like they were a few months ago. This situation is already bad enough.

The wolf whined and pawed at its head before shivering violently. Bones began to snap and alter, and within a minute, a naked woman lay on the floor. She tipped on her side, hugged her knees to her chest, and cried. The other wolves fell into the same routine until Dave had one woman and two men who were in varying states of disbelief. The enormous lion that rivaled the size of Hudson's beast twitched his paw.

Hudson completed the same ritual, finding an enormous tattooed male in place of the lion.

"Help me," a woman's voice cried from the huge hole in the floor. Dave and Hudson leaned on their fronts and each offered a hand to the woman beneath, they dragged her out with ease and rose. She fell into Hudson and wrapped her arms around him with a sob. She was a curvy bronzed bombshell with blonde wavy hair that touched her ass. A naked woman was hugging my mate, and a flare of jealousy burned hot in my veins. Hudson's gaze snapped to mine and he peeled the woman's arms from around him and took a step back.

She spun and wrapped herself around the naked male lion shifter. "Josh, what happened?" she asked in a whiny voice that grated on my nerves. *That's right, hug your own boyfriend, and keep your mitts off mine.*

"I have a van on the way," Dave said. "You guys can take the Escalade, I'll get them to the pack and give them a crash course in the factions and what their lives now look like."

One of the wolf males started to argue, and I decided I had enough supernatural drama of my own without dealing with the fallout from my grandmother's experiments.

Hudson followed me out of the town hall, leaving behind the sheriff who was busy spinning a tale to the residents about a freak earthquake that had occurred in their little town. It was sad to think that to be in our circle, you had to tell all these lies.

I nodded to him just as Aunt Sophia appeared from outside with a plate. "Cabbage rolls," she explained to Robert. "These will help your bad day."

"We are heading out," I explained. "Dave will take the others affected with him."

Aunt Sophia nodded. "I'll catch a ride back with the sheriff."

"You want to stay?"

She shrugged. "I can help with any lingering doubts the residents have. Sebastian left already in an Uber."

Umm, I guess that was a good reason, but something told me my aunt was giving me and Hudson space to talk before we arrived back at the house and everyone could hear everything we said.

I was both grateful and annoyed. I didn't want to hash out anything else that had occurred here—my life saving blood, Hudson's embrace with a naked woman, or my grandmother's plan that had crystallized into startling and terrifying clarity. Hudson side-eyed me as we approached his abandoned car that still had the doors open. Wow, he must have been in a hurry. There was no way I was getting out of this round of twenty questions. I slid into the passenger seat, clipped on my safety belt, and closed my eyes as the engine rumbled to life, then we were off. Perhaps I could feign sleep?

"We need to talk," Hudson rumbled. *Cora Roberts - daughter of death and queen of wishful thinking.*

# CHAPTER TWENTY-SEVEN

*Shifting parameters and soft apologizes.*

I fiddled with the radio stations, finding it to be one of those moments where everything was an advertisement or a catchy but irritating jingle. Hudson reached down and turned it off, leaving us in the awkward silence I'd been trying to avoid. 'We need to talk', was never a good sign.

"This has to stop," he said as his hands tightened on the steering wheel.

"What has to stop?" I asked carefully, because if he'd reversed his decision to be my mate, I wasn't sure Indigo would let him go unscathed.

"The constant running off into danger without me and without back-up."

My shoulders relaxed. "I had back-up."

He glanced at me as we shot past the sign wishing us a safe journey onto the main road connecting us to White Castle. "I'll rephrase, you need adequate back-up."

"I'm a terrifying Nephilim with unearthly power, what is it you think is going to happen?"

"You offering your throat to the vampire for starters. That could have been avoided."

"It was my wrist and would you have bled for him? Maybe Dave has a crush I'm not aware of?"

"If I'd been there, I would have had control of the shifters and he would have never been injured in the first place."

Huh, well, I couldn't argue with that.

"Thirty minutes, that's all I needed you to wait and we could have met these threats together."

"Robert was insistent."

"And you've just pointed out who you are and what power you hold. Try to keep your line of argument straight."

He was using my words against me and I was losing. He was right. I should have waited.

"I'm sorry," I whispered.

"Pardon?"

I glared daggers into the side of his head as his lips twitched. "I'm sorry, and you are correct." Damn, that hurt.

"You are forgiven, and as long as the vampire doesn't develop a thrall bond, he'll be safe—this time."

I sucked in a breath, held it, and then let it out slowly, along with all the anxiety in my stomach.

"Now that we have that out of the way, let's talk about what's happening in the pack that has you and Dave worried."

His thumbs tapped on the steering wheel as I waited for him to tell me it wasn't any of my business. Then I'd be the one wrapping his words in knots around him.

"There's unease," he started.

"You command thousands of beasts with their own conflicting priorities and agendas, I imagine unease goes with the territory."

He cast an amused glance my way as I twisted in my chair to face him. "True enough. However, this is more serious—an organized coup. And in my absence, I've allowed it to gain traction."

"I thought the alphas supported our mating?"

"The majority do, but while they can instruct their members, it doesn't account for the idiots that enjoy dissension and chaos. They will exploit a weakness and use it as a springboard to claim their own alpha status. You have to understand, we walk and talk, just like you, but underneath… the urges that drive us are entirely different. Shifters will always look for a weak link and strive to climb the ladder."

"Not sure how different we actually are."

Guilt gnawed at me, I was the reason he'd not been with the pack. In my selfishness, I'd distracted him from his people, and in return, they'd turned against him.

"Stop," he said. "It isn't your fault. You'd think after a lifetime of constant commitment from me, they'd be able to afford me a few months of down time. I don't take vacations, I've rarely divided my attention before now. I have put blood, sweat, and tears into uniting the different packs as one. To make us less vulnerable, a collective not to be trifled with. What do I get in return? Infighting and back stabbing with loose and weak plans to usurp me as their leader." He shook his head. "Sometimes, I think I should just let them have it. They think they have it all figured out, and none of them know the true extent of the power it takes to hold everyone together."

"What stops you?" I wondered. I could see the pain of betrayal written in his tight features. This had hurt him deeply and I hadn't been in tune with what was happening beneath the surface of my own mate. I needed to do better, be better, be the woman he deserved.

"Right now? The only thing stopping me is the greatest threat I've seen in my lifetime."

"My grandmother."

"If I leave and a power struggle ensues, there will be nothing to stop her from wiping them out. They'd be easy pickings while their backs were turned from external threats as they kept their eyes on the proverbial circling wolves."

"You know I don't expect you to give up being The Principal, just as I don't believe you expect me to sacrifice part of myself to be with you."

"And yet, without sacrifice, we can't make room for each other."

I stewed on that for a few minutes. "You're right, we need to find a middle ground, figure out what's important and how we can make this work."

He glanced at me and a little light shone through the darkness on his face. "Let's deal with your grandmother, then we can tackle some fundamentals like where we live, work, and eat."

Because right now, it was all in my territory, and that couldn't remain the case. His mate would be expected to be visible and accessible to the pack. I'm sure it came with responsibilities and a host of 'mate of the Principal duties' that I wouldn't care for, but I would do it for him.

"Okay."

He arched a brow. "Okay?"

"Yes. We end this threat and then we work out a schedule. I can be based anywhere for my doctor work, but I would insist on continuing to be available to see loners."

"I can work with that."

"The day-to-day business of the bed and breakfast is mostly run by Maggie and Rebecca. I don't need to be there full time."

He grinned. "Is this you compromising?"

"It is."

His hand left the steering wheel and settled over my thigh, the warmth of his palm penetrating my skin and settling my soul. "So let's start with what the hell happened back in Chatsham."

Ugh, and with that, all my happy warm fuzzy feelings were gone. "We believe my grandmother is stealing magic from the demons and using it via a spell in the Red Dragon to turn humans into elementals."

He frowned. "And the shifters?"

"Aunt Sophia thinks they have some shifter blood buried in their genetics, so the spell awoke that side of them."

"But humans aren't elementals."

"Apparently, I'm missing something important which would explain that, but we were too busy reversing the spell to have story time."

"You think she's building an army of elementals?" he checked.

"Humans are terrified of the unknown, they will always look for leadership and explanation."

"So the newly turned will flock to your grandmother and she will teach them all the ways of the factions as seen through her own eyes."

"Yes, and if she turns enough of humanity, the elementals will become impossible to beat. They may even turn against their own kind."

"That's a disturbing plan," he settled on just as we pulled into the drive of Summer Grove House. He cut the engine and turned to face me, savoring our few moments alone. Perhaps if we split our time between here and the pack, we might be able to steal more time together. It was an awesome thought.

"We need to stop her," he said as he leaned closer.

I nodded and got lost in his hazel eyes. His gaze dropped to my lips. "We do," I breathed. "But right now, we need to regroup."

"Hmm, regroup, that's right."

Our lips touched in the barest of caresses. His tongue flicked out and sought entry. I closed the distance and sunk into the intoxicating and wondrous sensation, that I would never get enough of. We broke away panting. "Just remember, whatever happens, my heart beats in tandem with yours."

"And I can find you anywhere," I finished for him.

The door to the house opened and Rebecca popped her head out. She waved and was then joined by a scowling Aunt Liz.

"Seems we are wanted," I grumbled.

Hudson leaned away from me and opened his door. I jumped out and began to follow him up the steps.

"What happened?" Aunt Liz asked. "Was it my mother?"

Hudson ducked inside the house, not needing to hear this tale again. I'd just made it to the porch when my feet froze, and my skin began to burn. A ring of fire erupted around me, a pentagram forming in the center.

"What's happening?" Rebecca shouted. She rushed forward and the flames roared higher, preventing her from reaching me.

Agony swept through my body as something powerful tugged in my gut. It felt like I was going to be ripped in two from the inside. Hudson came barreling out of the house toward me, his eyes wide in panic, his mouth shouting words I couldn't hear above the roaring of my pounding blood.

My vision darkened, and for a blissful yet terrifying moment, I thought I'd reached my end and was getting ready to meet my maker. What happened to Nephilim when they died? Did we get the same rights as the factions? Or did we sink out of existence?

Hudson's roar shook my body and then everything disappeared. I groaned as agony pulled at my flesh. It felt like being beaten by a hundred fists at once. I rolled onto my side and forced my eyes open. Outside of a familiar glass box, a silver-haired woman smirked with pure evil.

"Welcome, Granddaughter, to your destiny."

Fuck destiny, fuck fate, and fuck family. My heart thudded in my chest painfully. I placed a hand over it but knew deep down, wherever my grandmother had taken me to, no being on earth could find me.

# Chapter Twenty Eight

*The betrayal burns.*

I should have expected this level of betrayal from my grandmother, but somehow, it still hit me like a Mack truck doing ninety on the freeway. I sucked in breath after breath, trying to find my equilibrium after such a jarring teleportation. I hated to admit it, but Lucifer does it better.

"I could kill them all," Indigo said with a growl.

"Stay put. I don't know what she wants or why we are here." Even as I spoke the words in my mind, I knew I was lying to myself and to Indigo.

The symbols on the glass pulsed faintly and a tug on my magic made me grit my teeth.

"Why?" I asked my grandmother, who had not one ounce of love or affection in her gaze. The mask was off, and the true Eloise was present.

"I need power," she answered.

I rolled to my side and onto my knees, making my head swim and the room spin. "You were summoning demons for that."

She grinned. "Yes, I taught you a little too well. Really, it's my own fault. You shouldn't have been able to discover my intentions. I did cover my tracks."

"With sloppy Satanic rituals? You should know better."

Her jaw ticked. "The mess in Peach Tree wasn't my doing."

"So you didn't attempt to turn the residents into elementals using a poisonous plant capable of delivering a powerful spell?"

"That, I'm responsible for, and the cover up was to lead the authorities down a route to call in The Order. But those eyes? That wasn't me. What would be the point?"

I'd been wondering the same thing, and she had no reason to lie while she had me trapped. Which left me with a gaping hole in the narrative. Who or what had burned their eyes, and who had sent Caleb my way? Someone who knew what I could do. Which was a short list of people. Someone close to me was playing dangerous games.

"The demons we summoned burned out pretty quick," she carried on. "Chatsham was a success, but I need to expand, and that requires a greater source of power, one that will replenish so I can drain it over and over again. Once I acquired the Red Dragon, thank you for that by the way, I was able to level up the summoning, finding creatures more suited to my needs. Plus, I no longer needed fragile methods of delivery. That book, Cora, has the most potent of spells and is a gift to me, a sign that the world is ready for a shift in power. It's time to take back control of the earth, and return it to us. We were here first, after all."

She was talking in riddles, we weren't here first. My grandmother had lost the plot. "Humanity will continue to outnumber us, not even you can change that many people."

She shook her head and smirked. "I don't need to change the majority, I just need the strong, a selective process which weeds out the weak and converts the strong. If I control those, then everyone else will follow."

She wanted to build a race of strong people, parameters set by her mind. The scenes my father had shown me flashed through my head. Eloise was a dictator with a god complex, and that didn't only make her dangerous, it made her terrifying. I pushed from the ground and stood. Damn, everything hurt, from my fingernails to my toes. Indigo was poised to explode from my body, should we become more threatened.

"You're delusional. We live in a world of freedom, with equal rights. People will fight back."

"You're mistaken, we live in a world of illusion. People think they are free, but we force them into the acceptable molds of civilized society. They are told when to eat, when to sleep, when to work. From a young age, we are given rules and boundaries. If I offer them a world without those boundaries, then the strong will flock to me."

"You are missing an important point," I said as I glanced at the unfamiliar circle surrounding me. The runes etched into the floor were unlike anything I'd seen before.

"What's that?"

"The importance of human connection, the power of a bond of love, the desire to help and support those around us."

"Love makes you weak."

I shook my head sadly at the woman before me. She had so much knowledge and power, she could change the world for the better, but she was choosing a path of evil.

"Love makes you vulnerable," she asserted. I used to believe this, but Hudson had shown me a different way.

"Vulnerability is the bridge to belonging. If you open your heart, you can experience joy, love, courage, and hope. These are the things that mark our souls with light. If you can't be vulnerable, then you will always live in the dark."

She scoffed. "I see he has you hoodwinked into believing this, Granddaughter. You still believe you will be at his side in the pack? They would never accept you, and sooner or later, he would need to choose. What do you think his decision would be? A strong pack he built from the ground up, or a Nephilim who brings chaos and destruction into his world?"

I smiled sadly. She couldn't understand because she believed power brought her joy. It didn't, and it would never be enough. By the time she understood this, it would be too late. I'd never been stronger in my conviction of Hudson and I, and a bitter old woman's ramblings would not shake the faith I had in us.

"I pity you," I whispered. "You have a loving and wondrous family at your fingertips. You shape and command the direction of our faction, and yet you are unable to experience the contentment that should bring."

Her face twisted with rage, then smoothed out as she caught herself. "Enough," she snapped. "I need you to change so I can access the power your creature holds."

I laughed. She thought us separate beings, but I could access everything Indigo had and vice versa.

My grandmother sighed. "You won't like this if we have to do it the hard way. You hold more magic than any other being on earth, and all the demons. The creature has access to the power of heaven, and as far as I can tell, it will replenish your magic with time."

I kept my mouth closed and folded my arms. Perhaps I did need to keep Indigo locked down, if she truly had a link to the power of Heaven. What this party didn't need, was the angel of Death making an appearance. There was already enough disappointment being aimed my way.

Her gaze narrowed. "I don't want to hurt you any more than necessary. If you cooperate, you are much more likely to survive." Sure, so I can be drained over and over again. I don't think so, I was calling her bluff. "Fine, hard way it is."

Glad we established that I was expendable. My heart tugged in my chest at her words. I wanted to believe she would never do anything to truly hurt me.

That belief shattered into a thousand pieces as Michael Glaister emerged from the shadows, his oily magic coiling into the room. Indigo bared her teeth inside me. He would be losing his life before we ended this, even if it was the last thing we did.

Gas began to stream in from the vents in the top of the glass, connected to tubes. I pushed my hand over my nose and mouth as the sickly, sweet scent suffocated the room. My vision blackened at the edges and my limbs became loose, then I fell to the floor as I lost control.

"*Now?*" Indigo asked.

*"No, it's what they want. If I had to guess, I would say the runes are keyed into you specifically, probably an altered spell to summon our father. Stay down until you absolutely have to."*

A section of glass to my right slid up and Michael stepped inside, holding long lengths of chains and restraints that he let drag dramatically on the floor. I was about to be tortured by the Hound and it took everything I had to not let Indigo take over and shield me from the promise of agony dancing in his eyes.

He hooked the chains to anchors in the four corners then approached me slowly. I couldn't move, I couldn't even speak. Whatever they'd pumped into my body had rendered me defenseless. Indigo rumbled her disapproval. Okay, not defenseless, but if we went angel on his ass, and it didn't work, we had no cards left to play. I had to believe I would survive this, mine and Hudson's story had only just begun.

"Last chance," my grandmother cooed as the first heavy manacle wrapped around my wrist. A little of my control returned, and I turned away from the woman who should be protecting me and focused on Michael. At least he never wore a mask; he enjoyed inflicting pain, asserting control, and breaking people. He never hid that from the world.

When my limbs were shackled, he pulled the chains taut. I stuffed the whimper back down my throat. If I started to fold now, it would all be over in ten minutes. Michael smirked as he withdrew a blade from a sheath attached to his belt. I refused to close my eyes and hide from the horror. The psychopathic son of a bitch would have to look me in the eyes as he tortured me, because when I ended his life, I wanted him to return the favor.

The glass slid closed, making me turn my head once more. My grandmother folded her arms. "Pain will heighten the power discharged, but your aim is to get her to shift into the creature. Then we can really begin. Don't kill her."

With those comforting words, she turned and her heels clicked on the floor as she disappeared, leaving me and the Hound alone. I swallowed the painful lump in my throat and fisted my hands as pain pierced my soul. It didn't matter what Michael did to me, my own flesh and blood abandoning me would be the greater pain.

"You ready for this?" he asked.

I glared at him. "If I said no, would you give me a break and we could pick this up another time?"

He grinned. "Unlikely."

"Then hit me with your best shot, so we can both be disappointed in your abilities when you fail."

He shook his head. "Game on, little angel. Let's see if you bleed red like the rest of us, or if you're made of angel dust underneath all that pretty creamy skin."

I lay somewhere between agony and a strange blankness. The agony was unbearable, but the empty cavern terrified me, that way lay a broken mind to go with my broken body. I'd lost count of the slices Michael had taken, the fingernails he'd pulled, and the bones he'd broken. But through it all I'd clung to the pain and used it to keep my heart beating. I'd locked my power down tight, which meant no healing, no defense, and definitely no blacking out, allowing my crazy alter ego to run the show. If she did that, we'd be drained dry and my grandmother would have the power to enact her master plan. It was time for me to protect Indigo for a change. But with each new injury, my body was getting weaker.

Hours, perhaps days, had passed. Occasionally, they led a healer into the glass box of pain and fixed me up enough to continue. A dead Nephilim was no use to them.

Michael walked around the outside of the box, fingers stroking his chin as he thought of new and inventive ways to make me hurt, frustrated with his lack of progress. I spat red onto the stained floor, sticky with my spilled blood, and grinned at him. "What's wrong, Michael? Fresh out of torture techniques and agony afflictions? Is that the best you've got?"

It hurt to speak and breathe. I was fairly confident I had broken ribs that had punctured a lung.

Michael froze directly in my eyeline. "You think you're safe because you are her flesh and blood?"

I laughed which turned into a hiss. "This is your version of safe?"

"You know, I've left that pretty face of yours unmarred, perhaps it's time to give you a makeover."

"Aww, are you going to braid my hair too?"

"Tear it from your head, perhaps."

"*He won't be touching our face,*" Indigo asserted. She'd remained quiet but present, shoring up my strength as best she could.

"*I'll heal.*"

"*I don't care, he won't be touching our face.*"

Michael's gaze narrowed, like he'd overheard our internal argument. My heart stuttered in my chest. He'd done a number on me in the last round, and I think I was bleeding from some vital organ, but he'd not called in the healer yet.

He pressed a button on a small remote and the glass slid open once more. He appeared a minute later, his hands covered in leather gloves and carrying two flasks of clear liquid with a manic look plastered on his face. This was going to be bad.

He placed the flasks on the floor and leaned over me, tearing my shirt and bra in half to expose my chest. He tilted his head as he studied the bruising and blood stains, like an artist contemplating where his next brush strokes should go.

He grabbed one flask and tipped it over my breasts. A scream ripped from my throat and I tried twisting away, my wrist snapping in its restraint.

He grinned. "Sulfuric acid," he said with glee as he grabbed the other one. "This one is a little diluted." His fingers dived into my mouth and pried apart my lips. The first drop of the liquid made bile rush up my throat, but it had nowhere to go as he forced me to drink the acid. He was going to kill me, I realized. Perhaps it was for the best, I was never meant for this world. I wondered who would meet me at the pearly gates. Let's hope it was someone more sympathetic than my father.

Harry burst into the room and his face went slack in horror. "Miss Roberts."

Ha, now I was delusional, seeing my ghostly side-kick before I died. "*No dying. Not here, not like this, and not today*," Indigo growled. She pushed on my mind and I found I no longer had the fortitude to hold her back.

"Hold on, help is coming," Harry said. Then he disappeared. It was truly cruel to taunt a dying woman with false promises of rescue. It was worse than the torture being inflicted on my body.

Michael tore at my pants and the last of my resistance melted away, and with it came the sweet relief of emptiness.

# Chapter Twenty Nine

*My heart beats for you alone.*

I was dreaming I was trapped inside a zoo at night, with the terrifying roar of a tiger rumbling around me that rattled my bones. The blistering, consuming pain was hovering at the edges of my consciousness. Indigo was doing her best to shield me from the worst of it. Whatever happened, we couldn't let Michael believe she was in charge. The second that happened, my grandmother would move to drain my power, the gentle tug on my magic from the siphoning runes would become unbearable, and then she would be unstoppable.

I'd lost the contents of my stomach earlier, but it still twisted, causing my body to jerk in the restraints as tiny concentrated amounts of bile tried to escape.

"He's going to kill us," Indigo snarled in my mind as I vaguely registered a searing pain in my shoulder. Another roar tore through my mind and I sunk into the comforting delusion that my tiger would be rescuing me. My heart thudded erratically in my chest, a twin phantom beat that kept me strong, kept me alive. It was a wonderful thought, but with hope, came that vulnerability I'd been so adamant was a strength, and with that came the crushing knowledge that I was alone.

"What's happening?" Michael said.

I pushed through past the shield Indigo had formed in my mind and stared at a scowling Michael, who was towering above me with steel in his spine and metal in his hand. I guess he'd abandoned his acid attack.

Movement caught my attention. Outside of the box, shadows moved. My grandmother's face came into view as she shouted instructions to her minions who were running around like there was a fire burning their asses.

She pointed at Michael. "Stay in the box and guard her." Her gaze landed on me. "Your mate has overstepped coming here. He will die, plunging the pack into chaos." She grinned like this was wonderful news and I briefly wondered how on earth I could be related to such a bitch.

Then her words sank into my mind. Hudson was here? Endangering himself. Again. Oh, you complete idiot. Indigo snarled inside of me and threatened to break free. Michael's gaze shot to mine. He knelt at my side and an evil smile spread across his face. "We've been going about this all wrong. You'll never break from my pain, but from the agony of watching your mate suffer? That will draw your creature out, as surely as the sun will rise tomorrow."

"Try it," I ground out. The metallic taste of blood in my mouth made me gag.

Michael licked his lips. "Oh, I will. I can push him harder than I have you, we don't need him to survive."

Indigo raged inside my mind at his words. I grinned. "As I said, try it. You're weak, you can only torture females who are strapped down and at your mercy. In a real fight, you will lose every single time."

I was provoking him to do something stupid, like step outside of the box to prove himself. He tilted his head and smirked. "Nice try."

My grandmother shouted louder and then disappeared into the shadows. I watched as elementals ran around outside the box, blood covered some of their faces and they looked like they'd just met Death and he'd uttered their fate in their ears.

"Protect Cora," my grandmother snapped from somewhere in the darkness. The shaken elementals converged around the outside of the box, their backs to us. Didn't they know the biggest predator was behind them?

A giant wolf shot out of the darkness, causing a panicked elemental to shoot fire from his hand. The fire spread over the wolf's fur like it was resistant and harmlessly dissipated. The wolf responded by lunging at the elemental and sinking its teeth into his abdomen. Familiar eyes slid over me. Dave. A blonde female rushed toward another male elemental, who was ready for her with a spell meant to kill. It bounced off her like she was inside of a bubble. She lifted her hands and tore the head from the elemental. Her horrified gaze landed on me before lifting to the cause of my torment.

Rebecca grinned. If I could have moved, I might have shrunk back. Rebecca had left the safety of my house to come rescue me? Sebastian joined her and together with Dave and another unfamiliar wolf, dispatched the barrier of elementals surrounding the glass box. My grandmother had so few people here, clearly believing wherever she'd held me was secure from major threats.

Sudden pain pierced my stomach, ripping a scream from my throat. My eyes shot to the cause, Michael's hook sat in my stomach.

"Stop," he roared. He wasn't concerned with his fallen comrades, but he'd seen the writing on the wall for his own fate as my friends closed in.

Aunt Liz and Aunt Sophia walked inside the room. Their faces dropped two shades paler when they spotted me.

"I will gut her if you take another step closer," Michael said. The hook moved in my stomach, but I gritted my teeth against another show of the pain he'd inflicted.

My aunts parted and between them my grandmother stepped forward. For a terrifying heartbeat I thought they'd teamed up, and that betrayal almost wrecked me before Hudson emerged from behind Eloise, and my heart roared to life. He'd come for me. Even if I didn't make it, the knowledge that I was enough, that he'd come for me when I needed him, it was everything. He pushed my grandmother forward. His hand was around her neck, claws extended, and rivulets of blood trickled down her flesh and stained her cream blouse. Lenson and Rockhard flanked my aunts, they must be responsible for the shields the vampires and shifters had.

My grandmother's fisted hands were clamped in metal cuffs that shimmered with power. They'd managed to null her power, but it wouldn't last. Hudson was restraining himself as he carefully avoided looking over my body. I knew if he took in the extent of my injuries he'd murder Eloise, and that put my life in jeopardy.

"A simple exchange," he gritted out. "Your precious president for my mate."

Michael went preternaturally still as he weighed up the deal. For a horrifying moment, I thought he would prefer to murder me and sacrifice himself and my grandmother.

"Michael," my grandmother snapped. "Take the deal. We can live to fight another day."

Michael's hook slid free of my stomach and I sucked in a breath. I just had to keep on breathing. Keep my heart beating.

"The remote is in my pants pocket," Eloise snapped. I'd give it to my grandmother, to still sound strong and pissed in the face of such terrifying power, was a skill.

Aunt Liz dug inside her mother's pocket and withdrew the tiny black remote. The glass door slid open, and Michael took a step toward it, then paused. He seemed to realize something at the same time as myself. They would murder both him and my grandmother the second I was safe. There was no political etiquette here, they'd committed horrors which had no excuse. They would be executed.

He retraced his steps and leaned down to unlock my manacles from my wrists and ankles. My muscles spasmed after being pinned down for so long in one position.

He hooked an arm around me and forced me to my feet, my legs like limp noodles, refusing to hold my weight. He dragged me out through the open glass door, my vision darkening at the edges as I fought a battle with my body to stay in the moment.

With me as a shield, he stood before the impressive line of my family and friends.

Hudson let his eyes travel down my body and my grandmother cried out as his claws extended further.

"Everyone needs to leave, except for me, Cora, Eloise, and the Principal," Michael snarled.

My head lolled forward and I blinked, trying to stay awake. "Not happening," Hudson growled.

"If we exchange hostages with the power rolling through this room, there's still nothing to stop you from murdering us," Michael said. "Which means I need to level the playing field."

Hudson's instinct would be to protect me before killing them. It was a good plan, but I didn't like it. "Alternatively, I could just kill her and take my chances. And for every minute you delay, she draws closer to death." His hand pressed against my stomach, and for a few seconds, I lost the ability to breathe.

"Fine," Hudson snapped. Murmurs of disapproval swept around me before the supernaturals filed out of the room, leaving the four of us.

"On three," Michael snapped.

There was a count, then my body crumpled to the floor as Michael released me. Strong warm arms caught me before I hit the hard tiles. "I got you," he murmured into my ear as he hoisted me up and against his chest. My vision wavered as he ran with me down a long dark tunnel. It felt like hours, and at the same time, mere seconds before we emerged into the blistering sunshine.

"Put her down," Lenson demanded.

My body was carefully placed on the ground. "Save her," Hudson snapped.

"Give us room to work. Keep her heart beating, Principal, that's your job," Rockhard instructed. Hudson ran his hands through his hair and stalked around the people working to fix my broken body.

The potion masters hovered above me. I could feel them doing things to my body, but there was no pain. I'd become numb, and that wasn't a good sign.

"You need to let yourself feel it, it will help them find your injuries" Aunt Liz instructed. I tipped my head back, finding her on her knees behind me. Tears streamed down her cheeks as she cupped my face. "I know it hurts, Cora, but pain means you are alive. You have to feel it to fight to stay."

"I can give her my blood," Sebastian shouted. I couldn't see him. The figures were shadows as they circled me.

"Not a chance," Hudson roared.

"You'd rather she was dead?"

"Don't fight," I whispered.

"Your blood won't be enough, and it isn't a match for what we can do," Rockhard snapped.

"Can't she just transform?" Sebastian asked.

"I think she's too weak," Aunt Sophia said. "She has to fight this battle as Cora."

"Let the pain in," Aunt Liz coaxed.

Someone squeezed my hand and I found a very pale Rebecca at my right. Someone else grabbed my other hand. My head twisted, finding Aunt Dayna there, her eyes full of sympathy. Aunt Sophia moved closer and knelt at my feet, she laid her hands on my ankles and nodded. "We can help, Cora. Let the pain in and we will be here to catch you."

Indigo was pacing in my mind as the elementals worked around me. "*Let me out,*" she snarled. "*I can heal us.*" But her voice wavered like she wasn't entirely sure of this conviction.

Letting her out would mean another two people would know exactly what I was. Seeing it on video was one thing, but confirmation in the flesh of their suspicions was another. My circle of people was widening, but I needed to be cautious. Not everyone would take the news of a Nephilim in their midst in their stride.

I drew in a steading breath and unlocked the shields in my mind. Synapses sprang to life and my back bowed as my family and friends absorbed some of the agony. I clung to their strength and felt Hudson clutching my heart, keeping it pumping, giving me life when it would have sputtered out.

I let in the heartache, the betrayal, the searing pain, and I fed it to my soul. I would live and I would take my revenge. Michael Glaister and Eloise Roberts needed to be stopped.

I writhed beneath the power skittering over my flesh as it listened to my body's signals and sought out my injuries. I clutched the hands of my family, both blood and chosen, and fought to stay with them. Time moved like molasses.

"We've done all we can," Lenson murmured. He sounded so far away. My body ached. "The rest is up to her."

Warm arms picked me up and cradled me. Hudson's scent surrounded and comforted me. My eyes seemed to be glued closed, but I curled into him with a sigh. Lips brushed my forehead.

"How did you find me?" I wondered.

"I told you, my heart beats with yours. I can find you anywhere on this earth, because the closer I get, the stronger it beats."

"I was saved by a romantic version of hot and cold?"

He grinned. "Exactly. Now rest, heal, and come back to me," he murmured. "I will keep your heart strong."

Blackness washed over me once again, but this time, there was no pain. Only love and acceptance.

# Chapter Thirty

*Just when I think I've got everything figured out, someone flips my world upside down and inside out.*

Healing from physical injuries was simpler than recovery from the psychological. Time would beat the bumps, bruises, and breaks, but the crack in my psyche might be permanent. That's the wound that weeps with heartache and disbelief. Heartache that another person was capable of inflicting such horror onto another, and disbelief that my own blood had ordered it.

To recover, I needed to cling to the fact that I had people who showed up for me regardless of the danger they were facing. That had kept me breathing each and every day since, and three weeks in, I was starting to venture farther from my rooms, albeit in small doses. Much of the time I was secluded in my sitting room, which had gained a TV, due to Hudson's insistence that I needed something mindless to distract me.

They hadn't left me alone for one minute since my rescue, other than to use the bathroom, and even then someone waited outside the door, talking drivel to me. It was as if they were afraid I'd shatter into pieces and they wanted to be there to put me back together. I was eternally grateful, but as I had started gaining confidence to leave my safe place, they needed to begin leaving me alone to build up my resilience.

Indigo had been suspiciously quiet, no demands for retribution or soul sucking. Like me, I believed she was licking her wounds in her own way.

I twisted on the sofa, flopping from lying on my side to my back. Bella grumbled from her position on the back of the sofa. She'd also made it her business to watch over me.

Hudson squeezed my feet and I groaned, because damn, I'd discovered I'd do anything for a foot rub.

He tore his eyes away from another show about the Bermuda Triangle. Apparently, it's a portal to another dimension.

"You need anything?" he asked.

"I could murder for some of Aunt Liz's fried chicken."

"I'll call down."

"Could you go and get it for me? Perhaps get Maggie to rustle up a batch of triple chocolate cookies?"

His thumbs pause in a particularly sweet spot in the arch of my foot. His gaze bore into mine, and he seemed to get the unspoken need. With a sigh he lifted my legs and stood.

"Don't move," he said.

"I'll not leave the house," I promised, but I needed the toilet, so moving was important.

He bent and kissed my forehead. This was something else that needed fixing. He was treating me like I would break into a thousand pieces. He'd surrounded me with warmth and love, but any attempt on my part to make things physical was shot down.

He exited the room, closing the door behind him with a soft click. I swung my feet to the floor and sighed. See? Nothing bad was happening. I could do this. I made my way to the bathroom, relieved my protesting bladder, then sauntered back into the kitchen, grabbing a soda from the refrigerator.

On the counter top was a pile of mail that needed to be dealt with. I collected it and opened my door as I held my breath. Nothing happened. I was safe, I reminded myself. I made it to the ground floor and Maggie waved at me with her eyes comically wide. Rebecca and Sebastian strode from the parlor with careful smiles. I rolled my eyes.

"I'm fine." I waved the post in their faces. "I need to go and pay our bills before the electricity company cuts us off."

Hudson strode from the kitchen looking like he was about to carry me off. I held up a hand. "I'm going to my office. Alone."

He shook his head. "I'll come with you. In fact, I will pay those for you."

"Please?" I whispered. I needed to do something to start to restore my confidence.

He crossed his arms and sighed. "Fine, I'll be right here. If you shout, I will come."

I nodded gratefully and made my way to my office, leaving the door open so he could hear me moving around. I knew I wasn't the only one scarred by recent events. He had nearly lost his mate; that would have a profound and long-lasting effect.

Sitting in my chair, a long sigh left me. I opened my drawer and removed my laptop. I started making my way through the huge pile of mail, placing the bridal magazines to one side for later. Perhaps it was time to start facing the fact I would need them. Ugh, shopping, even for this, wasn't fun. I would delegate it to Rebecca and Dayna.

I grabbed Lucifer's business card from my top drawer which was next to the stack of weird little black cards I'd been receiving. I dropped him an email, keeping to the facts. Eloise was behind the demon summoning and was responsible for syphoning their magic. We'd interrupted her operation which was to build herself an army of elementals, but she'd escaped, and by all accounts was holed up in The Order's headquarters behaving like she'd not ordered the torture of her own granddaughter. I left that last part out. Lucifer wasn't interested in my welfare.

There were so many unanswered questions. Who had sent Caleb to me? What or who had burned the eyes from the residents of Peach Tree? In the grand scheme of things, this didn't seem important, but I think someone behind the scenes was pulling my strings, guiding me in a direction of their choosing. Whether their intentions were good or bad remained to be seen.

I lifted the stack of little black cards and placed them on my desk, spreading them out in the order I'd received them. I searched through the pile of mail I had yet to tackle and sure enough, another card slid out. This time a vertical line, with another line attached to the top, dropping down at a forty-five degree angle to the left. On the reverse were the words, 'The dawn has risen'. What the hell did that mean? There was a niggling memory buried somewhere deep about a clandestine organization, but it was just a legend. I flipped the card and ran my hand over the lines. The faint magic tingled against my fingers.

No amount of staring was helping my brain put together what these meant. I stacked the cards together and tapped them against the desk to even the edges. Power splashed in the room, sizzling against my flesh. My gaze flicked to the cards just as Hudson's shout came down the stairs. The cards fused together and the lines formed two familiar runes. My molecules began rearranging themselves, and I glanced up just as a frantic Hudson burst into the room.

My vision darkened, Hudson's hand whipped out and passed through my body. "Cora!"

The office swung around, like a switch had been flipped. I rose from my chair and my mouth fell open at the scene before me.

The sky was painted in breathtaking shades of pink, orange, and red. The landscape was a series of grassy hills, and on the top of the tallest one sat a blossom tree in full bloom. Underneath that tree was a round table, surrounded by six high-backed wooden chairs. I began walking toward the tree, the figures coming into focus the closer I got. I climbed the hill and the closest figure turned to face me, and I blinked. Sebastian's mother, Aira, looking as ethereal as ever smiled at me. Dave folded his arms and stared. Harry hovered over a chair like he was able to actually sit, and

Aunt Sophia offered me a welcoming smile as she continued to crochet.

The final familiar figure tilted his head and smirked. "Welcome to the Serpents of the Dawn, niece," Lucifer said.

*Cora Roberts - mistress of missing the big huge fat clues.*

Thank you for beginning Cora and Hudson's journey…

If you want to stalk me you can find me here –

Facebook reader's group – Adaline's Warriors (where you will find a group of the most awesome, like-minded people who are currently sharpening their knives).

Instagram - @adalinewinterswriter (my main hangout because of all the amazing, supportive people there).

Email – adalinewinterswriter@gmail.com

# Acknowledgments

I'm over two years into this author adventure and I'm entirely grateful for my badass team.

***Liberty***, my unicorn. You manage my crazy, hold my paper bag, and roll with every single insane idea I have. You are one in a billion. Everyone else, go find your own unicorn, she's taken.

***Michaella,*** you always make time for me, you make my words shine and I couldn't do this without you. I'm incredibly lucky to have you as my alpha, but more importantly as my friend.

***Shauni,*** I have found my soul sister for food. You are never too busy to lend a kind word or offer support. That has meant the world to me these last months.

***Jamie, Shauni, Shawna, Stephanie, and Tanya.*** Thank you for reading my raw words and your passionate comments to help bring it to life. You are an awesome team of betas and I am so lucky to have found you.

**Keyboard whores.** You know who you are. Thank you for pushing me to be better every single day. Special shout out to **Ruby** for endless optimism and being slightly scary, and to **Maddison** for telling me when I'm being nuts. That's quite the task, as I'm often being nuts.

***My readers.*** I am in awe at each and every one of you that takes the time to read my books.

And lastly ***my family.*** I love you. Always.

Adaline x

## *Serpents of the Dawn*: The Playlist

Set Free the Devil - Nick Kingsley & Daniel Farrant
Feral Hearts - Kerli
I believe in a Thing Called Love - Delta Goodrem
Still Breathing - Veridia
Here Come The Monsters - ADONA
Begin Again - Alex Ray & Randall Jermaine
Warfare - Katire Garfield
On The Surface - Jo O'Meara
Count the Saints - Foxes
I Want Your Love - Eduard Romanyuta
Say You Love Me - Theo Chinara & Craig Hardy
All Is Lost - Katie Garfield

Printed in Great Britain
by Amazon